HIGHLAND FLING

by

Anna Larner

2017

HIGHLAND FLING

ISBN 13: 978-1-62639-853-5

This Trade Paperback Original Is Published By
Bold Strokes Books, Inc.
P.O. Box 249
Valley Falls, NY 12185

First Edition: April 2017

Credits
Editor: Ruth Sternglantz
Production Design: Susan Ramundo
Cover Design By Sheri (graphicartist2020@hotmail.com)

HIGHLAND FLING

Visit us at www.boldstrokesbooks.com

Acknowledgments

A novel isn't the work of one person but the joyful result of many people's contribution.

A heartfelt thank you to the BSB team, in particular, Len Barot, Sandy Lowe, and Ruth Sternglantz.

To my awesome beta-readers, Bridget, Jen, Kay, Lis, Rita, Sue G, Sue L, thank you from the bottom of my heart for your amazing support.

To my wonderful family and friends—thank you for your love.

Highland Fling would not exist without my partner, Ang—for whom thank you is not enough.

Dedication

For Ang

CHAPTER ONE

Hottie alert! Two o'clock." Roxanne ran her hands through her hair and brushed away the debris of prawn-cocktail flavoured crisps from her chest.

"Where?" Eve looked around the heaving pub, trying to tease out individuals from the entangled mass of jeans, T-shirts, and hair gel.

Roxanne grabbed Eve's arm. "Don't look round."

"Right, so I'm supposed to look without looking?"

"Uh-huh. That's right, Evie—like how you get dressed in the morning," Roxanne said with a smirk.

"Yeah. *Anyway.* Don't let me forget to give you my spare keys. Rox?" Eve poked Roxanne in the ribs to get her attention.

"Ouch. What?"

"My holiday. You haven't forgotten already, have you?"

"Oh, yeah." Roxanne flicked at the rings of wet on the table, spritzing Eve in eau de lager.

"Nice, Rox, really nice." Eve screwed her face in disgust at her beer-stained shirt. "Remind me again why I'm letting you stay in my flat while I'm away."

Roxanne shrugged, her gaze straying, like a tomcat, in the direction of the hottie. "Because you feel sorry for me living in nurses' accommodation and you need someone to water your plants."

"Yeah, one of those is true. So you remember what we discussed? No sex in my bed." Eve watched a mischievous smile break across Roxanne's face. "Bin day's Tuesday. Best to put the rubbish out Monday night as they come, like, super early. Oh, and Rox, the funny noise you hear when you run the bath—"

"Completely normal."

"Exactly. Oh, and the washing machine door—"

"Sticks and I'm not to overwater the cactus, or leave the television on standby, or flirt with the neighbour but one, or forget to check your postbox, blah-blah-blah."

"Well…yes—"

"Oh God, she's coming over. Casual, Eve, casual." Roxanne's voice strained to an octave higher than usual.

The approaching woman was somewhere in her twenties and had chosen to complement her cropped vixen-red hair with a low-cut blouse and denim skirt, which every so often she tugged at to prevent from riding up.

"Oops, nearly." The woman giggled, smoothing her skirt back in place, as she perched one hip on the edge of their table.

Roxanne was enthralled. Eve suspected by Roxanne's wide eyes that she was thinking, *Please God let her drop something.*

Roxanne cooed, "Hi, gorgeous, how's things?"

Eve raised her eyebrows at Roxanne, who ignored her.

"I just thought I'd say hi. So *hi.*" The woman dragged out *hi* as if she was striking the first note of a song. "I'm Belinda."

"I'm Roxanne—feel free to call me Roxy."

Eve couldn't help but notice that despite a valiant effort to make polite eye-to-eye conversation, Roxanne couldn't quite manage to raise her eyes above Belinda's ample chest line.

"And I'm Eve, pleased to meet you." Eve gave a closed-mouth smile in Belinda's direction.

"Well, it was nice to meet you both. So, see you around." Belinda winked at Roxanne, drifting her hand across Roxanne's shoulder, the tips of her fingers lightly caressing the nape of her neck.

Utterly spellbound, Roxanne's entranced stare followed every hypnotic sway of Belinda's curvaceous hips as she slipped back into the crowd.

"Wow," Roxanne gasped. "I need another. You're nearest. Two more pints and don't forget the crisps."

"Oh my God, Rox, I can't even see the bar."

Roxanne glanced at the thronging, pressing crowds and then at Eve. "Elbows out and show no fear."

Standing on tiptoes, Eve shouted her order to the barman. Her trip to the bar left her dishevelled and mildly traumatized. Eve looked back at the crowds, at the faces she saw each Saturday night.

It wasn't that The Brewer's Arms was the only gay pub in the Midlands, it just seemed to be the place everyone gravitated towards, the familiar life-worn face in a world of strangers. It felt like every important event, each birthday, any cause of celebration in Eve's life had been marked by a pint in The Brewer's. And now Eve was older and so was her favourite pub. Eve looked at the carpet, which once had a pattern of sorts and now appeared plain. The uneven walls, once bright white, would likely be described in Farrow & Ball's paint chart as Tobacco Yellow. Tufts of royal blue velour fabric, sticking out from between seat and arm, merely hinted at the luxurious upholstered seating of the past. And the loos—well, Eve sighed—in many ways it was a shame that the toilet in best repair was the one without the lock. And if it was Saturday night and you had not claimed a seat by nine o'clock, then Eve was all too aware that you'd likely be standing, leaning on something sticky, for the rest of the evening.

She was thankful for Roxanne's unstinting dedication to drinking and to watching Saturday afternoon sport on the pub's television, for this meant that more often than not they secured their favourite booth in the bay of the front window.

A slow smile drifted over Eve's face, as she wondered what she would do without her best mate.

Eve Eddison had first met Roxanne Barns at the age of nine. Roxanne had shown her precisely where she could hang her pump bag, which teacher was nice, and who to avoid. As they grew older, it was Roxanne Eve turned to with her worries—she was her ally against the mad world.

Eve, in turn, had always been there for Roxanne: from homework and job applications; to food and frequent shelter; to gentle words of consolation, many mornings after many misspent nights before. Eve knew they were more than just best friends, they were family.

Eve weaved her way back to her seat, crisp bags dangling from her mouth, her cheeks tingling with the concentration of carrying two overflowing beers.

Eve slid next to Roxanne. "I swear there's more beer in my shoes than in the glass."

"Yeah, whatever. We, my lovely, are hatching a plan."

"Really? That sounds exciting." Eve was intrigued, if a little nervous as to what exploits she was about to be dragged into.

"To find you a woman," Roxanne firmly asserted.

"What, I mean, why?" Eve felt herself blush and took a long glug of her beer.

"When did you last have a date?"

"A date?"

"Yes, a date. You know—agree to meet someone. Have a drink, meal maybe. Go back to theirs. Lez on."

"Lez on?" Eve giggled. "Well, a couple of months back—you remember, Janie. You know, Gym Janie, who can lift her own body weight with one arm." Eve proceeded to give an impression of someone lifting weights. "Although, come to think of it, it was less sexy than wrestle-y, one-*er*, two-*er*, three-*er*." Eve shook her head at the memory.

Eve had always joked about the women she had fancied. On reflection, she could never imagine falling in love with any of them. Romances had ended before they had begun and Eve worried that she'd spoken with more affection about her childhood pet goldfish than any former lover.

It didn't help that Eve was also absolutely oblivious to those who fancied her, prompting Roxanne to often tease Eve for her lack of gaydar skills. Conversations would frequently end with Roxanne exasperated, complaining, "What do you mean she's just being friendly. She didn't offer to buy *me* a drink."

Seeing Roxanne's *I can't believe you bought us cheese-and-onion crisps when I've just pulled* expression, Eve said, "They're my favourite. I'm sorry, Rox. I didn't think."

Roxanne shook her head. "That's not your problem."

"What's not my problem?"

"Not thinking. You think too much," Roxanne declared in a spirit of intervention.

"I don't get you." Eve crunched in reply.

Roxanne moved the crisps away. "You think too critically about the girls you like and not enough action. You're too, how can I put it—"

"Appropriately selective?" Eve suggested with a shrug.

"Reticent."

"Reticent!"

"You overthink things, mate—you seem to be looking for the one, when you should be looking for the *many*."

"Well thank you for that observation, Nurse Barns," Eve said, smiling.

"Don't you go thinking that that advice is free, just because I work for the NHS. It'll cost you a pack of *plain* crisps."

Eve went a little quiet, serious.

"Look, I have a fab idea, Evie. Let's list down what you want in a woman. You know—physical features, personality, et cetera." Turning over a dog-eared beer mat to the less stained side, Roxanne divided the small card space into two, with looks on one side and personality on the other. "Right, what do you want her to look like? Her, of course, who is one of many."

"I don't know, Rox."

"Think, Eve."

Eve could discern a certain frustration in Roxanne's voice. "Okay, well…I don't know, maybe—"

"Spill," Roxanne asserted. "This is no time for shyness."

"I quite like an older woman." Eve spoke the words into her beer. It felt very much as if she was revealing the details of a guilty crush.

"Please don't say Nigella Lawson, as I can confirm there are no Nigella lookalikes in this bar this evening."

Eve shook her head slowly. She thought Roxanne's game was kind of fun.

"Right, well, older woman, that's a start." Roxanne looked at her two columns.

"It'll probably need to go into both," Eve suggested, as she leant over her friend's shoulder.

"Will she have her own teeth?" Roxanne added without a hint of a smirk.

Eve gave Roxanne a withering expression in reply.

Roxanne held her hands up. "Just checking, mate. Okay, hairstyle."

"Curly."

"Curly? Since when has curly been a hairstyle?"

"What can I say, I like curly hair."

Roxanne gave Eve a look that said *You'd better not be taking the piss.* "Right, old with curly hair—that's narrowed it down, narrowed it down to my gran's care home."

"I didn't say *old*, I said *older*. And I like someone who's brave and intelligent, yet intriguing and private." Eve could sense Roxanne was already getting bored. "Rox?"

"Yep." Roxanne nodded as she wrote the words under the right-hand column.

Eve continued, "Sort of broody, maybe, with a clear sense of herself—but not a sulky big gob. And she has to be kind, and honest, and trustworthy." Eve nodded to herself.

Looking down at the list and doing a surveying sweep of the room, Roxanne quipped, "I think hair straighteners are in."

Eve looked around. "Okay, I don't want to alarm you, but I reckon we are amongst the oldest in this bar."

"Nonsense." Roxanne shook her head, as if refusing to accept any suggestion that they were past it. "We're only twenty-six."

"I didn't know you were nearly thirty," Belinda remarked with a surprised tone, reappearing at their table as surreptitiously as the draft from an open door.

"Like I said, we're twenty-six and in the mix." Roxanne clambered from the booth, slung her arm over Belinda's shoulder, and gave her a squeeze, adding, "What are you drinking?"

Belinda slipped seductively into their booth as she requested, "Cider—a pint, honey."

"I'll come with you to the bar," Eve said, taking care to tuck the heavily inked beer mat into her pocket.

As they waited to be served, Eve leant in to Roxanne to confess, "I like outdoorsy types—Land Rovers, that kind of thing."

"Really?" Roxanne giggled and then looked puzzled, shortly followed by an expression of concern. "What, like the Queen drives? Oh my God. Please don't tell me you fancy the Queen."

The barman looked at Eve.

"*No.* Why would I fancy the Queen?" Eve spoke as much to the barman as Roxanne. "In any case, I'm not overly keen on corgis."

"You're a worry, Eddison." Roxanne shook her head, paid the barman, and took a deep intake of breath in Belinda's direction, exhaling, "I'm going in." Before she could add, *You can have my k.d. lang collection if I don't make it out alive,* Eve was turning away to head to the loo.

Although the toilets of The Brewer's Arms were not a place to loiter any longer than absolutely necessary, what Roxanne had suggested was making Eve linger and think. She couldn't help but wonder: Was she too reticent? She really liked women, and it wasn't that the women out there weren't fun, or nice, or in any way not good looking, it's just that they left her feeling kind of empty.

The dim lighting in the toilet just about gave Eve enough light to check her look in the cracked full-length mirror. She couldn't decide whether the twenty-six-year-old woman looking back at her would be considered good-looking or not. Was her short brown hair, with side parting, too tidy to be trendy? Did her favourite scarf, casually draped around her neck, evoke dusty travels across Asian continents or the onset of middle age? Eve couldn't decide. She thought her fitted grey T-shirt, white linen shirt, faded blue jeans, and beaten-up canvas shoes looked kind of cool, and gave her just enough of the confidence she needed to step back out into the crowded bar.

Their table was now packed with Belinda's friends. Roxanne and Belinda were pinned up a corner—not that they seemed to mind. The thought of staying any longer, the third wheel once again, was frankly depressing.

"I'm going to head off." Eve nodded to the door. "I've got packing and stuff to do. Rox?"

"Yeah, I'll call you later," Roxanne said, without taking her eyes off Belinda and her low-cut top.

Pulling on her jacket, the doors of The Brewer's Arms swinging closed behind her, Eve made her way out into the street. A few yards down the road she heard, "Eve. Evie wait."

Eve looked behind her to see Roxanne striding up the street towards her.

"Hey, Rox. You didn't want to stay after all?"

Catching her breath, Roxanne said, "You forgot to give me your keys, plonker."

"Oh shit, yeah." Eve dug deeply into the pocket of her jeans, separating her spare set of door keys from the remnants of a tissue. "Thanks for looking after my flat."

"No worries. I may not have a chance to see you before your hols, so have a good time. Oh, and say hi to your mum and dad for me and tell your sister, Gary's a prick."

"Thanks, Rox. I'll say you say hi. Mum thinks the holiday will help Esther, what with the divorce and everything, and she didn't want her to be bored—"

"And yet you still got invited?" Roxanne grinned broadly.

"Yeah, nobody's laughing." Eve looked around the empty street. "See."

Smiling, Roxanne asked, "So you're looking forward to it?"

Eve nodded. "Uh-huh." *At least, I think I am.* The memory of her recent phone call with her mother came flooding back.

It'll be good for us all, darling, to have a break, in any case. It's been quite upsetting all round. Divorce. Just awful, awful. Your poor sister, it's really taken its toll. Oh, and at her age, so unfortunate. Well, I knew you would want to help your sister by joining in. It would be no fun for Esther with just your father and me. And the

Highlands, well, they're just a delight at this time of year. A delight. So you'll come. Yes, marvellous, I'll confirm the booking with the agent.

At no point had Eve's mother, Lillian, paused to draw breath or to allow Eve to comment, or indeed implied by her tone that anything she said was a question that Eve might wish to answer. In any case, Eve could not remember specifically agreeing or, for that matter, speaking at all, beyond *Hello, Mum* and *Goodbye.*

"You'll be fine." Roxanne's reassurance interrupted the memory. "It will go really quickly. You'll be in The Brewer's boring me—sorry, telling me all about your hols before you know what." Roxanne eye's glinted with mischief.

Eve looked back towards the glowing windows of the bar.

"So, yeah…'night Rox. I'll text you when I get there."

"Take care, Evie Eds."

Just as she was about to step back into the bar, Roxanne hollered, "Oh, Evie. Don't do anything I wouldn't do."

Eve shook her head, turned, and walked away, the dog-eared beer mat warm against her thigh.

CHAPTER TWO

It had been at least fifteen years since Eve, as a child, had last visited Scotland. Gazing out of the back seat window, her head rested against the glass, the Scotland of Eve's memories gave way to the vivid wonder that surrounded her. Eve turned to glance at her sister and couldn't help but feel that the journey to the Highlands, past glinting lochs and the majestic ice-sculptured slopes of Glen Coe, would gladden the saddest of hearts and renew the weariest of souls.

It was almost six o'clock on the last Sunday in May when the Eddison family drove up the steep, winding road to the Highland hamlet of Newland.

Loch View. Eve's tired eyes traced the mesmeric swirls of the hand-painted wooden nameplate, which hung, weather-beaten, against the cream render of their holiday let.

Rather than follow her bustling family into their accommodation, Eve, feeling decidedly travel sick, pulled on her coat and walked the short path down the side of the house, and stood at the top of a long garden. She could not have expected the sight that greeted her.

With eyes saucer wide and lips parted in wonder, Eve gasped. "Okay. Wow. This, this is seriously cool."

A barely tamed lawn unfurled before her into meadow, where wisps of grasses dropped breathlessly away to reveal the distant rippling waters of Loch Ness, shining, dark, and beautiful. At the edges of the loch dense pine woods fringed rocky slopes of green, veined grey with hillside tracks. Clouds shadowed and broke to conceal and then reveal the drama of snow-capped mountains endlessly repeating themselves into the distant disappearing horizon.

It was quite simply the most beautiful view she had ever seen. Standing motionless, absorbed in the scene, it was as if sketchy, monochrome memories were being redrawn with a palette of intense colours and sensations that left her reeling.

"What the…?" Eve tipped her face to the sky, tracing the urgent flight of house martins, as they swooped and surprised in the air above, effortlessly cutting wing-shaped silhouettes against the evening sun. She spun around several times, her senses straining to absorb every pine-scented enchanting detail.

Eve's gaze eventually settled on their holiday accommodation. Nestled on the steep hillside, Loch View stood impressively in its grounds. Traditionally finished in cream render, with a sweeping slate-grey arched roof, it struck a striking architectural note. Sets of french doors opened out into the garden from both the living room and dining room, and a short run of three wide steps led to the grass below. By the living room window, a large bird table was crowded with feeding tits and finches.

To the right of Loch View was a further collection of discreetly situated holiday lets. To the left, a larger house, covered with climbing roses and ivy, sat informally, languidly on the hillside. A barn building, attached to this neighbouring property, reinforced the rural setting. If she was honest, the neighbouring house looked a bit ramshackle. It was clearly not a holiday let. Hens could be heard clucking and various sprouting veg on climbing stakes could be seen waving in the breeze from above the boundary fence.

"Eve, Eve! Can you help your father? Otherwise we shall be unpacking in the dark." Like the shock of a dropped glass, Lillian's high-pitched call shattered and broke upon the enchanting scene. The sudden crashing and charging of a rhino in a rainforest would have been less startling.

"Sure, coming." Eve took a long last gaze at the seductive view.

From the front of the house, lapping at the boundaries of the driveway, green rich views of hills and woodland washed away any lingering images of glass buildings and concrete horizons. The city, grey and fast-paced, felt like another world.

"It's beautiful, don't you think, Dad?" Eve said earnestly, as she diligently made the many trips from car to house, with bags, cases, raincoats, and wellingtons. "I mean, really amazing. I think it's going to be good being here."

"Excellent, Eve. Excellent." With these words, Henry grasped Eve and bear hugged the air out of his younger daughter's lungs.

Over his shoulder, Eve caught sight of a red Land Rover driving past, heading towards the neighbouring houses. She could not clearly discern who was driving, but if she was not mistaken, it seemed to be a woman. How cool was that?

"Right, that's me, Eve. Anything remaining will have to be dealt with in the morning. I'm ready for a gin and a sit."

Eve stood motionless staring out at the woodland view.

"Eve? Are you coming in?" Henry asked, the gin bottle clasped to his chest.

"I can't take my eyes off it."

"Yes, that's some view. It'll be there in the morning though."

Eve heard Henry chuckle. "Unlike this bottle of gin," he said as he disappeared inside.

Eve's sister, Esther, decided that she wanted the room at the front of the house with the woodland view. She told her family that the room facing the loch would be too bright. Since the finalization of her divorce, Esther had declared that she liked to sleep in the pitch dark. Although Esther would have had her family believe that her statement was one of confident independence, Eve suspected that the darkness helped mask an empty bed. Eve was pleased, not of course that her sister was sad, but that this meant that the bedroom overlooking the loch could be hers. It was a fab room. Eve loved it. Set in the eaves of the house, it had a little en suite with a bathtub, and a small window seat on which to sit and admire the views. The bed linen was a pretty yellow and blue check, cut from the same cloth as the curtains and lampshades.

Eve unpacked just her pyjamas, dressing gown, slippers, and toiletries. The other unpacking, Eve reasoned wearily, could wait until tomorrow or indeed whenever.

Sitting on her bed, Eve texted Roxanne. *Arrived safely. Cottage super nice with ace views. Will text again tomoz. E X*

Like a distant beacon signalling from a remote land, Eve's phoned beeped and blinked, *R X*

CHAPTER THREE

E ve slept more soundly than she had done for ages. She did not dream or wake for a wee. Before she knew it, her bedroom was light and she could hear the clucking and flustered flapping of hens from next door. It was nine o'clock. With some effort, Eve pulled on her dressing gown and yawned her way downstairs.

Patting sticking up bed-hair into place, Eve stared out the french doors to the garden.

"Morning, Eve. Here—tea," Esther said, holding out an earthenware mug.

"Thanks, sis. So what's the plan for today?"

"Well, Dad's suggested a walk. Mum's not sure. It does look quite hilly out there." Esther nursed a mug of tea at her chest and directed a frown at the view outside.

"Hilly?" It took all of Eve's slim reserves of maturity not to add, *And you expected it to be flat because...?*

Esther sighed. "You know what I mean. Anyway you'd better hurry up. There's talk of leaving by ten." Esther held up her watch, lifting her wrist awkwardly at Eve, to make the point. "Ten. Oh, and wrap up, Mum's heard the forecast and it's changeable."

Eve nodded. "Absolutely. I'm a welly away from ready. Is there any toast?"

Esther pointed to the toaster and walked away, shaking her head.

❖

It was midday when the Eddisons emerged through the woods to the car park of the Newland Forest Trust.

Their first walk had been hilly and hot. Meandering hillside tracks, where tadpoles scooted in the puddles of the ruts left by tractor tyres, gave way to steep moorland slopes. With each promise of a summit came a further rising hill. And with the exertion of each new hill, Eve took off a layer of clothing, wrapping the discarded item around her waist. Her back felt damp underneath her rucksack and her rain hat kept tipping in front of her eyes obscuring her view.

The relief to have found the car park, and what they thought to be toilets and a café was palpable. The relief was also short-lived.

Covered in grass, the two wooden toilet huts rather caught Eve off guard. Had she not been bursting for the loo, she would have given them a miss. For whilst there was a toilet seat, there was no toilet as such, merely a hole in the ground, where according to a note pinned to the wall, if one had the stomach to look, organic composting was taking place.

Eve hovered over the toilet, feeling the pain of tired calf and thigh muscles. She did her best not to look for spiders, convincing herself that if she could not see them, they were not there. Eve emerged having left any tucking in of clothes until she was outside the loo.

"I'm holding on," Esther whispered to Eve.

Eve nodded in agreement. "On balance, advisable."

Eve looked at the large wooden building in front of them. It had something of the Swiss chalet about it. Logs created the walls and roof and it had a carved wooden veranda, with stilts to the floor.

The whole set up—the loos, the chalet, the trails, the wooden benches, and carvings dotted around—had the feeling of something organic. It was very much as if the place and its contents were made from, and spoke of their environment.

"I imagine their carbon footprint to be quite low," Esther said. "What d'you think?"

"Yep. It's really cool isn't it?" Eve adjusted the rain hat on her head and retied her raincoat around her waist. She watched as her parents disappeared inside the chalet-style building. Shielding her eyes with her hand and tilting her head to one side, Eve observed, "There's no ice cream sign."

Moira Burns looked up from her work, surprised at the unexpected arrivals at the education centre. She glanced across at her colleague, Alice Campbell, who appeared equally taken aback. It was not that the sight of a family of four was rare. It was rather that the appearance of this particular group of individuals was less... usual.

The male of the group, who, if Moira was not mistaken, was the father, stood tall, mopping at his forehead with his cloth hanky. He was scanning the room with an expression that suggested he was absolutely delighted by the forest hideout they had stumbled on. The older of the three women, the mother, Moira presumed, appeared rather underwhelmed and seemed to be scanning the room for a seat. Her hair, swept high above her head in a silver beehive, resisted any movement. A leaf, daring to have fixed itself to the side of her head, was the only indication that any physical exertion might have taken place. Of the two younger women, one stood awkwardly with her arms folded and her legs crossed—she looked more than a little on edge. The other, the youngest of the group, appeared to have what looked like nearly all the clothes she had once been wearing tied around her middle. Her beaten-up rucksack, slung over her shoulder, was covered all over in brightly coloured badges. Moira noticed that she seemed particularly shy, embarrassed perhaps.

"Did you want something?" Alice's question to the visitors was more cold accusation than warm welcome.

Moira smiled warmly at the gathered group, quickly intervening with, "Hello. Welcome to Newland Forest Trust's Education Centre. I'm Moira Burns, and this is my colleague, Alice Campbell. How can we be of help?"

Henry stepped forward and firmly shook Moira's hand. "We're very pleased to meet you. I'm Henry Eddison, this is my wife Lillian, and our daughters Esther and Eve. We're on our holidays and have just enjoyed our first expedition—"

Eve looked up. "I'm sorry did you say education centre?"

Moira smiled and said gently, "Yes." She watched Eve swallow, and her flushed cheeks glowed to an even deeper red.

Lillian could not conceal her disappointment and hopelessly blurted out, "We were rather hoping for a skinny cappuccino."

Before the Eddisons could apologize and leave with what little dignity they had intact, Moira was filling the kettle and asking how they took their coffee.

Henry shook his head. "Oh gosh, that's not necessary, really, we're—"

"Gasping. Yes, milk no sugar." Lillian finished Henry's sentence very much as if she had started it.

"We've no milk," Alice said, abruptly. Her tone suggested that the sentence continued in her head with *so you may as well go.*

Mugs were filled and Moira handed the coffee around.

Eve stared at the floor, fixing her gaze away from the humiliating scene.

"Here." Moira handed Eve a biscuit.

"Oh, no, thank you." Eve raised her eyes so as not to be rude.

Meeting Eve's glance, Moira smiled, asking, "Are you sure?"

Eve felt a rush of self-consciousness, nodded, and blushed. To her increasing embarrassment the woman seemed a little slow to move away and Eve could see that she was looking at her, at her outfit.

"I wasn't expecting the sun." Eve shrugged in the direction of her wellington boots.

"No, it's okay, I wasn't…" Moira paused.

Eve thought she saw the woman's cheeks colour.

Moira continued, "It doesn't always rain in Scotland, you know."

"No, I know," Eve said, quickly, removing her rain hat and patting her hair into place. "And I also know you don't have midges all year round."

Moira nodded and broke into a smile again.

Impressing herself with her expert knowledge, Eve suggested, "And you probably don't wear kilts. Or eat haggis."

Moira replied diplomatically, "Well...some do."

"Oh, of course," Eve said, flustered. "I'm sure that it's a delicious favourite." *Oh my God. Stop talking. Stop talking now.*

Henry piped up, beaming with pride, "We've just come down from the mountain."

Alice and Moira looked quizzically at each other.

"Oh, you've come over the hill," Alice said, with a flat, decidedly unimpressed tone.

There was a pause, as the Eddisons took in the news that the mountain they had just bravely conquered was considered by the locals to be less of a Ben Nevis and more of a Murray mound.

Henry looked deflated.

"Yes"—Eve cleared her throat—"that's right. Although I think we all feel like we've climbed a mountain."

"Well, it's good that you are enjoying the walks here. Are you staying locally?" Moira directed her question back at Eve.

Before Eve could reply, Lillian gasped with pride, "Yes, oh yes, Loch View, Loch View." Lillian held her hand to her throat as she spoke, as if the thought of the magnificence of their holiday accommodation had momentarily all but overwhelmed her.

Eve watched Alice smirk into her drink. Somewhere in her early twenties, Alice was pretty and her long straight blond hair was scraped back in a plaited ponytail. She was tall and rested one hand on her hip as she spoke. She was casually dressed in jeans and a cream jumper and trendy outdoor shoes. She looked kind of mountain ski-style cool. Eve was certain Roxanne would approve.

"Yes. It's a lovely spot," Moira said. "I live next door in Foxglove Croft—the building attached to Foxglove, the main house."

Eve felt a tingle of recognition at Moira's reply. *The Land Rover driver?*

Eve braved a glance at Moira. With unkempt greying curly hair, bearing the imprint of having been wearing a cap, Moira appeared to be in her forties maybe. She wore lightweight black walking trousers and a grey fleece. Each pocket of her trousers seemed to contain something. Eve could see twine dangling out of a leg pocket and what looked like a piece of twig emerging from the left pocket at her hip. A whistle hung loosely from her neck. She was clearly dressed to work in the woods, to walk the hilltop bogs and the heather moors. Her muddy walking boots confirmed Eve's suspicions. She was obviously the more outdoorsy of the two women. She was dressed for action, Eve decided, rather than for the superficial whims of fashion.

Action woman, hey? Eve caught Moira's eye. Eve immediately took a *was definitely not checking you out* gulp of her drink. Moira shifted slightly and resettled.

"Oh, how lovely," Lillian said, resting both hands at her throat. Her eyes flickered over Moira.

Eve suspected her mother was trying to place their neighbour on the lawn at six, with Moira valiantly negotiating a bobbing olive in her pre-dinner martini.

Alice scoffed, "Yes, *amazing* isn't it, given that holiday lets normally push out the locals to steal the best views." Alice leant back slightly, her arms folded unapologetically in front of her, her eyes avoiding Moira's.

Lillian's expression turned to one of horror at the thought of being complicit in a crime. "But surely," she stammered back at Alice, "I would imagine tourists are important too?"

"Oh yes, we're very pleased to welcome visitors to Newland," Moira quickly intervened, "of course." As she said this, she glanced at Eve, who smiled self-consciously in response.

At that moment two children bustled in, nets in hand. Moira promptly told them to leave their nets against the wall and to wash their hands at the painting sink. With this interruption, the Eddisons took their leave.

❖

Moira found it difficult to sleep that night. She gave up trying and stood waiting for her stovetop kettle to come to the boil. She filled her mug with camomile tea and leant against the worktop. A hen squawked and she instinctively looked at the kitchen window, which by day, revealed the beauty of the hills and loch, and by night, became a black mirror. Moira looked at the reflection of the woman looking back at her. The curls of her hair, wild, the creases around her eyes signalling the pathways of past expressions. Her mouth, sad perhaps, she thought, turning down at the edges. The white letter *S* on her black T-shirt stood out, illuminated by the kitchen light. The surface of the letter was cracked and worn. Moira placed her hand over the letter in an urgent way, as if she was checking that it was still there.

Staring back absorbed by her reflection, Moira felt the years rushing back towards her youth. She was twenty again, dancing in her T-shirt, moving with the crowd, looking up at the stage, her heart beating strong and fast with the rhythmic music. Moira felt her head spin and opened the kitchen door to seek relief from the warm night in the hope that it would still her heart. In doing so, she disturbed a hen.

"*Shh* now, *shh.*"

Moira looked at the windows of Loch View, worried that she might have disturbed her neighbours. She found herself smiling again at the thought of the Eddisons, at the thought of Eve. She recalled Eve's face, her smiling, shy eyes, and instinctively reached again for the *S* of her T-shirt, resting her hand once more across her chest.

The blinking headlights of a car travelling along the road on the opposite edge of the loch intermittently illuminated the dark surface of the distant water. She watched the moving light, the flickering movement inducing a trancelike state and the beginnings of sleep.

Moira took one last look at the windows of Loch View. She wondered how long the Eddisons were staying. The dark curtained windows gave no clue. Shaking her head, closing her kitchen door firmly, Moira chastised herself. "What does it matter to you, Moira Burns, what does it matter?"

❖

Eve kept playing the scene at the centre over and over in her head. *I can't believe we thought it was a coffee shop, oh my God, how embarrassing. Wait till Rox finds out—I'll never hear the end of it.* Startled by a hen squawking, Eve looked across to the window, just visible in the moon-lit night. She nestled down into her sheets and closed her eyes. She called to mind the two women at the centre, the aloof hot blonde and the friendlier neighbour. Eve's mouth felt dry and her body hot. She swallowed, pulled the bedding down from her torso, and reclosed her eyes.

In that private, blurry space between awake and asleep, the friendly neighbour stood smiling, drawing Eve towards her. Aroused by the unexpected images conjuring themselves in her head, Eve moved her left hand across her chest; she could feel her heart beating. Thoughtlessly, sleepily, her right hand slipped beneath the sheets. She imagined herself undressing slowly, deliberately in front of the woman, who kept smiling, beckoning, and inviting...

A hen squawked again and flapped outside. Eve rolled over. "Eve Eddison, it's your Land Rover fetish." And with this giggly thought Eve drifted off to sleep.

CHAPTER FOUR

E ve woke to her phone beeping with a text. *Just got back from night shift (yawn) had patient in A&E tell me that he had seen the Loch Ness Monster. Thought of you. R X* Eve pulled on her dressing gown, drew back the curtains, and sat heavily on the window seat. Squinting from the bright morning light, she dialled Roxanne's number.

"Och aye the noo!"

Eve moved her ear briefly away from the speaker as Roxanne's voice bellowed down the phone.

"So, bored, eh?" Eve asked with a giggle.

"Absolutely not," Roxanne said, with a serious tone. "I have watered your plants, eaten the last of your custard creams, and graded each *BBC Breakfast* presenter's outfit out of ten."

"Wow, hectic. And? No, let me guess. Carol the weather girl, top marks again?"

"No, she looks a little frazzled."

"I know how she feels. We did this long hilly walk yesterday. It was good, but Rox, I'm knackered today." Eve could hear Roxanne munching. "I thought you'd finished the custard creams?"

"Yes, I have, but now I've moved on to your ginger nuts." Roxanne failed to suppress an immature snigger. "I know strictly speaking there's nothing funny about ginger nuts but…"

Eve could hear the clucking of next door's hens. She could also hear the voice of her neighbour calling the hens to feed.

"Why can I hear chickens?" Roxanne asked. "You sound like you're on a farm."

"It's our neighbour—she keeps hens. We met her yesterday in fact. She works for the Newland Forest Trust. She's nice."

"The what?"

"The land around here's owned by the local community, she works for them."

"Oh, right. You seem to know a lot about her."

"No, not really," Eve said, matter-of-factly. "Like I said, we bumped into her yesterday."

"Okay. So any Highland McTotty?"

"I've only been here a day, Rox, give me a chance."

"Well you seem to have got to know all about Newland and the chicken woman already." There was a pause. "Is the chicken woman hot?"

As Roxanne spoke, Moira came into view. She was dressed in blue cords and a green and blue chequered shirt.

Eve watched as Moira's shirt blew in the wind, hugging against her with each gust. Whether it was because Eve had fantasized about Moira the night before, or whether she was not expecting to see her, Eve found she couldn't take her eyes off her.

"Eve?"

"Huh? Sorry, Rox."

"So, this neighbour, worth asking for a private woodland tour?"

"No, I mean, I don't know. I mean, I need a tea. I've just woken up. Oh my God." Eve ducked below the window.

"Eve, what?"

"She saw me looking at her."

"Why are you whispering? Who saw you looking?"

"The neighbour. Oh my God, she's going to think I'm a perv."

Roxanne asked, with complete seriousness, "Why? Is she naked?"

"Naked? No. Why would she be feeding her hens naked?"

"Well then, why would you think she would think you were perving? Unless, of course, you were. Oh my God, *you were.*"

Eve over-protested, "No."

"Okay, just one question will settle this. Has she got curly hair?"

"I don't know, I can't remember."

"Can't remember? As if. Have another look."

"What? No. I can't look again. I'm going to have to crawl out of my room. That's what I'm going to have to do."

On her knees, Eve crawled underneath the window, emerging from her bedroom onto the landing, with her phone pressed to her ear.

"Morning." Esther, freshly showered and immaculate, looked down at Eve, somewhat confused.

Eve quickly said, "It's my back, it goes sometimes." She eased herself up, held the small of her back, and stretched. "There, that's better. You look a little tired, you okay, sis?"

Esther nodded, and with an amused, somewhat suspicious smile, said, "Tea? Mum and Dad have gone to the local shop for supplies for a barbecue tonight."

"Sounds cool. Yes, please, to tea. I'll be down in a sec. I'm just on the phone to Rox."

Eve watched Esther disappear downstairs.

"Your back? Don't you mean your mind?" Roxanne asked through a mouthful of ginger nut.

"Yes, thank you for your morning input, Rox."

"Pleasure. Oh, and Eve, keep me updated on the naked curly-haired chicken neighbour situation."

"She wasn't naked."

"Yeah, whatever you say."

"I'll give you a ring tomorrow, Rox. See ya."

Roxanne, despite the teasing, always made Eve feel good. She also, Eve was certain, had a way of knowing when Eve fancied someone, whether or not Eve herself was yet to realize.

Eve opened the french doors from the kitchen. She drank her morning tea seated on the steps to the garden, gazing sleepily at the softly shifting waters of the loch. She couldn't imagine a more beautiful place.

Eve glanced across to the neighbouring fence. All was quiet.

With tea in hand, accompanied by the odd yawn or two, she took a leisurely, sleepy stroll around the garden.

The garden of Loch View was orderly and yet kind of wild at the same time. Rocky mounds were littered with border plants and areas of grass were allowed to grow long for meadow flowers to flourish.

Eve let the smooth grasses and soft flower heads run through her fingers. Rain in the night had left a reviving, sweet, oxygenated air. Eve could smell coconut. *Okay, odd.*

As she pottered by the lower part of the neighbour's fence, she was startled by a kerfuffle at the bird feeder, on the other side of the garden.

Eve spluttered, "No way. That's so funny."

A pheasant had managed to land itself on the feeder, which rocked precariously.

Before Eve could fetch Esther, she heard a familiar voice from over the fence observe, "They're not the brightest."

Eve jumped.

"I'm sorry. I didn't mean to startle you," Moira said, standing facing Eve, spade in hand, smiling.

"Oh, no, it's okay. Hi." Eve felt herself blush as she tried to gather herself together. Should she mention perhaps that she was just taking in the view from her window? No, on reflection that sounded…pervy. She could say, *I wasn't looking at you earlier*, but then no, that would be rude. Eve desperately searched for something to say that wouldn't give Moira the impression she was weird.

Looking over to the birds, Eve said, "They're very pretty though, I mean the colours and everything. It's the male isn't it, that, you know, looks the prettiest?"

Moira nodded. "Need to look their best to attract a mate, poor things—a lot of pressure really for them."

"Yeah," Eve said with a shrug. "It's not like they can just hang out in their dressing gown and slippers, I mean, it's not like they'd have much chance to pull like that."

There was a slight pause.

Moira briefly glanced up and down at Eve.

Eve felt her stomach drop. *Oh my God.*

Eve looked at her slippers, placed her mug on the ground, and wrapped her dressing gown more closely around her.

"No, indeed"—Moira cleared her throat—"although, of course, you don't see that many pheasants in their dressing gowns."

Eve said emphatically, "Well, my point exactly, we know why."

Moira looked down and shook her head in amused disbelief that she was engaging in a conversation which she knew to be completely ridiculous but at the same time felt peculiarly insightful.

Before Eve could politely excuse herself, a second pheasant, a female, joined the first.

"Really?" Eve puffed out her cheeks. "Something's gotta give."

Sure enough, the feeder toppled, causing an ungainly flap of feathers and the spilling of seeds onto the lawn and nearby step. The smaller birds let out a united chirp of disapproval, as the two culprits strutted nonchalantly away.

Moira leant against the fence, elbow propped, left hand casually supporting her chin. She was watching Eve who was captivated by the pheasants.

"Blimey, they're a hazard aren't they?" Eve said, her gaze falling to Moira's hand. *Okay—no wedding ring.*

"Yes, troublesome. Need some help?" Moira pointed to the fallen bird feeder.

"Oh." Eve felt a little panicked. "I don't know, I don't want to trouble you."

Moira gestured towards her vegetables. "The beans can wait."

"Well, if you're sure, then, yes, thank you. I'll let you in." Eve felt herself blush again. She suspected that she had been blushing for most of their conversation.

"Okay, I'll get my toolkit." Moira fixed her spade firmly into the ground and headed to her croft. Stopping at the door to bang her boots free of mud, she glanced back at Eve.

Without thinking Eve waved goodbye. She had no idea why she was waving at her. She was seeing her in a few minutes.

Moira nodded in acknowledgement and then disappeared into her croft.

Turning towards Loch View, Eve paused. *Toolkit, eh?* Eve looked back towards where Moira had stood. *Nah, it's her job isn't it? Not everyone is gay, Eve Eddison, not everyone. I mean straight women can be good at DIY can't they? I mean, there's...* As Eve walked towards the house, her reflection in the french doors reminded her, once more, that she was in her dressing gown. *I'm such a tit!* "Esther." Eve called her sister for help. "Our neighbour's coming over to help put the bird feeder back up."

"What?" Esther called in confusion from the kitchen. "What's wrong with the feeder? Eve?"

Eve bounded up the stairs. "You'll need to let her in."

Eve, rushing, pulled on her jeans and her favourite FatFace blue hooded top. Giving her bed-hair a ruffle back into shape, she checked her look in the mirror.

"Okay you're behaving like a fool. Why do you care what she thinks? She's just the nice woman from next door. It's not a date, calm it down." Eve tried to breathe slowly in and out. "Calm it down."

❖

"Hello again." Reappearing in the garden, Eve spoke as nonchalantly as she could manage.

Moira looked up from working on the fallen feeder. She wiped her cheek with the back of her hand, tucked a curl of hair behind her ear, and replied with a smile, "Hello again."

"Here you go, milk no sugar, right?" Esther emerged, balancing three mugs in her hands. "It's Moira, isn't it?" Esther asked, handing Moira her tea.

"Thanks. Yes, that's right. I'm sorry, are you Esther or Eve?"

"I'm Esther, Esther Roberts." Esther paused, her eyes, for no apparent reason, filled with tears. "Pleased to meet you."

Eve rubbed her sister's arm. "It's okay."

Looking anxiously at Eve, Esther frowned. "Should I be using Eddison now?"

Eve shrugged, taking her tea. "I don't know how it works. All I know is that he was a complete bastard for cheating on you and you did absolutely the right thing dumping him. No question about that."

Esther thrust her shoulders back, stuck out her chest, and took a deep breath. "Anyway—what does it matter?" Esther directed the question at Moira, who gave a blank look in reply.

There was an awkward pause in the conversation.

"I'm sorry about that whole coffee thing yesterday. You must have thought we were bonkers," Eve said.

"You weren't the first to make that mistake and you won't, I'm sure, be the last, although"—Moira blew over her tea to cool it—"you were admittedly the first to request a skinny cappuccino."

Eve placed her hand over her face with embarrassment.

"It's our mother's favourite, you see. Sorry about that," Esther said, chuckling at Eve's reaction. She placed a protective arm around Eve and gave her a squeeze. "And this is my sister, Eve Eddison. Right, I'll leave you guys to it. Nice to meet you, again, Moira."

"Yes, you too, Esther."

Behind Moira's back, Esther gave Eve a wide-eyed knowing look.

Eve returned the glare with a look of exaggerated puzzlement.

When Roxanne had let slip to Esther that Eve was a lesbian, Esther had not commented either way. Eve sensed there had probably been much discussion about what the Eddisons should do about the *gay thing*, which Eve had been grateful that she had not been party to. Eve had noticed, however, that since the revelation, Esther would, now and then, give her sister the knowing wide-eyed glare, after spotting that Eve liked someone or that someone was paying Eve particular attention. Esther's gaydar was, however, somewhat unnervingly hit and miss. After all, less than a month ago, Eve had explained to an earnest Esther that no, the lollipop lady didn't fancy her, because unless Esther hadn't noticed, she stopped the traffic for everyone. Esther had taken the opportunity to suggest to Eve that she should be open to all possibilities.

Moira gave the feeder a nudge. "It's not going anywhere for now, but it probably needs concreting in. But that's for the owner to do."

"Okay. Right." Eve stood looking fixedly at the feeder, with her hands on her hips. She hoped her stance suggested knowledgeable consideration, but she rather feared Moira could tell she was in fact thinking, *Yeah, I haven't a chuffing clue*. "Thanks, Moira."

Despite having mended the feeder and finished her tea, Moira did not seem to be in any particular hurry to return to her beans. She continued chatting happily with Eve. She pointed out the names of the hills, lochs, and hamlets Eve could see from the garden.

It was becoming clear to Eve that, effortlessly and without a hint of arrogance, Moira Burns could likely identify each flower, fern, shrub, and tree that blanketed Newland. Eve felt certain that the landscape of Newland was as familiar to Moira as the face of her dearest friend.

Eve enthused, "It's so beautiful here, Moira, really, so beautiful."

Moira blushed in response.

"Refill?" Eve held out her hand for Moira's mug. The Eddisons' car could be heard pulling into the drive.

Moira looked towards the driveway. "Best get back to my beans." Seeing a fleeting look of disappointment on Eve's face, Moira added, "I'm leading a walk tomorrow afternoon, if you, and your family, of course, want to join in. It's just through the woods. It starts at two, if you can make it, that is."

"What starts at two?" Henry stood smiling broadly at Moira.

Moira held out her hand. "Hello again, Mr. Eddison."

Henry shook Moira's hand firmly. "Henry, please. Thank you for your hospitality yesterday. Much appreciated by all. So, what's happening at two tomorrow?"

Eve said, smiling admiringly at Moira, "Moira's leading a woodland walk."

"Yes, from the centre," Moira said, smiling back at Eve. "Just sturdy shoes will be fine. Unless, of course, it rains, then walking boots would be better." Moira looked at Henry's sandals.

"Well, that sounds great—count me in." Henry beamed at Moira.

"Great, well, I'll see you then." Moira turned to Eve, and said softly, "Thank you for the tea and the chat."

Eve blushed. "See you tomorrow."

Chapter Five

Eve arrived fifteen minutes late for the woodland tour. She had missed the introductory talk, which had helpfully included orientation, and caught up with the group at a collection of wooden totem poles. Eve stood partially hidden behind the small gathering of two couples, listening to Moira's instructions.

"The wildlife here in Newland is quite used to us humans." Moira addressed her walking group with a relaxed, open, and confident demeanour. "That said, remember to take care to stay on the designated paths as we walk. We will stop regularly to take a break. Ask any questions that occur to you as we go along."

One couple, German and well suited to the outdoors, had explained at the start that they could sadly only stay with the tour for a short while, as they were completing the West Highland Way to Inverness. The other couple, young, from Surrey and on their honeymoon, kept looking furtively for lovemaking spots. The group soon lost them by a grassy mound.

"Right, shall we carry on?" Moira cast her eye over her walking group, her gaze briefly resting on Eve.

Eve felt herself blush and raised her hand to wave hello.

Moira simply looked away without acknowledging their brief exchange.

Eve looked quickly down. She felt mortified and leapt to the conclusion that Moira had only invited her on the walk to be polite. Just the sight of her had obviously made Moira instantly regret her offer.

"Are these willows?" The German husband squinted into the canopy above.

Moira nodded. "Yes, that's right, Otto, these willows are part of our diversity plan, along with the Scotch pine and downy birch." Moira then pointed to the forest floor. "The brash piles between the trees provide excellent habitats for invertebrates."

Moira's voice was smooth and lyrical. Eve could have listened to her all day.

"Everything is really vibrant," Eve chipped in, "really green, almost fluorescent."

"Yes. I agree with that statement." Otto's wife, Gertrud, held Eve's forearm tightly, in a gesture of physical and intellectual togetherness. "Nourishing. Yes, it's all very nourishing."

Moira made no comment as she guided the group further into the woods.

Eve pulled up the hood of her raincoat, stuffed her hands into her pockets, and gave a sharp sniff. She regretted talking so much yesterday, certain that Moira was thinking, *Better not encourage that loon to start talking—never shut her up.*

Looking up into the trees, Moira pointed above her. "You will see that we have been working hard to thin out the denser pinewood, to allow more light onto the forest floor. We have already seen that this method is producing a better diversity and quality of forest flora."

Eve tipped her head back and squinted into the canopy of soft hazy green. The sunlight shone through the trees, dissolving their definition, breaking them down into shining, intense colour. Eve held her hand over her eyes, shielding them from the sunlight, and watched as the space between her fingers glowed orange.

The sting of Moira's rejection smarted in her chest. Eve closed her eyes, the impression of the trees imprinted on her closed lids, and for the briefest of moments she was sixteen again, zipped up in a sleeping bag, blinking into a bright light, and trying her best not to care.

"No—not yet, Evie Eds. Okay, I'm dressed. You can look now."

Eve dropped her hands from her face and looked straight into the blinding light of Roxanne's torch.

"You're sooo easy to play pranks on, Evie." Roxanne tucked herself into her sleeping bag as Eve blinked until her vision became less green.

"You're sooo dead." Eve shoved her pillow onto Roxanne's face, smothering her briefly. She stopped, let Roxanne take a breath, and then smothered her again before she could speak. Eve could hear a muffled sorry *through the cotton and feathers. "What's that? I can't hear you." Eve removed the pillow and grinned mischievously at her best mate.*

"Sorry." Roxanne spat out a feather with her words.

Eve lay on her back in her sleeping bag, looking up into the triangles of stitched canvas. The tent roof, propped perilously off the groundsheet with large sticks, still with the odd leaf attached, was, well, more droop than roof.

Eve mumbled apologetically, "Sorry I forgot the tent poles."

"Uh-huh."

"I thought Mr. Pugh was going to burst something. Did you see that vein on his temple throbbing?" Eve attempted to deepen her voice, sounding less like Mr. Pugh and more like Scooby-Doo. "Eve Eddison. You are sixteen. How on earth are you going to get through life, let alone through your Duke of Edinburgh? *I mean, that's not very encouraging is it?"*

Roxanne said, matter-of-factly, "He's a prick."

"Not a fan of pricks then?" Eve giggled, pulling her sleeping bag up under her chin.

Roxanne said flatly, "No."

Eve rolled on her side, to face Roxanne. "I'm now lying on the zip. Yeah, I'm not very keen on camp—"

"I like girls. Not boys. Girls." Roxanne turned her head to Eve, who gave a short series of blinks in reply. "It's okay, you're quite safe. I don't fancy you. I mean, God, no." Eve blinked again. "Look, just forget about it. I'm knackered. Goodnight." Roxanne turned over, away from Eve.

Eve lay on her back looking at the silhouette of branches casting their eerie shadow on the canvas roof. She flicked the torch off. Why wouldn't you fancy me? I mean—what's wrong with me?

"Shall we?" Moira pointed to a series of small steps which meandered down a slope dotted with clusters of clover.

Eve blinked into Moira's smiling eyes. She pulled down her hood and looked around, feeling slightly startled, like a person woken suddenly from sleep.

"It's just us," Moira said, gently. "I'm afraid we've lost our walking companions. And it seems we lost a few before we began."

Confused, Eve said, "I'm not sure, you see I missed the beginning of your talk and then—"

Moira clarified, "Your family?"

"Oh, yeah. Esther was ill in the night. Dodgy sausage. We had a barbecue last night. We may have overdone it with the firelighters. Everything was overdone before it was done." Eve shrugged.

Moira nodded, biting her lip, no doubt to stop herself from laughing. Eve wondered whether Moira had seen the billowing barbecue smoke from her croft.

"So, well, my parents have stayed with her." Eve folded and unfolded her arms as she spoke, before settling on shoving her hands in her pockets.

"Right. Well I hope Esther feels better soon. Have you enjoyed this afternoon?" Moira asked, with an uncertain tone.

Eve had found being ignored by Moira anything but enjoyable. Eve said cheerily, "Yeah, great. Thanks."

"I would normally carry on my tour for a bit longer but as it's just us you probably want to go home." Moira dropped her rucksack from her shoulders. She bent down, reaching for her water bottle.

Eve watched as Moira took a long drink. Her gaze fell to Moira's lips pressed tightly against the rim of the bottle, then to her throat, her neck, the curls of her hair brushing against her collar. Eve's eyes trespassed their way down to Moira's shirt, her buttons stretching the cotton against her chest.

"I don't mind. I mean whatever you...whatever you...think."
Eve knew she was talking, just not what she was saying.

Eve looked up from Moira's chest straight into Moira's quizzical expression. *Oh my God, caught looking at her boobs.* Eve quickly looked at her boots.

Moira asked, "No wellies today then?"

"Nope. I borrowed these boots from Esther. They're a bit big. I'm wearing two pairs of socks."

Eve bent down to show Moira as if showing her would be the only way Moira would believe her. When Eve glanced up, she saw that Moira quickly looked away down the path to watch the German couple disappear into the distance.

"I think it's best if I walk you to the main road, Eve, and then it will be easier for you to make your way back home."

"Great, thanks, Moira." Eve felt her heart sink with disappointment.

The path to the main road was just wide enough for two people to walk side by side, and every now and then, Moira and Eve would rub shoulders to avoid a rock or tree trunk. When this happened, Eve felt Moira's body intensely. Eve could not tell whether Moira felt this too—she appeared to be focused on the path ahead.

The air was heady, sweet, intoxicating almost. Now and then, Moira would comment on a flower, or mention an interesting fact.

"I love that you know so much about the natural world," Eve said.

Moira shrugged. "You get to know over the years."

"You've lived in Newland long?"

"Born and bred. I studied horticulture in Ayrshire for a few years and then lived and taught in Inverness in my twenties, but really I'm happiest when I'm here."

"Yeah, I bet." As Eve said this, she was looking around her, at the trees, the glimpses of views of distant hills, and the mountains. "The air's so sweet, so fresh." Eve caught a smell of coconut again. "This is going to sound odd, but now and then, I can smell, I don't know, coconut?"

Moira pointed to a yellow spiky bush. "Gorse flower."

Eve walked over to the bush and breathed in the familiar fragrance. "Wow, that's so cool—weird, but cool."

"And this?" Moira reached into her coat pocket and held out a thin branch with delicate yellow flowers.

Tentatively, Eve leant forward and half recognized the smell. "Okay. I know it, let me think."

Moira watched Eve frown.

"Leave it with me," Eve said, with a nod. "I shan't be beaten. Challenge on." Eve took the flower from Moira and tucked it into her pocket. "I really like cut flowers. I buy them from our local market in the city. I love tulips—yellow ones are my favourite, although they've got such a short life. I put a two pence piece in the water, it seems to make them last longer but…"

Moira watched Eve as she walked beside her, happily chatting, turning now and then to Moira and smiling. It seemed as if Eve brought with her warmth and light, thawing the coldness, banishing the darkness by her presence.

"Yeah, I'm not keen on carnations. I mean they last like weirdly ages but I don't know. The Queen hates them apparently so, well, enough said. So yeah. Do you have a favourite flower?"

Moira tilted her head in thought. "I suppose the flowers remind me of the seasons. I find I notice the first snowdrops and I like to see the bluebells in the woods."

"I bet it's really beautiful here all year round." Eve stopped to look into the woodland, staring silently into the many shades of sun-misted green.

Speaking towards the woods, Moira said, "It constantly changes. I don't think, even after all these years, I've seen the same view from one hour to another."

"Yeah, I can see that. Oh, my lace. I'll just…there." Eve sat down to tie her bootlace. Immediately, she spotted an ant scooting across her shoe. "Oh my God, ant." She flicked it away.

"Eve, you need to stand up," Moira said, with an urgent tone.

"I'm sorry?"

Moira grabbed Eve's arms and pulled her up.

Moira saw that Eve was blushing. She felt Eve's hands at the sides of her shirt as Eve steadied herself. She could feel Eve's body pressing against her. She struggled to find her breath with the intense sensation that rushed through her body in response.

"Eve"—Moira swallowed hard—"you appear to have disturbed a termite nest."

Moira might just as well have said, *There's a bomb strapped to your trousers*, given the speed at which Eve, having spotted a rash of ants at her crotch, took her trousers down.

"Really? I'm not at all keen on ants, or for that matter anything that wriggles, you know spiders, snakes, and things."

Moira bent down to untie Eve's laces.

With one hand resting on Moira's shoulder for balance and the other wrestling with her boots, Eve managed to wriggle out of her jeans. She shook them frantically.

"Is that all of them?" Eve was spinning around and desperately looking over her shoulder. "Please tell me it is!"

Moira slowly turned Eve around. "Yes, all gone."

Without warning, Eve dumped her rucksack on the floor and lifted her raincoat, revealing her shirt, and then bare torso. Moira wasn't sure where to look.

Eve gasped. "Really? It feels like they're all over me."

With a reassuring tone, Moira said, "No, they're all gone, don't worry."

"Are you sure?"

Moira nodded and smiled.

"Thank you." Eve looked down.

Moira rested her hand on Eve's right shoulder, as she asked, tenderly, "Did you want to put your trousers back on?"

"Hmm?" Eve looked into Moira's eyes.

"Your trousers—did you want to put them on, before you get a chill?"

But before Eve had a chance to react or reply, Angus McAlister appeared over the horizon of the path ahead, waving his walking stick in the air to announce his arrival. "Good afternoon, ladies."

Moira panicked, exposed by his sudden presence. Her heart raced and she quickly stepped away from Eve.

"Everything okay?" Angus was clearly trying not to look at Eve, who was scrambling back into her jeans.

"I sat on ants." Eve pointed towards the log seat. "Thank God, Moira rescued me. Hello. I'm Eve Eddison. I'm on holiday. Here. In Newland. I'm on Moira's woodland tour."

"Oh, I see. Hello, Eve. I'm Angus McAlister. I'm from here. Newland, that is."

To compose herself, Moira went over to the log bench and closely inspected the infestation, lifting leaves and twigs around the log. "I'll need to spray the area, best do it now. I'll collect some solution from the centre. The log will need to be removed for burning."

"I'll give you a lift to the centre—I've borrowed Margaret's ride. In fact, I can give you a hand." Angus nodded towards a wooded path.

Moira looked at Eve, who, every now and then, suddenly startled and slapped a part of her body. She couldn't help but smile.

"Can we drop Eve off on our way back here?" Moira gestured her chin towards a patiently waiting Eve.

"No, it's okay. I can make my own way home. Yes, I think it's that way to the main road?" Eve looked at Moira for confirmation.

The main road was in the opposite direction. "Yes, that's one way out, Eve, although perhaps you'd like to come with Angus and me."

"Well, yes, if you're sure." Eve smiled broadly at Moira.

"Right. Follow me." Angus saluted in the direction of a path that led out to a clearing. "Here we are. Now, where did I put the keys?"

"This isn't yours?" Eve stared at the red Land Rover in front of them.

Moira looked quizzically at Eve. "Mine? No, it belongs to Margaret, my neighbour a few doors down. Well, it's her late husband's. She lends it out to the centre now and then."

"Right," Eve said, somewhat forlornly.

Moira wasn't sure why Eve seemed so disappointed.

The road Angus took that led to the centre was less of a road and more of a woodland track. Where by rights there should have been tarmac, there were fallen pine branches, ferns, and flora. Where there should have been road signs there were bird boxes and what Eve deduced were education symbols. Every now and then the sun would haze its way through the woodland canopy illuminating the route and the trackside flowers that guided them. It was the most beautiful road Eve had ever driven on.

"So, how was your first Land Rover experience?" Moira held the door for Eve as she clambered down, on their arrival at the centre.

"How do you know it was my first?" Eve smiled.

"Ah, just guessing."

Eve suspected that not much guesswork had been required, as every time Angus had driven over anything a normal car couldn't cope with, she had gripped the dashboard with both hands.

Angus jumped down from the vehicle and disappeared into an adjacent shed. Eve followed Moira into the centre.

"Hello, Moira. Is that Angus? I was just shutting up. I wasn't entirely sure what your plans were," Alice said, looking at Eve.

"Hello again," Eve said cheerily.

"Hello." Alice's tone suggested to Eve that she was thinking, *And you're back again because now you want a hot chocolate?*

"I'll lock up. We're collecting termite spray, overalls, and the like." Moira looked behind Alice for the items she needed.

"I accidently disturbed them." Eve shrugged and smiled at Alice, who didn't smile back. *Okay. Rude.* "Moira saved me from them." Eve's words bubbled with admiration.

"Oh, I see." Alice briefly glanced at Moira, bent down at the cupboard.

"Yes. I mean, I think we got them off quite quickly." Eve was examining her clothes as she spoke, and when she looked up, Alice had already walked away towards the door. *Oh my God. What is your problem?*

"Oh and Moira, Mr. Hughes rang for Dad. I told him he'd be back again this weekend. Moira?"

Without looking up, Moira said, "Right, thanks, Alice. See you later."

Alice glanced again at Eve before leaving. It was almost as if in that briefest of moments she was deciding whether Eve was important and then quickly made up her mind that she wasn't.

"I'm sorry about Alice," Moira said.

Eve hadn't realized that Moira had noticed Alice's unfriendliness. "I get the sense that I'm not her favourite visitor." Eve shrugged her words towards the door.

"Yes, she's not the most tolerant of people but then—masks and overalls, ah yes." Moira stood from reaching into the cupboard. "Well, life hasn't been that kind to Alice. Not that that excuses her rudeness. I fear that if she's going to get through her work placement with us she'll need to develop her customer care skills."

"It's okay," Eve said, distractedly, not remotely interested in acerbic Alice, as she rested against a trestle table, waiting patiently for Moira, unable to take her eyes off her.

Moira asked, with a smile, "Are you staying in Newland long?"

"Two weeks. It's a bit far to come for anything shorter really. We're from the Midlands."

"Right, I see."

There was a moment of silence, a silence which felt sad.

"Here." Moira collected something from the reception desk. "To take back with you to the Midlands…to remember us. I didn't think you'd want the snake one."

"No." Eve giggled, looking at a leaf-shaped green pin badge with the word *Newland* embossed in gold lettering, resting in Moira's palm.

"You can add it to your badges, on your rucksack." Moira gestured towards Eve's bag tucked between her feet.

Eve felt her heart beating. Eve's badges were an out and proud collection of gayness. They featured rainbow colours, with slogans of *Glad to Be Gay, I can't even think straight*, and *Some people are gay, get over it*.

"I don't really collect badges as such," Eve said, stumbling slightly over her words. "My best mate, Rox, well, we agreed that we would collect a badge from every Pride festival we've been to. So between us that's about, wow, you know, at least eight. We've been to a few London Prides too. My rucksack is a fun place to display them I guess." Eve searched Moira's face for some sign of reaction. Nothing.

Had Moira guessed that she was gay? Eve wasn't sure how carefully Moira had read her badges. Was Moira familiar with Pride? Should she ask? Somehow it didn't seem right, and in any case if Moira didn't know about Pride, then that would likely mean that she wasn't gay, and that Eve would never...Eve swallowed and looked directly back at Moira. *Are you gay, Moira Burns? Everything about you tells me you are.*

"Can you?" Eve gestured towards the badge in Moira's hand.

Moira had expected Eve to take the badge from her and to pin it on her rucksack. Instead, Moira watched as Eve undid the zip of her raincoat, revealing her white linen shirt. She pulled the left side of the front of her shirt towards Moira. Moira leant forward and attached the pin, the edge of her hand resting briefly on Eve's chest.

Moira stood back.

"Thank you," Eve said quietly, adding, "for a lovely afternoon."

"My pleasure, Eve." Moira held Eve's gaze.

Eve broke their exchange by re-examining the badge resting against her chest.

Moira's eyes followed.

Holding the badge, Eve confessed, "I'll treasure it."

Moira swallowed deeply. Her beating heart choked at her throat. "Eve, I—"

"Okay, that's the solution loaded on board." Angus banged his feet on the coir matting as he entered the room. "Ready?"

Startled, Moira turned sharply to face Angus. "Yes. Ready."

Eve zipped up her raincoat.

Moira handed the masks and overalls to Angus. "I'm right behind you. I'll just lock up."

"No rush, no rush. Nice to meet you, Eve. Hopefully, you haven't been put off enjoying our wonderful woods." Angus extended his hand and Eve shook it firmly.

"No, no. I love it here. The woods and everything."

"Very good." Angus looked across to Moira and then briefly back at Eve before leaving, with the words, "Very good indeed," trailing behind him.

"Well…thanks," Eve said, turning away from Moira.

Moira wondered at the emotion in Eve's voice. "Eve?"

"Yep, bye then." Eve made quickly for the door.

Moira folded her arms and looked out the window, to watch Eve hurry away towards the main road. In the car park, Angus waved goodbye to Eve, who waved back. Just before she turned the corner out of view, Eve stopped. She was patting her pockets. Moira looked around the table where Eve had stood. She didn't seem to have left anything. When she looked out the window, Eve was walking back towards her.

Moira walked out into the car park to meet her.

"Have you forgotten something?" Moira glanced across briefly at Angus, who was leaning into the boot of the Land Rover. "Eve?"

Eve's face had turned pink. "Vanilla."

"Vanilla?" Moira asked, confused.

Digging into her pocket, Eve pulled out the yellow flower of the broom bush. "It smells of vanilla." Eve handed the flower to Moira, in a manner that someone presents a flower to someone they are declaring a passion for.

"Right, yes vanilla." Taking the flower from Eve, Moira felt her throat tighten again.

"Moira, I…I…"

Angus slammed shut the boot of the Land Rover. He called over, "Right, I'm ready to defend our woods from those munching invaders."

Moira turned around. "Okay, I'm right with you."

"No, no. I can cope on my own, Moira. You take Eve home. I think that's best. I'll catch up with you at the village meeting tonight."

Moira frowned. "Are you sure, Angus?"

"Aye, Moira." Tucking his empty pipe into his mouth, he started the engine and made his way back into the woods.

Moira returned her gaze to the flower in her hand.

"Sorry to make you walk me home."

Moira looked up at Eve, a slow smile drifting across her face. "Come on." Moira locked the centre and led Eve around the side of the building to the staff car park. Next to a red Fiesta was a blue-grey Land Rover.

"Yours?" Eve said, her mouth falling slightly open.

Moira nodded. "Well, I wouldn't want to disappoint you."

Eve said quickly, "I'm not disappointed—I mean, you don't disappoint me."

Blushing and looking down, Moira briefly glanced up to Eve. "I'm glad."

❖

Okay. You can do this—just get out of the vehicle. You have to go home now. You have to leave her. The prospect of leaving Moira's side was making Eve feel sick.

Esther waved from the kitchen window, attracting the attention of Lillian, who waved too. Moira and Eve waved back.

"Well..." Moira gave a long sigh. She sounded tired. The engine rumbled impatiently.

"Yes, see you later then."

Moira nodded in reply.

Eve clambered out of the Land Rover, holding her rucksack against her chest. She watched Moira release the handbrake. She was looking out in front of her. Eve closed the passenger door and watched Moira drive the few yards or so to her door.

"Moira!"

Moira was just about to step inside her croft when Eve rushed across the drive to her. She turned around.

Eve noticed that Moira wasn't smiling.

"I wanted to say thank you again, for helping me with the ants. I mean, I hope I wasn't too much of a drama queen." There was an awkward pause. Eve twitched and checked her sleeve.

"You may want to change your clothes, Eve. It will make you feel a bit more comfortable."

"Yes, good idea. I'm heading in for a long hot bath."

Moira nodded and turned to go inside.

Eve knew she should leave, that she'd said thank you and that with every second she stood there she was looking more of a nuisance.

"Have a good holiday, Eve."

Eve felt crushed, as if she'd been punched in the stomach. Moira might as well have said, *Get lost, loser.* She mustered self-control to say, "Yes, will do. Thanks again."

Just as Moira was about to close the door, Eve suddenly, and to her own surprise, blurted out, "I'm gay." *Okay, not keeping things to yourself then.*

Moira held the door in her hand. She looked serious for a moment. "I know, Eve, I know you're gay."

"Right, my badges."

Out of the blue, a woman called out, "See you at the meeting tonight, Moira."

"Yes, see you then, Margaret." Moira waved and dropped her arm heavily back to her side.

Eve turned around to see who had interrupted them. A woman carrying a wicker basket filled with sprouting veg was straining her neck to see who Moira was talking to.

Moira seemed to shift her feet impatiently.

"Well, I thought you might want to know for certain, I mean in case…" Eve stopped talking and swallowed.

Moira remained straight-faced. "I'm sorry, I don't want to be rude, but I've got a meeting to go to and I'm already running late."

"No, no, of course, sorry, of course." Eve turned around and walked towards Loch View. *Oh my God, keep walking, Eve. Don't look back.*

Eve let the front door bang shut as she hurried her way upstairs to her room.

"Eve? Eve, darling, is that you?"

"I'm having a bath and an early night. See you in the morning, Mum."

"What about your tea? Eve?"

"I'm not hungry, thanks anyway, goodnight."

"Is everything okay?"

"Yes," Eve called down with the most positive tone she could muster, before mumbling, "couldn't be better," under her breath.

❖

"Hi, Angus. It's Moira. Hi…Great, that's excellent. Thanks for doing the spraying today. About tonight's meeting—I'm afraid something's come up, I'll need to send my apologies…Yes, everything's okay…Yes, see you then…Okay, bye."

Putting down the receiver, Moira poured herself a whisky and sank heavily into her sitting room armchair. Her head hurt. She rubbed her tired face, breathing in the scent of vanilla on her hands. Digging into her coat pocket, she pulled out the slightly crushed yellow broom flower. Stroking the bruised petals back into shape, she gently placed it on the side table. She looked outside to her Land Rover parked in the driveway, gave a slow smile, and shook her head.

CHAPTER SIX

Eve was only just awake the next morning when her phone
rang. She spoke to Roxanne from underneath her duvet.
"It's not funny."

"No, of course, it's terrible." Roxanne snorted away her
laughter. "No, so, what happened again? I mean, what were you
doing to be sitting on ants?"

"I was on a walk. I was doing up my shoelace. How was I to
know that a colony of termites had taken up residence?"

"That's priceless, Eve, priceless. God, I bet your mum and
Esther freaked out."

"Well, that's another story. Esther got the squits from Dad's
barbecue, so they all stayed at home...Rox?"

Roxanne let out a whimper of pain from laughing so hard. "No,
no, I'm still here, just spilt my tea. Right, the Highland Shits? Well,
if it goes on too long, she'll need to see a quack. In the meantime,
Imodium, maybe?"

Eve yawned a muffled, "Okay," from behind her hand.

"You sound a bit tired."

"Yeah, I am."

"So it was a long walk yesterday?"

"Kind of. Well, it was a walking tour thing, although not many
turned up and it ended up being just me and Moira. And that's when
I made a complete tit of myself by sitting on the bloody ants."

"Moira?" Roxanne asked, a hint of intrigue in her voice.

"Our neighbour."

"What, the naked chicken lady?"

"Exactly, Rox, the naked chicken lady." Eve's sarcasm was unusual for her.

"Okay, mate, so she wasn't naked."

Eve paused. "I stood in my knickers and raincoat in front of her. What's more, I really like her, Rox, I *really* like her." Before Roxanne could comment, Eve continued, "I told her I was gay and she said she knew but then—"

"Stop, stop, stop. Back up. Why were you in your knickers?"

"I took my trousers off because they were covered in ants."

"Right. And was she pleased you'd taken them off?" Roxanne's tone suggested she was thinking, *Oh my God, what are you telling me?*

"Pleased? No, I don't think she was pleased. It wasn't a case of *Oh, thank God, I was desperate to see you in your knickers.* She seemed, I don't know, concerned."

"Concerned?"

"Yes, in a professional kind of way."

"Right, okay. Then how did the gay declaration come about?" Roxanne's voice betrayed her scepticism and growing concern.

"Well, we'd spent quite a bit of time together over the last day or so, and it felt, I don't know, Rox, it felt so easy to talk to her. It felt so good being with her, you know?" Eve's enthusiasm for Moira was met with silence, prompting Eve to conclude with, "It just sort of came out. She's really nice, Rox."

"I don't doubt it for a minute mate, it's just…"

"It's just what?"

"Nothing. So how did she take the gay thing?"

"Well, here's the thing, she didn't seem freaked out. She had a meeting to go to so—"

Roxanne said quickly, "Is that what she said, she had a meeting to go to?"

"Yes, she did, she wasn't just saying it, I mean…" Eve paused.

"So how did you leave things? When are you seeing her next?"

"I don't know. She wished me a good holiday and…"

Roxanne said, cautiously, "Right, okay, that's kind of non-committal."

"It's the kind of thing you say when you're not expecting to see someone again, isn't it?" Eve said, feeling pathetic and embarrassed. "She's not interested in me, is she?"

"Give her a chance, mate, you've only just met her. Although..." Roxanne spoke delicately. "She seems to be playing it a bit cool if she is, but you never know, you never know."

Eve was silent.

"Look, Eve, it's okay to flirt, there's no harm in it. She was probably very flattered."

"It isn't just about flirting." If Eve was honest, she wasn't entirely sure what it was all about.

"Right, well, of course, all I'm saying is, it's okay to like someone. It's just, well, she may not feel the same, that's all."

Eve fell silent again.

"Eve? *Anyway.* So you're never going to guess what happened to me at work last night. I stitched this patient's forehead wound up a little bit too tightly—left her looking like she'd just heard some surprising news—"

"Rox, perhaps, should I ask her out? Then I guess I'd know either way, wouldn't I?"

"*What?* Okay, who on earth is this chicken woman? And what spell has she cast on you? I mean, has she said she's gay? Eve, you're thinking of asking out a woman you've only just met, what, three days ago? And you don't even know whether she's into women or for that matter whether she's single. I mean, how old is she?"

Eve said quietly, "A bit older than me, maybe."

"And you say she's nice? She's unlikely to be single, mate."

Eve wanted to tell Roxanne that Moira didn't wear a wedding ring and that she thought Moira lived alone, but she knew that didn't help much.

As if suddenly remembering, Eve said, "She gave me a badge. She said it was for me to remember her."

"Is that what she said? For you to remember her?"

"Well, she actually said to remember us, but I know that she meant her, that it was a special gift for me." Eve started to have a terrible sinking feeling.

"That's nice, Eve. I'm sorry. I don't mean to piss on your parade. It's fun that you fancy someone on your hols, just take care, yeah? Don't do anything rash."

"I've lost it haven't I?" Eve asked, defeated.

"I didn't say that, mate."

"I've been coming on to some random Scottish woman. Oh my God, what was I thinking? I can't see her again," Eve said, with a mixture of adamant resolution and distress. "It'll be fine, in fact, there's no reason for me to see her again."

"You worry too much. Really, you do, Evie. Speak soon?"

Eve flapped back her duvet. The hens from next door squawked. "No reason at all to see her, no reason at all."

"Thank God you're up. I have to get out of here." Esther's eyes were wide with meaning. "Come on a walk with me?"

Eve looked at Esther's stomach. "Don't you still have the trots?"

"Let's put it this way: at this very moment, the prospect of shitting my knickers up a mountain is less painful and humiliating than listening to Mum tell me that she thinks it will be unsurprisingly hard at my age to find someone new. At my age? I'm thirty not eighty for flip sake."

Eve said, shaking her head, "I'm sure she didn't—"

"It gets worse. Despite that fact I nonetheless mustn't give up hope of finding someone *prepared* to love me." Esther pulled the door of Loch View firmly closed behind them.

Eve couldn't bring herself to look across at Moira's croft.

"*Prepared* to love me, for God's sake." Esther's voice strained with anger. "What does that flipping mean? What part of love requires *preparation*?"

Esther's fury had them striding out onto the main road. Eve watched Esther's face tighten as she visibly forced down her heartache into the ground with each step.

Esther briefly stopped walking and looked at Eve. "You know what the stupid thing is? I don't think I know what love is any more. I thought I knew."

Eve gave a sympathetic half-smile in response.

Esther continued with a sigh, "Maybe it does need preparation. Maybe I need to sit in a dark room chanting, opening up my chakra. What do you reckon?"

"I'm pretty sure I don't have a chakra," Eve said, her voice deadpan.

"No. I mean about the love thing."

Eve shrugged, shoving her hands into her pockets.

"Have you ever been in love, Eve?"

"I dunno," Eve said flatly, averting her eyes from Esther's questioning gaze.

Esther tucked her arm into Eve's. "Well that makes two of us."

Eve looked ahead, along the main road which was less of a main road and more of a grassy, gravelly track, snaking through the pastoral idyll of roadside crofts and cottages.

"Oh, Eve, this is a pretty cottage, look at the climbing roses above the door." No sooner had the word *door* left Esther's lips than she bent double, her face screwed up in agony, and her eyes desperate with alarm.

Eve gasped. "You okay? What is it? Do you need the loo? Is that it?"

Esther held the side of the cottage wall. She had begun to perspire.

"Oh dear, lassie." A soft, lyrical voice floated over the wall from the garden. "Can I help at all?"

"My sister's got an upset stomach," Eve explained to the kind stranger offering help.

The woman looked at Esther and repeated, "Oh dear," adding in a louder voice, "Angus, we have a young lady who needs our assistance."

"Hello again, Eve." Angus McAlister grinned broadly. "Come in, come in both. This is my wife, Elizabeth."

"The toilet's to the left, just by the stairs." Elizabeth shook her head in sympathy.

"Oh my God, I can't use their loo," Esther whispered into Eve's ear.

Eve shook her head. "I don't think you have a choice."

"Do we have some ginger, Angus? I'm thinking a warming ginger tea, yes?"

Angus nodded at her suggestion, and tucked an empty pipe in the corner of his mouth. He gestured for Eve to take a seat at their dining table.

"Thank you for your help," Eve said, blushing at Angus's smiling expression in reply.

Elizabeth filled teacups from a porcelain teapot decorated with blue and white flowers. The ivory white of the pot matched the hands that poured the tea.

"Eve?" Esther dug her sister in the ribs.

Eve's attention was drawn to the photos on the sideboard. "What?" She looked back to the table to find Elizabeth waiting with silver sugar tongs poised over a porcelain cup.

"Oh, no sugar, thank you," Eve said, returning her focus to the photos.

"She's eighteen there, Moira from the centre," Angus said. "Just about to go to college."

From within the brass frame, Moira smiled back at Eve. She was dressed in a red sweatshirt and blue jeans. Her soft freckles on the top of her cheeks and curly brown hair shone in the sun. The Newland hills were in the background. Moira looked happy and alive. *She looks beautiful.*

Angus picked up another photo of Moira chopping fallen trees with a chainsaw and handed it to Eve. "She was born to croft, to work the land. It's in her blood."

"Right," Eve said, with eyebrows raised. "They're big logs."

"Aye, we care for a variety of terrain. Our woodland is our particular joy."

Eve looked closely at Moira. Moira was older in the picture. She wasn't looking at the camera; her head was turned away towards the hills. She looked pensive, perhaps even sad. Eve looked towards Angus, who nodded back, as if absorbed in his thoughts, sucking on his empty pipe.

"Really, Angus, I'm sure Eve's not interested in our family photos." Elizabeth's cup softly knocked against its saucer as she placed it gently down.

"No, no. I mean…" Eve's cheeks tingled. She pushed her chair out from under her, the chair scraping along the tiled floor, and with care replaced the photo on the sideboard. "So is Moira your daughter?" Eve asked, her gaze lingering for a moment on Moira's photo.

Looking back at the McAlisters, Eve caught Esther's eye. Esther mouthed, *Stop being nosy.*

"In every way that matters," Elizabeth said, with a heart-breaking tenderness to her tone.

It struck Eve that this was an odd answer. She didn't like to ask what she had meant. Instead, she watched Elizabeth look at Angus and smile. It was a smile that seemed to drift from their lips to settle on shared recollections of times gone by.

Before returning to her seat, Eve cast her eye over the variety of other photos on the sideboard, filling the McAlisters' dining room with people, places, and precious moments in time. Angus and Elizabeth's wedding day. Angus stood tall, with Elizabeth's arm tucked in his. His tartan waistcoat and kilt declared his dedication to his country. His face, turned towards Elizabeth's, wore a soft, tender expression. Elizabeth's dress was delicate and demure. White lace sleeves ended at her wrists; intricate lacing ruffled at her neck.

Various picturesque Newland scenes adorned the polished sideboard. The McAlisters' cottage featured in many of the photos, taken at different times of the year. The garden appeared full of spring colour and then, in another shot, almost invisible against the white winter snow. Eve held one photo up to Angus. It showed a large group of people with spades and smiles. Eve recognized the landscape in the background as Newland's hilltop.

"We'd just got permission to set up a trust, to buy our own land," Angus confirmed with a proud nod.

"You're all looking very pleased," Esther said.

"Aye, aye. It just goes to show what a group can do as one mind, stronger together. We have so much to be proud of. And our work now extends out of Newland. We are becoming known for our pioneering outreach programme." Angus and Elizabeth shared a smile.

Putting back the village photo, Eve disturbed an unframed snap. A little dog-eared with a crease across it, and yellowing slightly at its edges, the snap was of a young woman in her twenties. She was shielding her eyes from the sun. There was a city scene in the background. *Inverness?* One strap of the young woman's blue dungarees had come undone. It didn't look like she cared.

"Iris Campbell." Elizabeth wistfully spoke into the room, almost as if her thoughts had formed themselves into words in the air.

Eve half whispered, "She's very pretty."

"Yes, she was very beguiling." Elizabeth's voice seemed to falter slightly. "A very good musician, mind."

Eve nodded. "Right."

Eve rested the unframed snap back to where it belonged against a framed picture of a smaller group, which included Moira and also a man with a full beard and mousey shoulder-length hair. Between them stood a young girl, curiously holding a large leek. The girl leant her head against Moira's side.

"The Campbells." Angus gestured his pipe towards the photo.

"Okay," Eve said, squinting with a frown. "Is the girl by any chance Alice, from the centre?"

"Yes, Alice, she'd have been…" Angus blew out his cheeks and scratched under his hat. "Well, let me think, she's twenty now…"

"Nine," Elizabeth said, tilting her head, "maybe ten."

"Well, I can't tell you how grateful I am," Esther said, gingerly getting to her feet. "We mustn't intrude on you any longer, must we? Eve?"

"Hmm?" Eve looked up and blinked. "Oh, no. Thank you." Eve smiled at Elizabeth, who smiled warmly back.

Accompanying them to the front door, Angus asked, "Are you staying long in Newland?"

"Yes," Esther replied. "We're staying a fortnight, aren't we, Eve?"

Eve nodded, "Absolutely."

"Wonderful." Angus smiled broadly. "Wonderful. And will we see you at the village dance, I wonder, this Saturday coming?"

"Village dance?" Eve's chest tightened. "I'm sorry, did you say dance?"

CHAPTER SEVEN

Why did you say yes to him, Esther? You know I can't dance." Eve held her hands in front of her face at the certain humiliation awaiting her.

At that moment everything felt too much for Eve. She was certain that she'd made a complete fool of herself over their neighbour. She felt sure her best friend thought she had lost the plot. And now, to top it all, she was expected to set aside her well-judged inhibitions to expose herself to the ridicule of complete strangers. And what was worse, her family seemed to think that that was okay.

"How could we say no?" Esther shrugged. "He looked so hopeful and they'd been so kind. In any case, it says they will show us how." Esther was rereading the leaflet Angus had given them.

"And that will improve my dancing in what way?"

Lillian entered the kitchen, apparently drawn by Eve's anguish like a moth to the flame. "I know dancing isn't your thing, Eve. I quite frankly have no intention of tripping the light fantastic." Lillian laughed at her own words, followed by the applause of her holiday flip-flops clapping against her heels as she crossed the room. "I can't make any promises for your father."

Eve caught a glimpse of Henry as he rehearsed in front of the hall mirror. He had his hands on his hips, working out which leg should be his lead leg for the *fling* part of the Highland fling.

"Ow." Eve gave Esther a look. *What the fuck?*

"Hold still then," Esther mumbled at Eve through a mouthful of hair grips.

Eve raised her eyebrows. "And the hat needs to be gripped to my skull, why?"

"You don't want to be worrying about your hat falling off do you?"

Eve wanted to say, *I'm worried about the hat staying on.*

"There, perfect." Esther stood back to admire her work.

Lillian and Esther had spent the morning cutting, sewing, and draping the fabric they had purchased the day before in Inverness. They had chosen to dress neutrally, in simple skirts and floaty blouses, finished off with a flourish of tartan sash draped delicately over their shoulder, and tied at the hip.

Since Eve refused to wear a skirt, her outfit had proven somewhat of a sartorial challenge.

Eve looked in the reflective cooker splashback.

"I'm sorry?" Eve glared at Esther, then at Lillian, and back at Esther.

"I've taken my inspiration from that Scottish seventies band—oh, now, what was their name again?" Esther looked to her mother.

"The Bay City Rollers." Lillian adjusted Eve's tartan beret as she spoke.

"Who?" Eve's voice strained with alarm.

"They were very popular, Eve. Your sister's been very creative."

To achieve Eve's outfit, Esther had fashioned tartan fabric into a floppy beret shape and hemmed the same material to artfully border Eve's trouser bottoms, collar, and cuffs.

"So, let's go. Henry," Lillian called out, summoning him from the bathroom.

Henry called through the door, "I'll follow on. You go ahead."

Eve was taken aback by how beautifully the village hall had been decorated for the dance. Bunting adorned the outside of the building, fluttering in bursts like the sound of birds flocking, taking to the evening sky above the heads of the revellers. Inside the hall, visible through the open door, large swathes of Highland tartan material billowed from the roof space.

"Gosh, that's really something, isn't it girls? We should have brought our camera." Lillian held her hand to her throat in evident wonder.

Eve grumbled to herself, "Yeah, a photo, that's just what we need—the memory of my outfit clearly not enough."

People had spilled out from inside the hall and were dancing, laughing, and sitting on the seats strewn around. An occasional wail of the bagpipe struck up. There were all ages present. Everybody seemed to know everybody else.

Eve saw Lillian look anxiously down the lane; there was no sign of Henry.

"Esther, you stay with me and let's find a table inside. Eve, darling, drinks." Lillian ushered a reluctant Eve towards the hall door.

The hall was crammed with people. Their excited chatter hummed in the room, now and then interspersed with startling shrieks of laughter. Eve found the drinks table creaking at its hinges under the array of home-brewed concoctions that greeted her.

The attractive, hand-painted label of Mrs. Mackie's prune and barley wine caught Eve's eye. Eve unscrewed the bottle, a sharp fizz escaped, and the sediment at the bottom floated, like a snow globe on the streams of bubbles. Eve risked a sniff. She felt the hairs in her nose burn and her eyes water. *One for Esther to avoid, maybe.* In fact, all of the homebrews on display, Eve suspected, would successfully clear a drain or at the very least one's bowels. "Oh, Jane's Jungle Juice." Eve raised her voice at the promising label.

"It's not local but it's very good." A voice came from behind Eve. She turned around. "It's cider, strong, mind." Angus McAlister was smiling broadly. "Good evening to you, Miss Eddison."

Eve was greatly relieved to see Angus. "Hi, Angus." Taking Angus's advice, Eve filled three plastic tumblers with the cider.

"And you've come on your own, good for you." Angus's grin spread warmly from ear to ear.

"Oh no"—Eve shook her head—"I'm with my family." Eve looked at the tumblers. *Oh my God, does he think I'm drinking all three?*

"Aye." Angus had not stopped smiling. "I will make sure I say hello. You and your family are very welcome, Eve, very welcome indeed."

Eve wanted to ask Angus if Moira was coming, but she couldn't bring herself to. She caught the eye of Alice. Eve raised her hand to wave only for Alice to quickly look away.

Angus noticed the exchange.

Eve felt her cheeks sting with embarrassment, as she said, "Everyone seems to know everyone."

"Aye, village life for you." Angus paused and lightly placed a hand on Eve's arm. "Lacks perhaps a little privacy at times."

"Right, yes." *Privacy? There's no way he can know I like Moira, can he?* "I better get this to my mum. You know—Dutch courage."

Eve was aware that people were looking at her. She could not be sure whether it was because she stood out as a tourist amongst the locals, or whether her outfit was attracting unwanted attention.

Balancing three Jungle Juices through the elbow obstacles of the crowd, Eve rejoined her mother and sister, who were perched on the end of a long wooden bench, in the corner of the room.

Groups of dancers were congregating on the dance floor. A clatter of cymbals and the trill of a tin whistle called Eve's attention to the gathering musicians on the makeshift stage. A pencil-thin violinist tucked a fiddle under his chin, and a round-bellied man squeezed himself onto the drummer's stool behind a drum kit. Every time he moved, which was quite often as his beer sat on the floor below him, his belly struck the lower cymbal. A wild-haired woman held a tin whistle to her lips. Eve half expected a snake to arise and sway at her bidding.

"John. Yeah, come on, John." The crowd cheered the latecomer on to the stage. Slinking through the throng, the middle-aged man quietly took his place next to the violinist. Eve thought she half recognized him. John's arrival had caused an excited ripple of appreciative noise from the gathered crowd. The band members exchanged a unified nod, the tin whistle was raised in readiness, and then John extended his elbows, drawing out the first high-noted breath from his accordion. The Highland dancing began.

"Impressive." Eve shrugged at Esther.

"Wow, they can really kick their legs high, can't they?" No sooner had Esther spoken than the hall door opened and Henry, dressed in a kilt, flung himself onto the dance floor. His arms were raised in the air, less of a Gaelic master at work and more like Adam Ant's Prince Charming.

"Oh my God!" Esther choked her words at a speechless Lillian. "No one knows we're with him, right?"

Lillian's, Esther's, and Eve's hopes of anonymity were soon broken by Henry waving and calling loudly over for his girls to join him. Everyone seemed to stop and look. Everyone, Eve came to realize, including Moira.

Through the bodies on the dance floor, Eve could see Moira standing with Elizabeth and Angus, and an evidently disgruntled Alice. Moira was dressed in normal attire—just a shirt and cords. Eve thought how attractive Moira looked. Elizabeth and Angus were laughing and clapping, and Moira joined in. Eve watched as Moira's group divided their attention and applause between the stage musicians and Henry.

Eve attempted to shrink into her seat. She was not sure at that precise moment what she was most mortified by—her father's flamboyant dancing and the occasional flash of Y-fronts or being in the same room with the woman she had outed herself to. *Oh my God. Oh my God. Okay, you need to do something.*

Eve stood to try and encourage Henry off the dance floor, but her exuberant father grabbed her and began to fling her around. Eve concluded that she had two choices: storm off and make a complete tit of herself; or stay, attempt a few Highland high kicks, and make a complete tit of herself. Making a complete tit of herself was the only certainty in the whole scenario. Suddenly they were not alone, as Angus had his arm in Henry's and Elizabeth had tucked her arm around Eve. They split into groups of two, and the floor filled with couples dancing.

"Do you think we pulled it off?" Eve breathlessly asked, leaning in to Elizabeth.

"Admirably." Elizabeth held Eve by both hands, swinging them in time with the music.

❖

Moira stood transfixed as she watched Eve dancing with Elizabeth. Eve was smiling, gesturing to her tartan beret and to the colourful trimming of her trouser bottoms. Elizabeth was laughing with her head thrown back in delight. Moira liked what she saw. She liked it very much. Eve's evident admiration of Newland and, if Moira was not mistaken, for her, had renewed a warmth in Moira's heart. She found she couldn't look at Eve and not feel joy.

Alice grumbled, "I don't see what's so fascinating about them." Alice directed her comment at Moira. "Why they thought they could just turn up at what is clearly an event for locals. I mean, really. That man is completely making fun of us."

"He's just enjoying himself, Alice." Angus dabbed his forehead with his hanky. "He certainly didn't intend any harm. And, for the avoidance of doubt, I invited the Eddisons. I like them very much indeed." As Angus said this, he looked at Moira. "Very much."

Moira looked down and felt herself blush.

Their group was joined by the accordion player. "That's it for me, these elbows can't take any more." As he dug around in his jacket pocket for his pipe and then his tobacco, Alice grabbed his sleeve.

"Come on, Dad." Alice said. "Let's show them how it's done."

John Campbell attempted a protest to no avail.

The dance floor refilled with more locals, as hands were shaken and arms roughly slung over shoulders. There was an infectious clan-like camaraderie.

Moira glanced across to the Eddisons, who were clapping in time to the music, watching the local families dance. She noticed that Eve was absent. She was caught off guard by the odd sense of panic that seemed to arise in response. She took a deep breath and walked over to her neighbours, thinking it would be rude not to say hello.

"Are you having a good evening?" Moira asked with a smile.

"Moira. Hi." Esther patted the seat Eve had left. Moira didn't sit down.

"Hello." Henry rose from his seat and shook Moira's hand firmly. "Excellent evening, excellent. Very much enjoyed by all."

"She's outside," Esther said. "Eve, I mean. I think she's outside." Esther grinned at Moira.

Moira felt taken aback and wondered at what point she had given Esther reason to think she might be looking for Eve.

"That is if you were looking for her, of course," Esther continued awkwardly. "Lovely, so, I'm going to check on Eve," Esther said, standing and gathering her belongings. "Then I think I'm ready for home—yes? So see you two outside."

Henry had his arm around Lillian, and they nodded in unison.

"You carry on. We'll be right behind you, darling," Lillian said, her cheeks tinged with a cider glow.

"Well, it's nice to see you all again. Enjoy your holiday, won't you?" Moira looked to Henry and Lillian, who were deep in conversation. As she turned away to rejoin her group, Moira thought she heard the words *groin strain*.

Eve had sensed that Moira had been watching her make a fool of herself. She could only imagine what Moira was thinking. She had kept her eyes firmly fixed on Elizabeth, not daring to look across to meet Moira's gaze. She had left the hall at the earliest opportunity, slipping unnoticed through the crowds.

"You okay?" Esther slung her arm over Eve's shoulder. "I've been looking everywhere for you." Esther had found Eve down the lane from the hall, not far from Loch View, leaning on the fence of a field of horses.

Eve shrugged. "Yeah, just needed some air—too much cider."

"Take your time, enjoy this beautiful evening." Henry called over to his daughters, as he and Lillian passed by.

Eve couldn't help but smile at the sight of her father in his kilt. Holiday memories had been made that night, and if Eve was not mistaken Henry's dancing would overshadow tales of the Loch Ness monster as the subject of local folklore for many years to come.

"You go ahead, I'll just hang out for a bit," Eve said, leaning forward to rest her chin on her hands which lay against the fence.

"Sure, although *the bit* didn't seem to be leaving anytime soon." Esther nudged Eve playfully.

"'Night then," Eve said, pretending she hadn't heard.

The setting sun had left a fading golden hue to dapple on the surface of the loch below. A soft dusky twilight would envelop Newland until morning. Eve could not tell how long she had stood and watched the waters ease and ripple. All she knew was that the horses were at the far end of their field and leant sleepily against one another. She had not noticed their departure.

Eve could hear in the distance the remnants of the dancers disperse. A group of partygoers walked down the lane towards her. She turned briefly around and caught Alice's eye once again. Alice's companions were the accordion player and Moira. *Moira. Oh my God, will this look like I was waiting for her?* Eve knew that to suddenly walk off to Loch View, now that Moira would likely have seen her, would look even stranger. *Shit.* Eve held her breath and looked down as the group passed by.

❖

"Okay. See you tomorrow. Goodnight." Moira waved her companions farewell, pausing at her door. She glanced back up the hill towards Eve, shook her head, and turned the key.

She stood inside her croft, leaning against her sitting room door. The twilight through the window silhouetted her furniture, her life, against the plain cottage walls. With only passing shadows for company, the room felt cold. Empty.

Feeling alone was nothing new to Moira. But that night, what was new was the nagging sensation that it shouldn't, needn't be that way. Moira's thoughts drifted to Eve standing outside. *Was she waiting for me? I should have said hello. She'll wonder why I didn't. She'll think...* Moira knew that there was only one way to find out.

She turned away from her sitting room and made her way out of the croft, up the lane, to the woman who she was finding it increasingly hard to ignore.

❖

As soon as Eve saw Moira walking towards her, she had feared the worst. *Oh my God, I should have gone in. Why didn't I go in? She'll wonder what I'm doing. What am I doing? Shit.* Panicked, Eve turned back towards the horses.

"So, how did you enjoy the dance?" Moira asked, her voice wavering with emotion.

Eve didn't say anything. It was as if she had no more words left. No quips, no funny anecdotes, no giggly jokes, no awkward apologies. Nothing.

Moira leant against the fence next to her. Speaking into the ground, Moira spoke quietly. "I'm sorry about the other day, if I came across..." She stopped and looked at Eve. "I was too tired to talk."

"Are they the Campbells?" Eve nodded in the direction of Foxglove.

Moira stood straight and then leant one elbow on the fence to face Eve. The question seemed to catch her off guard.

"Yes, Alice, of course and, and John, they live next door." Moira was looking intently at Eve, who was looking out again towards the loch.

"It's just I thought I recognized..." Eve paused and looked enquiringly at Moira. "I saw some photos in Angus and Elizabeth's place."

"Photos?"

"Yeah. Esther and I, we had tea with them, the other day."

"Right. Okay. They didn't say."

"Angus showed me photos of you in fact."

"I see."

Eve looked into Moira's eyes as they searched Eve's face.

"You were eighteen, about to go to college in one of them. You looked happy. And in another you were felling trees—impressive."

Moira blushed and looked down.

Eve became briefly silent again, focused on the view, before asking, "You must go back a long way together."

There was pause before Moira said, "Yes."

Eve stood silently with Moira looking out to the distant hills, beyond the loch. More partygoers could be heard laughing up the hill.

"Eve, it's getting late. Let's walk home, yes?"

Before they moved away, Eve pulled at her hat, trying to remove it from her head.

"They've gripped it on. Really, they treat me like I'm four." Eve struggled to remove the tartan beret. "I'm the easy-going, not-to-be-taken-seriously Eve, who will do whatever. I mean, look at me. I look ridiculous."

Eve was breathing heavily. Giving up on the beret, she leant her elbows on the fence. It was all she could do not to cry.

"Here, let me." Moira carefully removed the grips that held the beret. "All gone, Eve, all gone."

"Thank you," Eve mumbled into the ground, embarrassed at her outburst.

"I guess…" Moira leant on the fence again. "It's easy to live your life more for others than yourself. Although, maybe the situations we find ourselves in are more likely a result of our own making."

Moira's wistful words made Eve want to ask Moira if she had any regrets, but it didn't feel right.

"You're very wise," Eve said, admiration coating her words like honey.

"Wisdom is all very easy in retrospect, Eve. The most stupid of people can be wise after the event."

"I guess so." Eve could feel a stray grip down her bra. Pulling out her shirt, she peered in, and then fished out the offending object.

As Eve looked up, she slowly took Moira in. Moira's light blue shirt was untucked at her waist. Her shirt collar was crumpled slightly at her neck. The soft curls of her hair brushed against her collar. Eve could feel the effects of Jane's Jungle Juice blurring the edges.

"I like you." Eve looked directly at Moira. "I like you very much." Eve held the fence as she spoke, as if she needed to steady herself, as if the ground felt unreliable.

Moira didn't say anything.

She was looking at Eve with an expression that suggested she was trying to work something out, as if Eve was a difficult puzzle.

"Let's head home, yes?" Moira said again, tenderly.

Eve nodded. If she was honest, she didn't quite know what she expected Moira to say.

Reaching the gate of Loch View, Eve stopped. "Well, I guess this is me."

"Goodnight, Eve. Sleep well." Moira turned and walked towards her croft. She dug in her pocket for the keys to open the front door. Sensing that Eve hadn't moved, she looked back to Loch View. "You okay?" she called across. Moira glanced behind her at the main house of Foxglove. Both Foxglove and Loch View were in darkness. She walked back over to Eve. "You can't stay out here all night."

"Okay, I know this is going to sound weird, but I'm not a weirdo, I promise, Moira." Moira shook her head, confirming that she didn't think Eve was. "But if I go inside, then…" Eve paused and looked at Moira.

"Then?" Moira encouraged.

"If I stay out here, I'm still somehow in the same space, the same air, the same energy, that we are sharing now. I don't know, it's like you're still here somehow." Eve frowned and shrugged.

"Right." Moira looked at Eve, who was clearly fighting back tears, and then at her croft. "You want to come over for a bit? For a hot drink, before you go to bed?"

"No, I mean, it's okay, I don't want to put you out."

"No? Then what is it you want?" Moira hadn't meant for her words to sound so irritated.

"I…" Eve was looking at Moira's neck. Moira felt unsettled, exposed by the intensity of Eve's gaze upon her.

"Eve?"

"I—sod it." Without any further explanation, she placed her arms around Moira's waist, and hugged her.

In return, off guard, instinctively, Moira held Eve close against her.

"I'm sorry," Eve mumbled into Moira.

"It's okay, Eve. But—"

Eve released her hold. "Of course, I'm so sorry, Moira."

"Don't be sorry, it's just—"

A random blast of bagpipe echoed down the hill from the hall.

"I know," Eve said, nodding. "It's just you don't feel the same and that's okay, really. I won't bother you again."

"No, Eve—"

"It's okay, I'm sorry." As Eve said these words, she unhooked the gate, leaving it open to bang behind her, and rushed inside.

Numbly, Moira shut Loch View's gate and returned to her home. The words *I'm sorry* repeated themselves in her head. She walked into her sitting room, poured herself a whisky, and leant against her sideboard.

Feeling cold, she roughly rubbed her arms. It felt as if, when their embrace ended, Eve had taken all of Moira's warmth with her. Even though she had held Eve for just a few seconds, Moira's arms felt oddly bereft of her. A gust of wind blew against her door. Her heart raced; she couldn't tell whether she wanted it to be Eve or not.

Despite rushes of excitement, amusement, embarrassment, confusion, all Moira was left with was an intense feeling of sadness, a sadness that felt painful. Her whole body felt bruised. What Moira Burns would do, should do—if anything—about Eve Eddison, she simply did not know.

CHAPTER EIGHT

When Moira held Eve in her arms, she instantly recognized those intense feelings, the rushing sensation that overwhelmed her body, and for a fleeting second she was twenty, a third-year student at the Scottish Agricultural College, Ayr, and holding Iris Campbell once again.

"Hello, I'm Iris Campbell, from Inverness." Iris stood knee-high in a boggy stream, smiling back and holding out her muddy hand towards Moira. They were working on a project together to monitor the health of the local streams that ran through farmland into the River Ayr.

"I'm Moira Burns. I'm from Newland."

"I love tadpoles. I love to watch them scooting along. I love to watch them grow." Without drawing breath, Iris continued, "My mother has a phobia of frogs, we get loads in the garden. Our neighbour has a pond, and well, when they jump she screams the house down." Iris let out a loud scream to emphasize the point.

Moira jumped and looked around her to see if anyone had noticed.

"Right, yes, they're jumpy," Moira said hesitantly, not quite believing she was chatting with the infamous Iris Campbell.

Moira had seen Iris around the campus and at various lectures, but up until this project they had never spoken. This was mainly because Moira had spent the first two years of her course either in the library or working from home in Newland.

Towards the end of their first day together, Iris said, "I've seen you in lectures and stuff, you know, before today."

Moira felt her cheeks tingle. "Yes, I've seen you too."

"Well, I'm quite noticeable." Iris made jazz hands.

Moira could remember the first day she'd seen Iris. She had stood in the queue for coffee, in her first week at college. Iris stood in front of her chatting to a group of people. She was telling them that they *must* do *everything* to preserve their Scottish heritage.

"Everything you can do, you should do," Iris had emphatically declared.

Moira remembered that she had wanted to agree with Iris, to interrupt and confirm her support, but the words wouldn't come. Only a fortnight ago, she had sat behind Iris in a lecture. She had watched Iris making notes and coughing into her hanky, fighting a heavy cold. Moira had wanted to recommend a herbal remedy Elizabeth had made her, but for some reason she felt she couldn't. It was almost as if Iris was out of Moira's reach. And yet, here she was standing and casually chatting with her.

"You don't go to the Union much, then?" Iris asked, a curious expression on her face.

Moira was waist-deep in pond weed.

"No, I tend to just work, I guess, when I'm here. I socialize back at home, mainly." Moira looked at Iris who was smiling quizzically back at her. "So, no, I don't go often. I went in Freshers' week though—"

Iris raised her eyebrows. "Freshers' week? So not that long ago, then?"

Moira shrugged and looked away.

By the end of the second week, Moira and Iris had cleared the excess vegetation from the area of stream that they were to survey. They had agreed the methodology and had sketched out the plan for the next six weeks.

"I think we should test both the cleared area and repeat the test in some of the uncleared area." Moira was filling in her time plan as she spoke, resting the sheet on her knees. As she sat, she dangled her wellied feet in the river. "What do you think?"

Iris sat next to her, scribbling what looked like a poem in a well-worn notebook. "Yeah, sounds good." She looked up and squinted at the bend in the river further down. "It will need to be roughly in the same spot though. How about by the willow tree?"

Moira nodded, staring at the bowed tresses blowing in the wind. "It's been a good week. We make a good team, Moira Burns." Iris gave a broad smile.

Moira felt self-conscious at the compliment.

"But, well, all work and no play." Iris held out her hand to Moira and pulled her up from the bank. "They've created a new live music area in the Union, and I'm playing there tonight, with my band, The Bells."

Moira tilted her head, smiled, impressed at the thought of Iris in a band, and asked, "The Bells?"

"Yes, it's quite funny really. Three of us have the surname Campbell, but we're not related, at least not that we know about, anyway, so we thought we'd call the band The Campbells. But then, that made it sound like we were a family group, you know, like The Von Trapps. So, well, we thought that was a bit crap, so we shortened it to The Bells. Anyway, I was wondering…if you wanted, you could come and watch us. We start at about nine. We could have a drink beforehand. What do you reckon?"

Moira frowned. "I don't know. I usually go home, back to Newland on a Friday night."

"So ring your parents and let them know that you're staying at college tonight." Iris shrugged as if to indicate that this shouldn't be a problem surely.

"It's just my dad." Moira looked at Iris. "My mum's not alive, she died when I was young." Moira wasn't sure why she had just said that. She certainly didn't want Iris to pity her.

"I'm sorry, that must have been hard. It's just me, my mum, and my gran. My dad took off when I was a nipper. I think he went to sea," Iris said matter-of-factly.

"I'm sorry too."

"Don't be—by all accounts he was a drunken arsehole."

Moira didn't know what to say.

Iris nodded at Moira and encouraged, "He'll be okay for one night, though, your dad?"

"Yes, I suppose so."

Iris bent down, gathering her belongings, holding her notebook at her chest. "Look, it would be great if you can make it, but if you can't, then, well, I guess I'll see you Monday."

❖

The Union bar was packed, as usual, on Friday night. There was a five-deep queue to be served for a drink. Jimmy Somerville sang out loudly from the wall-mounted speakers. A group of students slurring along to "You Make Me Feel (Mighty Real)" clattered into Moira as they passed by. The room smelt strongly of cigarettes and beer. Moira's feet stuck to certain sections of the floor. She felt a rising sense of panic, and just as she turned to walk out, she felt a tug on her sleeve. It was Iris.

She hollered in Moira's direction, "I love him. He puts such passion into his music and he's got such a distinctive voice. Don't you think?"

Moira had no thoughts—she'd never heard of him.

"Jimmy Somerville," Iris said, with a smile.

"Oh, right," Moira nodded. "Right."

"Come on," Iris shouted into Moira's ear, as she led her out the main bar to the side entrance and back in again. They re-emerged behind the main bar and, directly addressing the barman with a slap on the back, Iris announced, "Hi, Matt, we'll have…" Iris looked at Moira, waiting for her to tell her what she wanted to drink.

Moira swallowed, cleared her throat, and said, "A cider. A half. Please."

"A pint and a half of Strongbow." Iris placed her order with a wink to Matt, who nodded and placed two glasses under the cider pumps.

Moira looked at the queue of waiting students they had by-passed. "So you know the barman, then?"

Iris nodded, handing Moira her drink. "I work here on Tuesday and Wednesday evenings."

"And you get free drinks?" Moira was amazed at such an awesome perk.

"What? *No.* I wish." Iris laughed. "They'll take it out of my wages—I'm not stealing, honest."

"Oh no, I mean, I didn't think you were. I mean you don't seem the type." Moira shut up quickly before she made things worse. She wasn't, if she were honest, entirely sure what type Iris was.

Moira knew that Iris had, by the third year of her three-year course, gained a reputation for what could be best described as eccentricity. Her quirky, independent appearance mirrored her carefree manner. She wore flared dungarees that, when ripped, which was often, she would patch with flower-patterned fabric. Iris's short spiky hair changed colour it seemed with each season. Iris stood out.

Moira had heard rumours about Iris's affairs with both men and women. However, Moira had never heard anyone speak badly of Iris. Her confidence and openness to exploring her sexuality, and her unapologetic approach to relationships and to life in general, made her an oddly admired college figure; she almost had a folkloric quality to her.

"Well, cheers, then," Moira said, with a smile.

"Cheers." Iris drank half of her pint down in one. "God, I needed that. Well that's the vocal cords lubricated. Come on, I'll introduce you to the band."

Iris's band mates were a trio of three skinny lads, dressed in black T-shirts and tight black jeans. In true rock and roll style they were clearly strangers to a hairbrush, razor, and soap.

"This is John, accordion, occasional piano. Hamish, strings. Billy"—Iris gave Billy a wink, prompting Moira to wonder whether Iris was dating him—"drums, he is the beat of the band." She clinked glasses with a beaming Billy.

"So, what type of music do you play?" Moira looked around at the instruments propped up on the stage.

"Traditional music of the homeland." Hamish dramatically placed his hand over his heart as he spoke.

"Gaelic folk," John said. He seemed irritated.

"Right, great." Moira's eyes flicked from instrument to instrument.

John hadn't looked up at Moira. He was intently cleaning his accordion. When he did look up, he seemed surprised by her, in a good way, Moira thought.

"You're not what I expected," he said, smiling.

"Oh." Moira felt herself blush. She didn't dare ask John what he was expecting or indeed what he had obviously heard about her from Iris. His smiling appreciation made her feel a little funny. She both liked the attention John was giving her, and at the same time she found it a bit creepy, intrusive.

On closer inspection, Moira could see that each band member's black T-shirt had the band name on the back.

"Here." Iris encouraged a reluctant John to lift his accordion from his chest to reveal the letter *E* on the front of his T-shirt. "They're the *L*s." Iris was nodding towards Hamish and Billy. "And you"—Iris handed Moira a black T-shirt—"can be my *S*. That is, if you want."

"Don't you girls want to be the *L*s?" Billy looked mischievously at John.

Iris shrugged and with a contemplative expression, said, "Maybe, maybe." Iris looked at John, who looked across at Moira and back at Iris.

Moira sensed that this intimate group of four had a certain amount of history together. That each look they gave one another meant something. But what, Moira couldn't quite tell.

Without warning, Iris disappeared behind the stage.

"Moira." Iris called up.

Moira jumped down and found Iris sitting on an orange plastic chair, pulling on a pair of tight black jeans.

"They're okay, you know, hairy, smelly lumps, but nice ones," Iris said, slightly breathless, as she stood to do up her zip and button.

Moira giggled in response and then blurted out, "Are you with any of them? I'm sorry, I don't mean to pry." Moira couldn't quite believe that she'd asked such a personal question.

"No, it's okay. Oh, you know boys." Iris blew at her fringe.

Moira nodded, although she wasn't sure what she was agreeing with.

"I'm sure, given half a chance they'd shag me, but well, I don't know." Iris looked at Moira and smiled. "How about you, do you have someone?"

Moira shook her head. She felt ashamed somehow. "I'm too busy."

Iris smiled, kindly, curiously in reply. "I'm surprised—you're lovely Moira, quite handsome actually."

Moira looked down, uncomfortable at such scrutiny, and focused on examining the T-shirt she'd been given.

"You don't have to play an instrument or anything. It's just, well, we're The Bells and there are only four of us." Iris shrugged. "You don't have to wear the T-shirt."

"No, I'd like to be your *S*, I mean…" Moira's heart raced as Iris smiled back at her, and a surge of emotion threatened to overwhelm her as Iris lifted off her jumper and dumped it on the chair, revealing her bare chest.

"I'd like that too." Iris blushed at Moira.

Moira tried to look anywhere but at Iris's breasts.

"Sorry, I didn't mean to embarrass you. I didn't think." Iris pulled on the band T-shirt. "Although, it's not like I have much to embarrass you with," Iris added, pulling out her T-shirt away from her. "I don't even think I've enough for a handful." She shook her head and looked back at Moira. Moira was holding her new T-shirt against her chest.

"I guess mine are a bit bigger," Moira said, swallowing hard. "But yours are, yours are really nice, I mean—"

"The Bells!" A loud introductory shout came from the stage area.

"Oh God, I'm on." The band began to play as Iris disappeared onstage.

Moira, still holding the T-shirt in front of her, pulled the chair to the side of the stage, and taking a large glug of her cider watched, entranced, as Iris and her Bells lit up the Union.

❖

Iris was already busy with her net when Moira arrived on Monday morning.

"Found anything?" Moira asked as she pulled on her waders.

"A rare, endangered Coke can." Iris held the dripping can in the air.

"Wow, a great find," Moira said, shaking her head. "Although, what it will tell us about the effects of farming on the wider environment, God knows."

"Moira, look." Iris was pointing to the sky. "It's their famous sky dance."

Moira looked up and shielded her eyes from the sun as it flickered and beamed, in and out, from behind white-grey clouds.

"There, there." Iris gasped, as she clambered out the river and joined Moira at the riverside. "Just above the trees—it's a hen harrier, do you reckon?" Iris beamed at Moira.

"Yes. It's an adult male, white body, black wingtips, yes." Moira returned Iris's beaming smile.

Iris pulled her binoculars from her yellow woven string bag and handed them to Moira.

"You go first," Iris said, her gaze fixed to the sky.

"Are you sure?"

Iris nodded.

As Moira tracked the bird's flight, Iris tucked her arm around Moira's back.

"Has he got something, Moira?"

"Yes, a vole."

"Wow, he'll need to land then soon, right?" Just as Iris said this, the bird dropped into the far trees. "Can you still see him?"

"No, he's disappeared for now. Let's record him, yes?"

Moira moved away from Iris, who remained standing where they had stood.

"I love birds of prey, their wildness. They seem free." Iris's tone had a faraway quality to it.

Moira gathered together the recording paper and clipboard. "Until the gamekeeper sees them, that is," she said flatly.

"I suppose. Maybe that's what makes them seem so awesome. Their freedom is so fragile, powerful, and vulnerable at the same time. It's kind of exciting. I like that, you know, how precious something becomes when it is inherently at risk, when it dares to fight for itself, its right to exist, in spite of the world around it."

Moira had the sense by the intense way Iris was looking at her that Iris was speaking in broader terms about life in general.

"I guess. Best keep our eyes out, maybe there's a family group." Moira held the binoculars to her eyes once more.

"Sure," Iris said. "Of course."

Over lunch on the riverbank, with their feet dangling in the stream, Iris said, "I had a really good time on Friday, you know."

"Yep, me too. You have a beautiful voice, Iris, haunting."

"What, like giving you nightmares?"

Moira enthused, "No, like spine-tingling, hairs on the back of the neck kind of thing."

Moira had spent the entire weekend back in Newland, humming tunes from Friday night. Her father had had to stop her at one point, saying, "Honestly Moira, you'll not sleep if you don't get that tune out your head."

For the last two weeks, in fact, Moira had found it difficult to sleep. She felt excited, really excited. She had abandoned her pyjamas in favour of her new T-shirt for bed. She couldn't get Iris out of her head. Iris was the topic of conversation, even when she had no place in it.

"Don't tell me," her father had teased. "Young Iris would do it differently. I can't wait to meet this lassie."

Feeling stupid and exposed, Moira quickly decided that she would try not to talk about Iris at home; it felt like the two worlds didn't fit somehow. It also, Moira realized, revealed her affection for Iris and she knew instinctively that this was, and should be, a personal, private matter.

"There's something about singing without all that overproduction, it's what I'm into." Iris threw a piece of bread into the stream. "I'm into pure experiences, you know."

Moira nodded, even though, if she were honest, she didn't really know what Iris meant by pure experiences.

As if Iris could tell, she said, "*This* is a pure experience, being here with you now, just talking, talking about what matters to us and sharing together."

"I like talking, and being with you too." Moira looked at Iris's notebook, clothed in purple fabric, adorned with hand-painted designs. "Are you a poet as well as a singer?"

"I write songs, which, I guess, are poems to music. I write about what's going on in my life."

"Right. So what do you enjoy more—caring for the environment or singing in the band?"

"Oh," Iris said absently, "singing."

Moira felt saddened by her reply, although she wasn't sure why.

Speaking wistfully, Iris said, "'Cause when I sing, I feel alive, on fire. I love to see people's faces enjoying the music. I like to make people happy."

"You do make people happy, Iris. Very happy."

Iris looked closely at Moira. "I hope so. I really do."

After lunch, when it was Moira's turn to record, she found herself watching Iris. Moira noticed that, endearingly, when Iris found something of interest, she did a little skip and clap of her hands. "Moira," she would shout, "look." With the thing in her net, she would wade towards the bank, flushed with excitement. *You look so beautiful. You're so beautiful, Iris.*

Now and then, Iris would look up from her scooping and catch Moira's eye.

"What?" Iris asked with a suspicious smile.

"Nothing." Moira looked down quickly.

Iris jumped onto the bank. "No, really, what were you thinking? Tell me, Moira."

Moira stared at the ground. She knew she could tell Iris pretty much anything, that she was unshockable, and that it was likely she wouldn't have been the first woman to say she was beautiful. Iris stepped in. "Were you thinking I looked stupid?" Moira shook her head. "Were you thinking I looked very hip in my waders? I've stuck a rose patch on." Iris showed Moira her knee patch. "Or…"

Moira looked up.

Iris looked directly in her eyes. "Anyway," Iris said quickly, stopping the conversation and sliding back into the stream.

As Moira took her turn to survey and collect, a lump of moss fell near her making her look up. There was no tree above her, no bird or squirrel. *Odd.* The second lump, which hit her on the head, made Moira suspicious. She deliberately ignored it. The third lump, Moira caught.

Iris squealed and splashed down the stream. "I'm sorry," she called over her shoulder. "It was a twitch."

Grabbing a handful of mud from the riverbank, Moira splashed after Iris, who had made a hopeless attempt to hide in the tresses of the weeping willow.

Iris screamed as Moira held her tight and shoved the mud squarely in her face, then dropped the caught moss down Iris's waders.

Before Moira could escape, Iris wrestled her back into the stream.

"Iris Campbell"—Moira spluttered—"there's no need to drown me."

Iris was smiling widely back and then her expression became serious. "What were you thinking?" Iris brushed back Moira's hair from her eyes.

Moira paused and caught her breath. "What?"

"On the riverbank—a moment ago, what were you thinking?" Iris's hand cupped Moira's wet cheek.

"That you were beautiful," Moira heard herself admit.

"I thought you were. You had that dopey expression that people always get when they like me. Another one bites the dust!"

"You shouldn't make fun of me, Iris."

Iris held her arm, stopping Moira from turning away. "I love that look," Iris confessed, turning Moira's face to look at her. "And I love that it's on your face. I want you to think I'm beautiful." Iris paused. "'Cause I think you're beautiful, I've thought it for ages. I coughed my way through my lecture the other week to get your attention. I actually ended up with a sore throat." Moira couldn't quite take in what she was hearing. "Whilst I'm in confession mode, I swapped with James to do this project with you. I'm meant to be on dune habitat surveying."

"Right, I see." Moira felt numb.

"My knickers are wet," Iris said, without a trace of emotion.

Moira's eyes opened wide; she felt her cheeks burn.

"Oh no," Iris giggled, "not because I'm turned on, although…" Iris giggled again. "I have a leak in my waders."

Moira laughed, her laughter tinged with embarrassment, as Iris shoved her playfully as they made their way to the bank.

Grabbing Moira by the hand, Iris pulled her out of the water and into her, bringing their bodies together.

Moira could feel Iris's ribs pressing against her stomach.

Iris lifted an errant twig from Moira's hair and ran her fingers through the wet curls.

Moira could hear sniggering from behind her. She turned to see a group of students pointing at them, laughing. She was mortified.

Iris tried to console her. "It's okay, Moira, we must look pretty silly, soaking wet and everything."

"It's not okay." Moira released herself from Iris's hold and began collecting her things together.

"Wait. Have you plans for tonight?"

"No." Moira felt sensitive and tried to keep her soaked jeans from her legs. "No plans, unless, of course, you consider making my tea and having a bath, a plan."

Iris held Moira by the arm. "Meet me at the Union, say eight?"

Moira looked at Iris, who was nodding to her to indicate it was a fab idea.

"Please," Iris said, the expression in her eyes pleading with Moira.

"Okay."

"Great. We'll make you a regular yet, young Burns." Iris gathered her things and left with a skip of delight.

Packing up her own things, Moira noticed that Iris had left her notebook, open, by the nets. Moira carefully picked up the book. A pebble, which had held the book open, slipped to the ground. The exposed page revealed a poem Iris had called "Highlander." Moira looked around her; it felt wrong to be reading Iris's work without her permission. There was no one about. Moira sat amongst her belongings by the side of the river and held the book in her lap. She looked around her one last time and then began to read:

> When I close my eyes at night, I think of you, my
> Highlander.
> You take me with you into the hills, to the woodland, into
> the deep sweet darkness.
> When I wake in the morning, I think of you, my Highlander.
> You take me with you down to the loch, to the water, into
> the deep sweet darkness.
> Take me with you, my Highlander, how I long to be with
> you in your deep sweet darkness.

Without reading any more, Moira closed the notebook, gathered it with her things, and headed home to her college room.

"Moira?" John offered Moira his tobacco pouch, lit his pipe, and took a deep drag in.

"Oh, no, thank you, I don't smoke."

"Good for you, Moira, it's a disgusting habit," Iris said, waving her hand to disperse the smoke in the air.

John looked suspiciously at Iris.

Iris averted her eyes from his gaze.

Debbie Harry sung out "One Way or Another" in the background of the Union bar.

"Billy not here?" Iris raised her voice against the music.

"Nah, girlfriend trouble." John exhaled, in between smoky inhalations of tobacco.

"Another?" Iris lifted the empty beer jug and tipped it, somewhat dramatically, upside down.

"I have a better idea." With a furtive clink, Hamish sneaked out a bottle of whisky, along with four chipped shot glasses, from his guitar case.

Moira giggled in disbelief. "Do you actually have a guitar in that case, or is there just cigarettes and alcohol?"

"I have the essentials, and my guitar, of course." To prove a point, Hamish pulled out his guitar and slung the strap over his shoulder. "Give us a tune then, Iris."

"Nah, I don't have my songbook tonight, my beauties." As she said this, she looked at Moira.

Moira took a guilty slug of her beer.

"Moira?" Hamish was handing Moira a shot of whisky. "It's the good stuff, single malt, early birthday pressie to myself, from myself."

Moira said hesitantly, glancing at Iris, "Okay. Happy birthday."

"Good girl." Hamish leant into Moira, slurring, "My birthday's not for another seven months."

"Right." Moira leant away from Hamish, her shoulder brushing against Iris's.

Out of view, under the small round table cluttered with their drinks, Moira felt Iris briefly place her hand on her leg.

"Moira?" Iris spoke softly.

Moira swallowed hard and fixed her gaze into the distance.

Iris removed her hand.

"Good health." Iris raised her shot glass in the air.

As a gesture of togetherness, the group of four drank down their whiskies in one go. Moira suppressed the urge to cough.

"Walk me back to halls?" Iris held out a hand to Moira.

Moira just looked at it. Her gaze traced Iris's fingers, to Iris's hand, to Iris's wrist, to Iris's bare forearm. She could feel the warmth of the whisky at her throat. She blinked at Iris as Iris used her outstretched hand to straighten Moira's crumpled collar.

"Let's go, yes?" Iris picked up her bag.

"Don't you girls do anything we wouldn't do." John said, with a smirk.

Iris winked back at John.

"He's really creepy sometimes," Moira said, just out of earshot of John.

"Oh, he's harmless, Moira."

"He's not harmless, Iris. What if he says something to someone else, outside the group?"

"So what if he does?"

"It's *private.*" Moira stopped walking. She could feel her cheeks burning.

"Moira?"

"Whatever's going on with us." Moira stammered slightly as she spoke. She felt her heart ache. "It's between us, no one else."

"But no one really cares, Moira, don't worry."

"*I* care." With this she carried on walking, silent and withdrawn.

"Well, this is me." Iris sighed and leant against the corridor wall as she looked for her keys to her room.

"I have your notebook, songbook, I mean." Moira reached into her pocket. "You left it by the river this afternoon. I didn't want to mention it in front of the boys. You didn't seem to want to sing."

"No, I want to…" Iris looked into Moira's eyes. "Go to bed."

In her angry state, Moira took this literally. "Well, I'll see you tomorrow." She turned away to leave.

"Did you read my poem?"

Moira couldn't decide whether she should tell the truth.

Iris said softly, "I left it for you to read."

With her back turned away from Iris, Moira spoke quietly. "It seemed quite intense, the darkness bit."

Iris gently turned Moira around to face her. "The deep sweet darkness," she corrected.

Moira nodded, only to be startled by two laughing students crashing down the corridor.

Iris reached for Moira's hand and, opening her door, she led Moira into her room. She didn't turn on the light. "The deep sweet darkness."

"You're being weird," Moira said, folding her arms against her chest. "You're making me feel nervous."

"I'm sorry." Iris sat on her bed.

Moira stood leaning against the door. Iris's curtains were open, illuminating the room with a street light glow. Iris's room was co-lourful, soulful, and welcoming; it smelt of sandalwood incense. A tissue-thin amber cloth was thrown over the table lamp by her bed. An SNP poster declared Iris's allegiance to Scottish independence and a CND poster declared her protest against war. An embroidered banner with a labrys at its centre hung next to her bed. Gaelic song-books were strewn on the floor. Iris's room embodied Iris: it spoke of nature, politics, patriotism, passion, and performance.

Iris kicked off her sandals and lay down.

Moira suppressed a strong urge to lie next to her. Instead she walked across to the seat by the study table opposite Iris and sat down. She mumbled into her lap, "Am I your Highlander?"

Without speaking, Iris stood. She leant past Moira and lit a single candle fixed onto a white porcelain saucer on the table. She then softly closed her curtains and turned to face Moira.

Moira watched Iris take a long, deep breath, then effortlessly unclip the straps of her dungarees and let them fall to her feet. Iris carefully stepped out of them.

"Iris?" Moira's mouth was dry and her heart was pounding. Moira could feel her heartbeat choking her.

Iris pulled off her jumper and let it fall to the ground.

"Iris? What are you doing?" Moira held the edges of the chair.

Iris took another deep breath and stepped out of her underwear. She stood naked in front of Moira, just out of reach.

Moira's heart and head hurt in a crushing ache.

"Do you want to be?" Iris quietly asked. "Do you want to be my Highlander?"

Moira looked at Iris, at her serious face flushed, the prickling rash of pink on her neck and collarbone betraying the depth of the emotion Iris was feeling. Moira looked at Iris's breasts, her nipples erect, tender. She followed the line from Iris's breastbone, past the ripples of ribcage, down to Iris's navel.

Moira gasped—"I'm sorry, I can't, I'm so sorry,"—and rushed out of the room. She got as far as the end of the corridor and stopped.

The image of Iris standing rejected and naked upset Moira. She wanted more than anything to hold Iris, feel her close, and kiss her. Moira's body ached for Iris, each step away from her physically hurt, and with the kind of compulsion that overwhelms reason, Moira turned around and knocked on Iris's door. The door opened. Iris had put on her dressing gown; a newly lit cigarette burnt at her fingertip. She let Moira back in.

"I couldn't leave, I'm sorry, Iris. I couldn't leave you." Moira leant against the closed door.

Iris raised her hand to Moira's face, resting her palm against Moira's cheek.

"Be with me," Iris whispered into Moira's ear. Taking Moira's hand, Iris led her to her bed and took a long last drag on her cigarette.

Moira watched the cigarette tip embers burn and glow, as Iris inhaled and exhaled.

Iris extinguished the cigarette against the porcelain saucer and blew out the candle.

"Have you done this before?" Moira spoke hesitantly into the darkness. "Been with a woman, I mean." Moira felt Iris's finger cover her lips.

"Shh, what does it matter about what we've done in the past? What matters is what we do now, Moira."

"I haven't though, I haven't been with anyone." Moira could feel herself shaking.

"It's not important." Iris lifted Moira's jumper over her head, letting it fall on the floor. "How does the sun know how to shine, Moira?"

"I don't know." Moira could hardly speak.

Iris unbuttoned and unzipped Moira's trousers, and eased them down. Moira stepped out of them.

"How does the wind know how to blow?" Iris reached around Moira's back, unclipping her bra, releasing it away from Moira.

"Oh my God." Moira half breathed, half spoke her words.

"How does the rain know how to fall?"

"It just falls, it just falls," Moira repeated towards Iris.

Iris eased Moira's underwear down.

"You'll know what to do, Moira."

Allowing her own robe to fall, Iris held Moira close to her. "I know you will."

CHAPTER NINE

Sunday morning had arrived far too quickly and brought with it the most awful panic, stifling fear, and nausea. Eve hadn't slept a wink, worrying about last night, worrying about the hug. *What was I thinking? Oh my God, what's Moira thinking? I can't believe I did that. What sort of person does that? A person who's definitely lost it, that's for sure—*

Eve's phone rang, startling her from her spinning whirlpool of regret.

"Hey, Rox." *Keep it together.*

"Hey, Evie Eds. How's you? I've just got off night shift," Roxanne said, with a loud yawn. "Just back at yours now."

Eve could hear Roxanne opening the main door from the street and the lift opening and closing. She could just make out muffled laughter.

"Is that my neighbour but one? Rox?"

"Erm…might have been."

Eve gave a heavy sigh. "Please at least tell me my flat's in one piece."

"Absolutely. It's pretty much just as you left it."

"Pretty much? Rox?"

"Yeah, not exactly sure what this mark is on your kitchen counter. It'll probably come off though."

"What mark?" Eve tried to sound vaguely normal but knew her tone held irritation, turning to alarm. "Don't use anything abrasive."

"Sure. Chill out."

"Chill out?"

"So, Evie Eds, what's the stalking latest?"

"I'm sorry?"

"You know—your holiday crush on your neighbour, any news?"

Eve was silent.

"You're not speaking to me from the police station are you? Don't tell me—they've given you a suspended sentence for indecent exposure."

"What? *No.*"

"I was joking, Evie. Anyone lost their sense of humour this morning? Or maybe it's just a bad hair day—although no, that's every day isn't it?

Eve heard Roxanne chuckle. "Yeah, whatever," Eve said flatly.

"So, no news?" Roxanne asked gingerly.

"No."

"Okay, well." There was an awkward pause. "You could send me a picture of her. I mean, I will be able to tell in an instant whether she's one of us lucky few."

"No, it's okay, thanks."

"Sure. Well send one through, if you change your mind. Eve? *Anyway.* So, well, your flat's fine. Nothing to report this end either, unless no loo roll classes as a major emergency."

"I hugged her."

"Who?"

"Moira." Eve could hear the flush of a toilet. "Rox, are we having this conversation with you on the loo?"

"No, I've finished. So what happened? I mean, what did you do?"

"I just couldn't leave her, Rox. It was like I was being pulled towards her. Really, it felt physical."

Roxanne gasped, "You'd been drinking right? Please tell me you were drunk."

"Yeah, I must have been, 'cause I've got a right thumper this morning. In fact"—Eve rummaged around in her suitcase, pulled out a pair of sunglasses, and put them on—"I just feel like staying in bed."

"Had Moira been drinking too?"

It felt very much to Eve as if she was a patient in A&E and Roxanne was trying to establish the severity of the injury. She was waiting for Roxanne to ask if she could raise both arms above her head. She said defensively, "I don't know, maybe."

"Okay. Good." Roxanne seemed reassured. "So what exactly were you doing together before you hugged her?"

"We'd been to a dance."

"What—you went on a date?" Roxanne asked, in evident disbelief.

"No, my family and, well, the whole village really—"

"Intimate."

Eve sighed.

"No, no, go on, I'm all ears."

"No, Rox, you're *all* mouth." Eve ignored Roxanne's guffaw down the phone. "Well, we chatted after the dance, just her and me. It was nice. She's really nice. There's something about her. Something special, you know?"

"Right." Roxanne cleared her throat. "So, okay, how exactly did the hugging come about?"

Eve heard the kettle begin to boil in the background.

"Well, it was about, I don't know, elevenish maybe, and we'd walked back to our houses after chatting, and then..." The kettle clicked off.

"And then? For God's sake, don't stop now."

"I sort of explained that I didn't want to go into Loch View, because then that would mean I wasn't with her."

"You know you're behaving like an intense crazy person, right? I almost dread to ask what she said to that."

"Actually, Rox, she invited me around to hers but I said no of course—"

"What do you mean, of course? She asked you to sleep with her and you said no?"

"No. She asked me around for a hot drink before bed."

"Yeah, right, some of my hottest sex has begun with the word *coffee*."

"Come to think of it, she did seem a bit confused that I said no."

"Okay and her confusion is surprising, why? One minute you're telling her you can't be away from her and the next minute you're declining an invitation for a hot drink around at hers."

"My family would have wondered where I was." Eve walked over to her bedroom door to check that it was properly shut. "It would be like saying I'm just off for an oatcake and an orgasm, don't wait up." Eve heard Roxanne snigger.

"Okay. But I still can't quite see how this leads to a hug."

"She asked me what I wanted."

"I bet," Roxanne said. "Your head checked," she added in a quiet mumble.

"I heard that."

"You were meant to. Please don't tell me you rambled on in front of her with some romantic shit." Eve was silent. "No, I mean, so you said, *I'd like a hug please, Moira?*"

"Well, not exactly, I just hugged her."

"Right, okay. So she hugged you back, then?" Roxanne asked with a tone of uncertainty. "I mean, it's got to have been a bit weird for her surely?"

"I don't know, I mean, yes." Eve paused. If Eve was honest, she couldn't remember whether Moira had held her or not. "I think she held me."

"You think?"

"I don't know if it was that she was just being nice though, sympathetic. She didn't seem that weirded out by it."

"So what did she say?"

Eve could hear the clinking of a teaspoon against a teacup.

"I can't remember."

Roxanne swallowed a large glug of tea, spluttering, "You can't remember?"

"Really, I can't remember. It's all a bit of a blur now."

"A blur? So do you remember how you left things? Are you seeing her again?"

"Well, that's the thing. I kind of ran out on her before we agreed to anything."

"You ran out on her? So let me get this right. You randomly hug her, and then, without warning, you up and leave on her. God, that's messed up. What's she supposed to think?"

"Oh, Rox, don't, I know, I feel like such a tit. What do you reckon I should do?"

There was a pause.

"You may need to let the dust settle a bit, mate. You know, see how she feels about everything. I guess, if she wants to see you again, she'll be in touch somehow."

"But what happens if she doesn't contact me? If I don't get a chance to see her again, what happens then?"

Roxanne was silent. "Rox?"

"Well, then you come home. We get you blind drunk and then we find you someone a bit nearer to home, yes? Eve?"

Eve wanted to say that she only wanted Moira and if she couldn't have Moira, then she didn't want anyone. "I guess."

"It'll be okay, mate, I promise. But," Roxanne said a little more softly, "it's just, you don't really know her, Eve, that's all. You don't really know what you're getting into. Perhaps don't hug her again until you have a bit more confirmation from her that that's what she wants."

"I've imagined her feelings for me, haven't I? Oh my God, she's going to think I'm some kind of weirdo."

"Eve, no, mate. Look, you're not weird. She would have been giving you signals. For Christ's sake, you're that bad at gaydar they were probably semaphore."

Eve sighed. "She's really hard to read, Rox."

"Then just let her tell you straight then, so to speak, if—when—she gets in touch. Let me know how it goes. In fact, why don't you, in the meantime, get some fresh air, take a walk, clear your head. Make holiday plans with your family."

"Okay, thanks, Rox, thanks for listening. And Rox?"

"Yeah?"

"I wish you were here."

"You'll be fine. I'm just a phone call away."

Roxanne flopped into Eve's armchair and placed the phone on the side table next to her. She played with the velvet arms, moving the grain of the purple fabric forwards and backwards. She hated it when Eve was upset. She felt a rush of exhaustion; it had been a busy night, without the opportunity for a break. She finished her tea and, yawning, went into Eve's bedroom and slumped onto the bed.

If Roxanne was honest, she was worried for Eve. She worried that things wouldn't be fine. She worried that Eve had confused the kindness of an outdoors-type woman with something more. After all, many an unsuspecting lesbian had fallen foul of the subtle and dangerous powers of a difficult to read straight woman.

"Dangerous women." Roxanne thumped Eve's pillow more firmly into place under her head. "Dangerous straight women."

Chapter Ten

Eve couldn't help but notice that, even on holidays, Sundays somehow remained distinctly Sunday. When she wandered into the living room, at a tardy midday, no one seemed to care. The impulse to consolidate the holiday's success, to plan the adventures for the week ahead, had not yet stirred.

Saturday evening's high kicks had taken their toll on the Eddisons. Eve glanced at Lillian, who was balancing a large glass of sauvignon blanc in one hand and a Catherine Cookson in the other, reclining on the sofa. Esther was curled up in an armchair fast asleep. Only Henry mustered the energy to stand at the window holding a pair of binoculars against his pale face.

Eve looked out warily across to Moira's garden. She felt sick with embarrassment. *Oh my God.*

She recalled Roxanne's advice to take a walk, clear her head, and make holiday plans with her family.

"So, anyone fancy a walk?" Eve asked, faking cheeriness and enthusiasm.

Without looking up from her book, Lillian said, "Darling, I've just poured your father and me a white wine."

Henry spoke from behind his binoculars. "Remember to take your phone, Eve."

"Right, okay. Will do."

As Eve set out on her walk, she replayed the previous night's hug again and again, desperately trying to recall the details of what happened and to second guess what Moira might be thinking. *I wonder if she's cross. Or upset. What if she's upset?*

Engrossed in her thoughts, before she knew what, she had climbed halfway up the hill. She looked back down the curling path, which revealed the journey she had travelled past black peatbog, blowing grasses, dragon-tongued ferns, and mystical fir trees. Eve leant against a tree and watched the shadow of clouds pass over the distant hills and mountains.

Eve could feel the effort of exercise reinvigorating her lingering hangover. *I could do with a sit.* Eve looked at the grass under the various trees. Everywhere she looked she thought she saw something wriggle or move. Eve took a large glug from her bottle of water. A shape amongst the trees caught her eye. Nestled amongst tree trunks and ferns was a circular hut, complete with grass roof.

Eve peered inside and saw a low wooden bench. The hut was clearly used for teaching and had various posters and handling objects scattered about. It was also clearly, with all its shadowy nooks, the ideal home for spiders.

Along with her mobile and her raincoat, Eve had brought with her, tucked into various pockets of her rucksack, a torch, a bottle of water, and two chocolate mini rolls. She had also shoved half a loo roll into her trouser pocket, just in case.

She clicked the torch on. Warily, she checked the hut, looking under the bench—*clear*—along the bottom edges of the hut—*suspect webs but no sign of spiders.* The hut smelt unsurprisingly of grass and old wood. The wooden frame supporting the roof had been carved to form the shape of a fifty pence piece, with struts at each angle meeting at a central point. Fir branches tucked between the wooden frame provided a rudimentary canopy.

Eve shone her torch and followed the struts along. She decided that she would just lie down on the bench for a moment and was pleasantly surprised by how comfortable it was. She undid her raincoat from her waist and tucked it under her head. For the next sleepy few minutes, Eve clicked the torch on and off, checking the suspect webs and the floor of the hut for any woodland company.

❖

When Moira arrived at the teaching hut to drop off items for Alice's session with the scouts, she felt as if she had stumbled across the most precious thing in the world.

Eve was sleeping on her side, with her face towards the doorway. One arm was wrapped around her, the other lay outstretched towards Moira. Her long-sleeved T-shirt had lifted slightly revealing Eve's torso. Moira looked at the sliver of bare skin exposed between T-shirt and jeans. Steadying herself against the doorway, she fought back an intense and powerful need to hold Eve. If there was any doubt in Moira Burns's heart as to whether she wanted Eve Eddison, it vanished right there. She knew she should wake Eve but simply couldn't bring herself to. She rested her jumper over Eve's sleeping body and turned off the lit torch which lay on the floor underneath the bench. She then stood for five minutes watching her sleep.

"There's so much I need to say, Eve," Moira whispered. "You make me feel alive."

When Alice arrived at the hut, she screwed her face in Eve's direction and asked, "What on *earth* is she doing?"

Moira briefly rested her hand on Alice's arm. "Shh, let her sleep."

"But I've got a class in here."

"Well, wake her before the group arrive. Will you stay with her? I've got mud bricks going off by the Whisky Still and they need to go in." Moira effortlessly feigned complete indifference.

"No—I mean, you wake her up, Moira. She's in the way."

Moira didn't reply.

Alice snapped, "This is ridiculous. She's ridiculous."

"She's not ridiculous, Alice. She's doing no harm."

"I don't know why you're defending her. Is that your jumper?" Alice looked directly at Moira, her face flushed, accusation burning in her eyes.

"I'll see you later, Alice." Moira folded her arms in front of her and headed towards the Whisky Still, towards the woodland, towards the constant, certain sanctuary of the Newland hills.

❖

Eve woke with a start. She couldn't tell how long she had slept; she only knew that when she woke she had somebody's jumper over her.

"Moira?" Eve spoke out loud, triggering a rustle from outside. In the doorway, lit like a shadow from the light behind, stood a slim figure.

"No, it's Alice."

"Oh, I'm so sorry, Alice, I must have dropped off. You should have woken me. I didn't mean to be a trouble." Embarrassed, Eve sat up and adjusted her clothes.

"I was about to wake you. We have a local scout group gathering here, any minute now actually." Alice was staring at her wristwatch as she spoke. "But Moira told me to let you sleep for a bit, so…" Alice shrugged and looked around her.

Moira? Feeling decidedly in the way, Eve quickly gathered her belongings together, pausing to take a look at her phone. There were no messages. It was two o'clock.

"I'd best make my way back home. Thank you for the jumper." Eve tried to hand back the jumper to Alice.

"No, it's Moira's," Alice said, somewhat defensively.

"Oh, right." *Moira's?* "Well, thank you again." Eve looked at the jumper in her arms and back at Alice.

Alice said flatly, "She's mending the Whisky Still."

"Oh, right. I'm not quite sure which way—"

Alice sighed heavily. "Down the hill, to the left."

From nowhere, suddenly, Eve was surrounded by togglewearing, khaki-shirted children, swooping around her like seagulls around fish-and-chip-eating tourists. As she weaved her way through the crowd, she looked back and caught Alice's eye. Eve waved her hand to say farewell. Whether Alice did not see it or whether she ignored Eve, Eve could not tell. Either way, Alice simply turned away.

So Moira found me sleeping and put a jumper over me? Okay. Despite the sun, Eve felt herself shiver. She felt oddly a bit exposed. She worried that she might have been caught snoring or, even worse, drooling. Eve wiped the edges of her mouth on the bottom of her sleeve and looked across to the Whisky Still, tucked down into a little valley by a stream. The historic landmark had been carved into the craggy hillside and was partly covered by a soft, dense moss. Eve couldn't see Moira, but she could see a variety of tools, and she could hear a digging noise.

Eve took a deep breath and called out, "Moira, hi, it's Eve."

She did her best to sound nonchalant, breezy, and not like the weirdo she felt she was. She was also hoping she wouldn't have to make her way down the steep incline. At first, there was no reply. It struck her that it might be better after all not to bother Moira and just to leave her jumper by her door.

"Hello." Moira popped her head briefly out the Still. She covered her eyes with her hand to shield them from the sun.

Eve felt relieved that Moira didn't sound particularly cross. Speaking cautiously, she said, "Hi, I've got your jumper, sorry to have bothered you by being in the hut. I didn't mean to fall asleep. I just fancied a walk, and I'm a bit tired from last night." She stopped herself, not quite believing that she was stupid enough to remind Moira of the night before.

"Sorry, Eve, I've got to finish this." Moira's head disappeared back inside.

Right. Eve wasn't sure what to do next. Did Moira want her to wait or to leave? Eve took a quick glance around her and as she gingerly made her way down the slope, she could feel the soft terrain giving way underneath her wellington boots. She used her hands to balance herself and finally resorted to sliding on her bottom. *Elegant.*

Eve stood waiting at the entrance.

"So, well, I've got your jumper. Moira?" Eve could just see that Moira was fixing mud bricks into holes in the wall. She was holding two bricks into place and searching behind her for the final one. Eve stepped inside and picked up the missing piece, handing it to Moira.

"Thanks. Sorry I just needed to finish that before it set." Moira turned to face Eve.

Handing Moira her jumper, Eve felt her stomach drop. Moira's cheeks and neck were flushed with the effort of her work. The top buttons of her shirt were undone. Eve watched as Moira tucked a curl of hair behind her ear and smoothed her palm over the front of her shirt. *You look so hot.* A rush of admiration for Moira swept over Eve so much so she couldn't help but enthuse, "You're very skilled, you know."

Moira smiled broadly. "I'm sure you are skilled in your field, Eve."

Eve tried to think of skills she could tell Moira about. "I'm a librarian. I work in the City Library, in Leicester. So I guess I'm good at orderliness." Eve rubbed her hands together to remove the remnants of soil.

"Nature's not very orderly or tidy, I'm afraid," Moira said, moving her work lamp to one side as she sat heavily on a roughly sculptured mud seat.

"I can't believe they make you work on a Sunday." Eve glanced around the shadowy Still.

"You can't really leave things that need mending, or easily limit access to the woods, not that we'd want to. So it's a seven day a week job. I don't mind—I like being out here."

"So it's vocational work, then, really," Eve said, her eyebrows raised with her suggestion. Eve felt sure there was something funny she could say about nuns.

Moira smiled and said, "Exactly."

Eve basked in the warmth of Moira's smile, only to realize that she was likely holding Moira's gaze just that little bit too long. She could hear Roxanne telling her that she was behaving like a crazy person.

"I'm sorry about, you know, hugging you last night, a moment of madness. I'm fully in control again, really," Eve said in earnest. "Really."

Moira nodded and looked down. Speaking towards the ground she said, "I just wasn't expecting it."

"Yes, of course. I don't know what came over me. I'm very sorry, it won't happen again."

"It's okay, Eve."

"I understand if you don't want to see me again. Really I do." Eve swallowed back her growing feeling of despair.

Moira smiled kindly. "It's okay, really, it's okay."

Eve heard herself say, "It feels like I'm on a roller coaster when you smile at me." *Okay, what was that?* "I said that out loud, didn't I?"

Moira nodded, amused.

Embarrassed, and feeling a nuisance, Eve mustered some self-control, and turned to leave.

"Eve."

When Eve turned around, Moira was standing in front of her. There was a pause.

Moira looked intently at Eve's face.

"I've mud on my face, haven't I?" Eve rubbed at her cheeks with her sleeve. "I slipped a bit coming down, you see." Eve lifted her shirt to reveal her muddy bottom.

Moira looked at Eve's bottom.

Eve saw her swallow. "That's a bit too much information, isn't it?"

Moira's expression seemed serious.

"Okay then," Eve said quickly. "I'll leave you to it."

"You don't have anything on your face, Eve." Moira was blushing. "Your face is, that is, you are..." Moira sighed heavily.

Before Eve had chance to wonder what she *was*, Moira leant towards her and kissed her cheek.

"You're very sweet, Eve," Moira whispered, at the same time moving away.

Eve felt her legs buckle, as she mumbled, "Uh-huh." Her cheek tingled where Moira had kissed her. She could still feel Moira's lips against her skin.

Tying her jumper around her waist, Moira turned away to collect her belongings.

"Don't go, please, Moira."

The voices of children could be heard outside.

"I've got to go." With these few words, Moira stepped out the Still.

Eve could hear Moira talking to the children. Then there was silence. Eve slumped onto the mud seat blinking into the half-light.

She kissed me. Was she expecting me to kiss her? Why didn't you kiss her? With her face firmly buried in her hands, Eve exclaimed out loud, "You're really crap at this." Eve didn't notice the Still darken.

"You need to know…" Moira stood in the doorway. Her voice broke as she spoke.

"Moira?"

Moira's hand covered her mouth, as she fought in vain to prevent her tears. "You need to understand, Eve, I'm not like you."

Eve held her breath.

"My life—it's not like yours." Moira seemed to be struggling desperately to control her emotion, as if it threatened to overwhelm her.

Eve sat motionless, staring at the silhouette of Moira. She simply didn't understand.

The natural process when you don't understand is to ask questions, but Eve couldn't bring herself to. Eve knew that Roxanne would just come straight out and ask Moira if she was gay, but Eve, looking at a distraught Moira, trying to explain, that she was not like Eve, couldn't distress her any more.

"I've no right to upset you, to make you explain yourself to me. I'll go home, Moira." Eve scrambled out the mud seat.

Moira bowed her head and began to cry into her hands.

"I'm so sorry, Moira." Eve gently, instinctively, placed her arms around Moira and held her close. Eve could feel the wet of Moira's tears on her neck. "I'm sorry."

It was as if the word sorry was reaching out beyond excusing Eve's rashness to soothing a deeper pain suggested by Moira's tears. As she released her hold, Eve kissed Moira's cheek. It felt warm and soft. Eve reached into her pocket, and with a smile and a shrug, she handed Moira the bundle of just-in-case loo roll.

Moira wiped her tears, the beginnings of a smile breaking across her face. "I feel stupid." She moved slightly away from Eve.

Eve held out her hand, and Moira took it. It struck Eve how easy, natural the action felt.

Moira looked at their hands, their fingers entwined, and asked, "What are we doing?"

"I guess we like each other. Or"—Eve shrugged—"we just happen to be the only two people in the world who like to hold hands in muddy caves just for the sake of it."

Moira shook her head. "That'll be it then."

Eve tucked a curl of damp hair behind Moira's ear, away from her face.

"I really like you," Eve whispered, moving close to Moira.

Moira smiled warmly. "I'd never have guessed."

Eve giggled. "Yeah, I've kept the admiring you thing in really well, haven't I?"

There was a pause. Eve looked at Moira's hand tucked in hers.

Feeling a rush of bravery, Eve cupped Moira's cheeks and kissed her gently on the mouth. Moira's lips felt cold. Eve kissed them again.

"Moira?"

Moira looked down. The mood became serious once more.

"Is this okay, are you okay?" Eve could feel Moira's chest rising up and down as she breathed. She was clearly trying to breathe deeply, to steady and to calm herself. Eve could feel Moira shaking.

"Here." Eve untied Moira's jumper from around her waist and lifted it to rest over Moira's shoulders. She moved her hands over Moira's back, soothing and consoling, holding her close.

In response, Moira held Eve, resting her face into Eve's neck.

Eve caressed Moira's hair, stroking through the soft curls, pausing to lift Moira's face and lips to hers, somewhat tentatively kissing Moira's top lip and then her bottom lip.

Moira opened her mouth slightly, allowing Eve to kiss her. With her arms tucked around Eve's waist, Moira repeated the same pattern with Eve's lips, and then they kissed together.

The sensation was so powerful, that Eve felt instantly weak.

Eve leant in to Moira, breathing her in with each kiss. Moira smelt of fresh air; she smelt of wildflowers, of earth, of gorse, and pine; she smelt of Newland. Eve held Moira's sides. She could feel Moira's shirt, the softness of the brushed cotton, the warmth of her. As their kissing deepened, Eve felt an intense need for Moira, a need to be close to her, to touch her. She gently slipped her hands underneath Moira's shirt; she could feel Moira's skin, soft and warm.

Moira was kissing Eve intently, urgently, pulling Eve into her. Eve's hands explored Moira's back, feeling Moira's bra strap under them.

Beep. Beep.

Eve felt Moira jump. She stopped kissing Eve.

Eve said breathlessly, "I'm sorry, it's my phone."

With their intense, delicate intimacy painfully shattered, Moira released her hold of Eve.

Eve retrieved her phone from her pocket and read the text. *U okay?* It was Roxanne. Eve shook her head. "It's nothing." Eve dropped her hand to Moira's hand and held it.

"You'd better go home—your family will be worried." Moira's voice sounded full of emotion, full of feeling.

"No, it's not from them. It's okay." Eve held Moira's hand tightly. "I could come later tonight? To yours." Eve searched Moira's face.

Moira said gently, "I'm sorry, I can't make tonight."

"Sure, yes, of course."

Moira stroked Eve's cheek, her expression tender and soft, as she said, "Tomorrow. How about tomorrow?"

"Yes—although I won't be able to come till late. I'll need to wait until my family have gone to bed. Say, eleven?"

"Tomorrow night then."

Moira let go of Eve's hand, turned, and walked away.

CHAPTER ELEVEN

S aturday night was fun, wasn't it?"

"Fun?" Eve raised an eyebrow at Esther's assessment.

"You know what I mean. In fact, it was good to see you relax, let your hair down a bit."

Eve was drying the wine glasses from Monday night's supper, whilst Esther washed up.

"Why, do you think I'm too uptight?" Eve asked, her head tilted questioningly.

"Well, perhaps not uptight, just careful. Not that that's a bad thing."

There seemed to Eve to be an incredible irony in the conversation she was having with Esther. She knew why Esther had formed that opinion. Up until this week, Eve would have agreed that she liked to be sure, that she would hold back her feelings. But, with Moira, she had been anything but careful, anything but uptight. *Moira.*

"Eve."

"Huh?"

"I think it's dry." Esther gestured to the glass in Eve's hand.

"Oh, right." Eve put down the glass she had polished to a brilliant shine.

Esther asked casually, "So, have you seen our neighbour since the dance?"

"What?" Eve pulled down her bottom lip and frowned as if trying really hard to remember who Moira was, let alone whether she had seen her recently.

"It's just, well, I saw you," Esther said, leaning in slightly.

"I'm sorry?"

"After the dance—with Moira."

Eve felt instantly exposed.

"I wasn't being nosy. I'd got up to get a drink and happened to look out the kitchen window and there you both were."

Eve nodded. "We were just saying goodnight, you know, a goodnight hug."

"A hug?"

"Yes—why, what did you see?"

"You seemed to be just talking. She hugged you? See, I *knew* she liked you."

Henry appeared from the living room, grabbed a lemon and a knife, and said, "Don't mind me, as you were."

Oh my God. Eve held the tea towel in front of her, as if it offered protection from Esther's probing.

"Seriously, Eve, I think she's got the hots for you."

"Really? Nah." *Oh my God.*

"Well, my bet is she's a fully paid-up member of your team."

Eve squeezed out, "My team?"

"You know—the girls' team." Esther nudged Eve playfully.

Eve shrugged. "I hadn't thought about it, maybe, who knows?"

Esther gave Eve a sceptical look.

The truth was that Eve didn't know. She didn't know if Moira played for the girls' team—at least, not whether she played full-time. She could tell from their kissing that she enjoyed being with Eve, but to assume that Moira was gay was perhaps assuming too much. She knew they could talk more tonight, that she could check before they...before they what?

"Eve?"

"What?"

"Never mind."

Eve watched Esther walk away, shaking her head.

Everything in that moment felt surreal. With every breath that she denied any feeling for Moira she could feel herself wanting her more. Moira was so present for Eve and absent from her at the same time. She looked at her watch. *I must get ready.*

In the hour or so leading up to eleven, Eve showered and tried on every outfit she had brought with her. She sat on the edge of her bed, half buried in all of her clothes. Even the clothes she had discarded to be washed were lying on the bed for outfit consideration. Eve let herself imagine a passionate scenario where Moira was lifting, say, her jumper off her, only then to imagine the likelihood of the jumper creating a static charge that left her hair alarmingly wild. No, she wouldn't wear a jumper. Eve complimented herself, that even in her fantasies she was nothing if not practical. A shirt then? Eve had set aside her travel home outfit. Could her light blue cotton vest and blue linen shirt be worn tonight and, perhaps, still be clean enough to travel home in? Eve held up her muddy jeans and gave them a sharp shake. They'd be fine to wear—wouldn't they? As a matter of habit, Eve briefly wondered whether she should ring Roxanne for advice.

If Eve was honest, there was something about Roxanne's reaction to Moira that had left her feeling hurt, her feelings called into question, undermined. The thought of telling Roxanne about what happened in the Whisky Still didn't feel right. It all felt too private, serious, and certainly not for the scrutiny, ridicule, or amusement of others.

Lying on her bed, waiting for eleven, Eve felt sensitive, hyperaware, kind of raw. She felt unsettled. It was almost as if Eve could feel the onset of change.

❖

As she waited for Eve, Moira drank two double whiskies and rearranged the cushions on her sofa at least three times. She changed her outfit twice. Her first outfit was formal—dark trousers, a white blouse, and a blazer. It looked, she decided, like she was about to go to an interview, rather than on a date. *A date?* Moira wasn't sure what this was. Was it a date? If it was a date, what did that mean? Did it mean they would kiss again? She absently traced her lips with her finger. She recalled what it had felt like to be kissed by Eve, to kiss her, to hold her. It felt really good, it felt right. Kissing Eve, holding her, it was what Moira wanted to do, and what she wanted to do again tonight.

And yet, as she chose her second outfit, Moira stood in front of her bedroom mirror, dressed just in her underwear. She should have gone out today and brought a fancier bra, just in case. Just in case what? Was Eve going to see her bra, her breasts? Was that what Moira wanted? Her heart had begun to race. Moira's bra was white, cotton, and mostly plain, except for a small bow in between the two cups. She looked at her knickers—also white, cotton, and plain. She should have bought new knickers too. Moira began to feel upset. She sat heavily on her bed.

She struggled to understand what Eve saw in her. Why would Eve fancy her? She looked at her body. What would it feel like for Eve if she touched her? She ran her hand over her breasts; they felt warm and soft, enveloped in cotton. She moved her hand over her torso, her stomach. Moira was fit, active, and yet age had shaped how she looked, and moreover, how she felt about herself. She wished she was more toned. She felt the curve of her stomach. Eve's body felt firm. Moira swallowed. What if Eve wanted to touch her, for them to be together? Moira's throat was tight, she felt panicked. What was she doing? Eve was so much younger than her, she lived miles away and she…Moira paused and took a long intake of breath. Her mouth felt dry. Her head ached. What on earth was she thinking?

Moira spent half an hour sitting motionless, in her single chair, a whisky glass resting in her lap, her sideboard lamp lit, staring into an empty hearth. She looked to her door at the sound of Eve knocking once, and then a second time.

Moira's heart ached at the thought of Eve standing alone, hurt, and confused as to why Moira hadn't opened her door. But she couldn't—she just couldn't. How could she have been so stupid in the first place to let things get this far? Eve deserved better, better than her.

She heard Eve call out, "Moira. Hi, it's me, Eve."

At the sound of Eve's voice, Moira approached the unopened door and stood numbly, silently, her hand resting on the handle, tears itching at her neck. She heard Eve call her name one last time and then her footsteps against the gravel as she walked away.

❖

When Eve opened her eyes the following morning, every movement of her body hurt. It felt like she had been beaten up. She had slept in her clothes, the imprints of zip and buttons marked pink against her pale skin, like tattoos of her despair.

She blinked blearily at the light at the window. Her bedroom curtains were open. Slumping in the window seat, she leant her head numbly against the cold glass. Moira's hens were loose and pecking at their feed but there was no sign of Moira. Eve tightly folded her arms, suppressing an impulse to shudder.

Eve knew she had to see Moira, even if just for a moment—just a moment to help her understand what had made Moira change her mind, if that's what had happened. Eve's thoughts raced, seeking out scenarios to ease her pain. Moira could have been called out to an emergency. Yes, or she got held up somewhere. She wouldn't have just stood her up. Would she?

Eve looked at her watch. It was eight o'clock. She rushed from the window seat, out of her room, and headed downstairs.

"I'm going to get some air, Dad."

Henry looked up from his morning paper. "You okay?"

"Yep." Eve pulled on her coat, glancing at Henry's puzzled expression.

Henry raised his eyebrows. "Take care then," he said. It looked like he wanted to say more but thought better of it.

Eve left with a brisk, "Bye, then."

Moira's croft gave nothing away, betrayed none of the heartbreak it had witnessed last night.

Please answer, Moira, please. Eve's knuckles ached from knocking in vain at Moira's door. She could feel herself becoming upset; it was all she could do not to cry.

Moira's Land Rover was no longer parked in the driveway. Eve tried to think what she should do. Should she try the education centre? She wouldn't need to disturb Moira for long. Just long enough for Moira to explain what had happened. Yes. And then they could arrange to meet again, couldn't they?

The journey to the centre seemed extra-long and hard. When Eve arrived, feeling hot and bothered, she could see Alice clearing some painting pots away, humming as she worked. Eve knocked on the side of the open door.

"Hi"—Eve took a deep breath—"I was wondering if Moira was about."

"Oh." Alice straightened herself up. It looked like an unpleasant smell had just wafted under her nose. "She's gone away for the rest of this week, to prepare for a wilderness education course we run in the Cairngorms. It was meant to be next week but…" Alice shrugged.

Eve's heart sank and ached painfully in her chest. She began to feel sick.

"Have I missed her, then?" Eve said, with a hopeless, desolate tone. She briefly placed her hand in front of her mouth. It felt like she was about to puke her heart up, leaving the bloody organ to shudder on the floor by the painting sink. "I'm going home in a few days, you see."

Alice swallowed hard. "Well, you can leave a message if you like." Not waiting for the answer, she turned away from Eve.

"No, it's okay, thank you."

Alice carried on with the work she was doing, as if Eve was not in the room. Eve numbly turned around and closed the centre's door behind her.

Eve could not remember walking back to Loch View. All she knew was that her coat and shoes had been discarded on the floor of the porch, and she was standing in the hallway in her stocking feet and thinking. Thinking about Moira.

*I could leave her a message. I'll write her a note, yes, a note ex-plaining that I'd like to see her before we, before I...*Eve swallowed down the upset at the thought of not seeing Moira again.

Furtively, tearing a page from the back of the visitor book, and using a worn-down pencil that wrote everything in a hazy double mark, Eve scribbled.

Dear Moira,

Was that too formal? Eve was determined to keep the tone of the note breezy. The last thing she wanted was to make Moira feel bad. Eve lingered over the white page, hovering pencil over paper as if waiting for the words to write themselves.

I am very sorry that I missed you. I go home this Saturday (11th).

Eve added the date in brackets, to avoid any confusion.

Hope to see you before I go. Eve

Eve decided that the note should be factual, rather than emo-tional in content, in case someone else should read it by accident. She would find a quiet moment to post the note through Moira's letter box. *What more can I do?* Her irrational heart told her to de-clare her undying love for Moira to her family that instant, and then to rush to the Cairngorms and rescue Moira from her life without her. Her rational head told her she didn't know what Moira was feeling, and how was she going to get to the Cairngorms, and where were they in any case. All Eve could do now was wait and hope.

❖

Friday came and it was the end of a long week for Moira. The time spent in the Cairngorms had not just been about teaching, it had been about decisions. Or rather, as Moira came to frustratingly realize, indecisions. Most evenings, sitting by an open fire outside her cabin, drinking drams of whisky, she would decide to be brave and to see Eve one last time. *We need to talk. I need to see her again.* But by the morning, in the daylight, she would change her mind and wonder at her madness for even entertaining further time alone with Eve.

Yet, driving past Loch View on her way home, Moira wanted so desperately to catch just a glimpse of Eve. And then finding Eve's note...*Hope to see you before I go. Eve.* Moira read the note four times as she sat, still wearing her coat and boots, in her armchair.

"What are you doing, for goodness' sake, woman? Enough." She repeated out loud, "Enough."

CHAPTER TWELVE

Moira knew when she heard the soft knocking at her door that it was Eve. She told herself that she hadn't been deliberately waiting, hoping for her to come, that routine tasks had simply kept her busy until late.

But what tasks? She looked around her living room. Her bag lay unpacked by her stairs, her post remained unopened on the table. Her boots that she'd only just removed were tucked by the side of her armchair. And her coat, still warm, rested in her lap, as she'd sat into the evening, consumed in thoughts of Eve.

Her week away had made nothing clearer. All she knew for certain was that if Eve came to her door one last time and Moira didn't answer, then it, whatever *it* was, would be over. Perhaps it was already. Perhaps Eve was just here to say goodbye. After all, Moira had stood her up, with no explanation or apology. Surely that was unforgivable.

Moira stood and walked to the door. She hesitated, her forehead resting briefly against the cold grains of wood. If only she could discern one emotion from all the conflicting emotions surging through her. Would should she do? Thoughts were hopeless. All she had left was her instinct.

Moira opened the door.

"I saw your light on," Eve said breathlessly. "I thought I'd check. I didn't know whether you'd come home or...hi."

"Hi." Moira folded her arms in front of her.

"I came over to knock for you, Monday night." Eve swallowed "I must have missed you or something."

Moira looked down.

Eve's voice faltered with the question, "Well, I left you a note. Did you get it?"

Moira nodded.

Moira's silence made Eve fear the worst. *You don't want me here, do you?* "Look, it's okay, Moira, if you didn't, don't, I mean, it's okay if you don't want to—"

"Do you want a coffee?" Moira asked, her question catching Eve by surprise.

"A coffee? Yes. Yes, please." Eve felt an overwhelming sense of relief. "Thank you."

Moira simply nodded in reply.

Eve stood in the middle of Moira's sitting room, feeling very much as she looked—unprepared. When she'd noticed, with a start, that Moira's light was on, she had rushed across to her croft, without thought to how she might look. The laces of her shoes were undone and the bottoms of her jeans were wet with dew. Her shirt was untucked, the sleeves unbuttoned at her wrists. Eve strongly suspected that she was channelling *vagrant* rather than *Vogue*.

Eve took a deep breath and said, "Alice told me that you've been working in the Cairngorms this past week. Did it go well—your work?" *Keep it breezy Eve, light and breezy.*

Speaking from the kitchen, Moira replied, "Yes, it was good. It was good to get away, to think."

"Right."

"I had some stuff to work out." Moira's tone implied there was more to say.

Stuff to work out? Eve looked into the kitchen, catching a glimpse of Moira through the half-open door.

"If this pilot goes well it could become a permanent course," Moira continued, her steady voice betraying no emotion.

Work stuff—so nothing to do with me. "Would it mean you moving to the Cairngorms?"

"No." Moira carried two mugs into the sitting room and gestured for Eve to take a seat on the sofa. "Newland is where I belong. They won't need me as often when they've got it up and running."

"Right. Cool." Eve wasn't sure why Moira's answer made her feel so relieved.

"You'll have to let me know if you want me to light the fire, I'm not quick to feel the cold," Moira said, nodding towards the hearth.

"I'm okay," Eve said, smiling, taking her drink from Moira. "Thank you."

From behind the steam of her coffee, Eve looked around Moira's sitting room. A dining room table with a drop leaf sat under a small window, which looked out onto the front driveway. A pile of correspondence and centre leaflets spilled across its surface. The curtains at the window had a pretty floral pattern which lent a soft contrast to the dark stained furniture and hardwood flooring.

"I'll close them," Moira said in the direction of the curtains.

Eve said quickly, "Sorry, I didn't mean to be nosy."

Off the sitting room was a small kitchen, and Eve could see the bottom of stairs which, she guessed, led to bedrooms and a bathroom.

"I have a sunroom." Moira nodded towards the other side of the sitting room. "It has the best view of the loch. Although it's used more as a greenhouse. I grow veg, tomatoes, and the like."

It was clear that Moira was incredibly green fingered. Various vessels in her sitting room had something sprouting and pretty in them. Seed packets rested against nearly every surface, and there was a faint sweet, herbal smell in the room, accompanied by a lingering undertone of woodsmoke.

"I like your painting," Eve enthused, staring at a picture of the loch and mountains hanging above the fireplace. The lamplight illuminated the raised surface of the oils, defining every brushstroke and contour. The dark burnt black oil paint, slicked with ochre and creamy whites, recreated the surface of the loch, so that it shined, rippled, broke against the embankments of the ornate frame.

"Yes? My father painted it," Moira observed, with a wistful tone. "I remember watching him as a child, the concentration on his face, his shirt smudged in paint."

"Your father was a painter? That's cool," Eve said with a nod, her gaze fixed, captivated, upon the painting.

"Not by profession," Moira replied. "He was a crofter. It's in our blood, like generations of our family before him. That said, his father broke with tradition and turned away to engineering. He did well—he had Foxglove, the house next door, built. Dad said it was as if his father needed to prove something to the community. He tried to get Dad to follow in his footsteps, but he never settled." Moira glanced across to Eve, who sat nursing her drink, listening patiently to every word. Moira continued, with a sigh, "When my mother died, well, Dad found consolation in painting. I've still got his brushes and paint pots somewhere. Daft really."

"No. Why's that daft? That's beautiful. Your home's beautiful, Moira."

Moira looked at Eve, her expression embarrassed and incredulous in the face of Eve's compliment.

"It's small, but, well, there's only me living here." Moira sank heavily into her armchair and took a swig of her coffee.

"It's only me at my place too. I rent a small one-bedroom flat in the centre of Leicester. Although"—Eve giggled—"I often end up sharing it with my best mate. She's a nurse and my flat's near the hospital so she often stays over."

Moira looked at Eve.

Eve shook her head. "No, I mean, we're not together, we just hang out a lot. I mean, I'm single." Eve was finding it hard to read Moira's expression.

Moira looked away from Eve, stood, and reached for a drinks decanter on the sideboard by the fireplace.

Eve noticed that there were no photos on the sideboard or, for that matter, anywhere else in the room.

"Do you have relatives in Newland?" Eve asked, casually.

"Want one?" Moira lifted an empty whisky glass to make the point.

Hell, yeah. "Yes, thank you." Eve glanced at her half-full coffee mug and set it aside on the floor by her feet.

Eve watched Moira with her back to her pour them both a drink. Moira was wearing a blue brushed cotton chequered shirt with dark blue cord trousers. Her feet were bare against the wooden floor. Eve's gaze fell upon the curls of hair at Moira's neck brushing at her collar. *I want to kiss your neck.*

Eve felt herself blush as Moira turned around and handed Eve her drink before leaning against the sideboard to face her.

"I'm an only child and my parents passed away some time ago now," Moira said, with matter-of-fact dispassion.

"Right, I see," Eve said, taking a sip of the whisky. It was sweet, mellow, and warming. "I guess it must be a bit weird, me being here—having a stranger in your home."

Moira gave Eve a quizzical look and, as if choosing her words carefully, replied, "You're hardly a stranger to me, Eve. If I'm quiet it's because I don't really know what to say. I enjoy your company, you make me feel..."

Eve encouraged, "I make you feel?"

"I guess it's having someone new to talk to. We're a small community and, well, it's nice." Moira drained her whisky dry and turned away from Eve to pour herself another.

Eve felt a sting of disappointment. *Nice?* Nice was sunshine on a walk. Nice was bread and butter pudding. Nice was not *Thank God she's come to rip my clothes off.* And what about their kissing? Surely Moira had not forgotten it already, was that just nice too? Eve, feeling hurt, wrapped her arms around herself, holding the whisky against her folded arm.

Moira turned back around, looked at her glass, ran her forefinger round its edge, and asked quietly, "How long have you known you were gay?"

Eve, startled a little, stumbled over her words. "I think I've always known. I mean, I never really had boyfriends, well, not properly. Being with a woman, I don't know, it just feels right to me."

Moira stood watching Eve, looking at her lips as she spoke, lip-reading the words as if deriving meaning from sound alone was not enough.

Eve did not know what she could ask Moira in return.

"Do you, I mean, have you?" Eve paused and looked down. "You seem to like me. I mean, I think you like me. You seemed to enjoy kissing me." Eve dared to look up.

Moira stood motionless, staring at her whisky glinting gold in her glass.

"It's okay, Moira." Eve shook her head. "I'm always getting things wrong. In fact, I'm really not very good at this at all, really I'm not. Ask my friend Rox. I'm hopeless at gaydar, I mean—"

"Gaydar?" Moira asked, her expression curious.

"Gaydar, well, I guess, it's a sense of someone's sexuality without it being confirmed by them either way. It's kind of gay guessing."

"Right." There was a slight pause. "And what did you guess about me?" Moira sat down as she spoke.

"That you liked me. And, by like, I mean fancy. And then, of course, you kissed me." *There, no going back now.* "And that's okay, because I fancy you too. I've thought about you constantly since we first met. Really I have." *Sod it.* "I've been fantasizing about you." Eve was on a roll. "About you kissing me, like you did before, and touching me, and me kissing you, touching you, making love to you." Eve ran out of breath, just managing to ask, "Do you feel that way about me too?"

"Yes"—Moira's voice broke—"but I can't." She looked at Eve. "I don't know what to say to you."

Eve moved from the sofa and knelt in front of Moira. "Then don't say anything. You see, it's okay, it's okay to want me. Really, it's okay."

Moira could feel herself trembling.

Eve's hands rested on Moira's knees, her left hand covering Moira's hand.

Moira felt the warmth of Eve resting against her, as she asked, "What now?"

Moira watched Eve's every move, as Eve lifted Moira's hand to her mouth and kissed the back of it, the side of it, the palm.

The truth was that Moira knew that the sensible thing would be to stop what was happening, to ask Eve to leave. But that night, feeling the intense sensation of Eve close to her, she could feel her resolve unravelling, collapsing, giving way to a deep, inevitable need.

Moira's gaze fell to Eve's shirt, to each button that led from Eve's neck, to her chest, to her stomach.

In response, Eve slowly undid the buttons of her shirt.

Moira shifted in her seat. She could feel her heart pounding.

"Is this okay?" Eve looked directly at Moira. Her eyes fixed upon her, questioning, seeking confirmation.

Moira Burns did not know Eve Eddison, but every instinct she had, all of her forty-six years of life, told her clearly that Eve was a good person. A good person Moira could trust.

Moira took a deep breath. "Yes." Tears gathered at her lower eyelids. "Yes. I—"

Before Moira could say anything else, Eve leant forward and kissed her on the mouth. As she kissed her again, Moira opened her mouth slightly to receive Eve's lips. Eve held the side of Moira's legs, her torso resting against Moira's knees.

Moira cupped Eve's flushed cheeks in her hands as they kissed.

At that moment, it felt to Moira that there was nothing in the world except them. No croft, no wood, no loch, no sky, no one else, nothing, just the intense momentum of their need for each other.

Eve let out an *mmm* as their kissing deepened.

In response to the signals of pleasure from Eve, Moira instinctively, thoughtlessly slid Eve's shirt off her shoulders, running her hands over Eve's bare shoulders and down her arms.

Eve was wearing her blue vest top that she often wore in bed. She was aware that her nipples had become pronounced through her bra and through her top. And Moira was looking at them.

Moira looked quickly up to Eve and blushed.

"It's okay," Eve said quietly, lifting the vest over her head and letting it drop to the floor.

Moira swallowed deeply. She watched as Eve reached behind her, released her bra fastening, and let her bra fall to the floor.

Eve was not sure where she was getting her confidence from; all she knew for certain was that she was with the person she wanted to be with.

Moira's eyes refilled with tears, as she confessed, "I feel a bit overwhelmed."

Eve nodded and tucked a curl of hair behind Moira's ear.

"Me too. But I want you so much, Moira." As she said this, Eve fought back her own tears.

Moira looked at Eve, kneeling in front of her, vulnerable and half-naked.

"You can touch me if you want." Eve blushed as she breathed the words of encouragement. Eve could smell the musk of whisky as Moira, a little hesitantly, leant forward and kissed Eve's shoulder blade, moving her way slowly, cautiously, keeping half an eye on Eve's expression for indicators of approval.

As Moira kissed her, Eve took Moira's head in her hands, caressing her hair, massaging, comforting, consoling, and reassuring with her touch. Eve drew in a breath as Moira closed her mouth around the tender flesh of her nipple, and a tongue flicked across as her lips formed a kiss as she withdrew.

Tears fell down Moira's cheeks.

Eve wondered how many restless nights, unrequited loves, unfulfilled longing years this woman had waited to be fully herself, to express and act on her deepest needs.

"Can I?" Eve whispered into Moira's hair. Finding the base of Moira's shirt, Eve eased it gently up.

Moira slowly began to undo the buttons. She stopped halfway and looked at Eve. "They're not like yours, I mean…I'm older than you. My body's different."

"To be honest," Eve said shyly as she glanced down at herself, "I was worried about what you would think about my body. Despite my apparent gay abandon, I'm not in the habit of stripping off." Eve swallowed down the emotion rising in her as she spoke. "But I really fancy you." She sat back on her heels and shook her head. "I guess I know now what all the fuss is about—you know, how someone can make you feel so…" Eve paused.

Moira was slowly undoing the remaining buttons of her shirt.

"You're beautiful, Moira." With these words, Eve kissed Moira's neck and as she kissed she repeated, "So beautiful," kissing her way along Moira's collarbone.

In response, Moira slowly slipped her shirt off her shoulders, allowing Eve to work her way down her chest, kissing Moira's breasts, enveloped in her bra.

Eve's naked torso pressed against Moira's bra as they kissed again. Tongues more urgently explored the insides of each other's mouth. Eve slipped her hands behind Moira's back and eased Moira from her chair down to the floor, to rest on top of her, at the same time uncatching her bra, releasing Moira's breasts. Eve took the weight of Moira's breasts, caressing them.

"Oh, oh." Moira deeply inhaled. "I...I, oh my God."

Eve's body surged with pleasure, as she gasped, "You feel so good."

Without thinking, Eve moved on top of Moira, her lips searching out each breast. Eve could hear soft groans of pleasure.

Moira's hands fondled Eve's bottom through her jeans, pulling Eve into her.

Eve's kisses made their way to Moira's navel and the soft skin below. Eve paused and looked up to Moira, asking, "Moira, are you okay?"

"Yes, yes." Moira's eyes fell once more to Eve's breasts and with the backs of her fingers she caressed the soft flesh.

Eve bit her bottom lip and swallowed, just finding the breath to say, "I want you so much, I've never wanted anyone like this, honestly Moira, I've never, I've never felt so..." Eve placed her hands over her face. She felt she would cry. *Hold it together, Eve, hold it together.*

"I know, Eve." Moira slipped her hands along Eve's thighs. "I know."

Eve leant over Moira, kissing her, her soft warm body covering Moira's. Purposefully, she released the top button of Moira's trousers, unzipping her fly, and moving off her slightly, she freed Moira to lift her bottom, allowing Eve to ease her trousers and underwear down her legs.

Moira reached up, pulling Eve on top of her, and as she did so, Eve felt Moira take a deep intake of breath. Eve kissed Moira deeply, their mouths working harmoniously to receive each other.

Following the momentum begun with the kisses, Eve's hands deftly explored Moira, her kisses caressing her torso, her breasts, her fingers tracing their way along the insides of her legs, pausing at the centre of Moira.

Taking a long, deep breath, Moira let go, giving in and dissolving, allowing herself to be consumed by the sensation of Eve inside her. Images conjured themselves in Moira's head. She was running, running hard through the woods, the ferns and leaves against her skin. She was running as if for her freedom, her chest beating hard, her body urging her forward.

Eve's fingers moved smoothly in a motion that mirrored the waves breaking on the shore of the loch outside—easy at first, then more intensely, sensing and responding to Moira's need.

Moira couldn't stop herself running, she was at the edge of the wood, at the edge of the hillside, on the edge, the precipice where land meets sky, she knew she would fall and she was powerless to stop.

Moira's body began to tense, to tremble, as her breath caught on the peaks of the intensity of each sensation.

Moira stepped from the edge and fell, below her the cool waters of the loch inviting her, bidding her come, and then she was flying, flying over the water, up, up into the sky, over the hills, away, free.

Moira's body shuddered and tensed for the last time, and then relaxed.

"Oh my God." Moira's voice trembled as she lifted her fingers to her mouth.

Eve whispered, "It's okay, Moira, everything's going to be okay."

CHAPTER THIRTEEN

Can you stay a while?" Moira asked with a hopeful tone.
Eve replied dreamily, "Yes, until sixish. My folks will want an early start." She watched as the delicate hairs on Moira's forearm stood erect at her touch.

"Eve, with the women you've been with before, was I okay?"

Eve knew that what she was feeling with Moira she had never felt before.

"I mean, should I have...?" Moira glanced to Eve's buttoned jeans.

Eve lifted herself up onto her elbow, her naked torso pressing against the sitting room rug, the woven wool surface brushing against her skin.

"I enjoyed giving you pleasure. To be honest, I tend more often to make love to the person I'm with, rather than them make love to me." Eve gave a short shrug.

Moira asked gently, "You like to feel in control?"

Eve frowned. "Not really, it's more I'm not very good at, well...letting go." Feeling embarrassed at her unguarded honesty, Eve lay back.

Moira wrapped her arms around her. "I see," Moira said softly. Without warning, Moira scrambled to her feet, pulled a throw off the sofa, and wrapped it around herself. She disappeared into the kitchen, reappearing holding a couple of blankets. One she handed to Eve, the other she rolled under her arm.

"I want to show you something," Moira said as she gestured towards the garden.

Eve heard the back door open. "Really? We're going outside? I mean, when I came over it was really quite chilly. Moira?"

Moira called through from the kitchen, "You'll be fine. I promise I'll keep you warm."

"Wait." Hastily misbuttoning her shirt and grabbing the blanket, Eve followed Moira out into the night. Nervously, Eve looked back at Loch View. It was dark and quiet.

"Eve, come on. It's okay, it's not far."

"I'm not sure. I mean…" Eve was looking around, searching out the features of the landscape through the strange, otherworldly half-light. Eve felt Moira slip her hand into hers. Eve's eyes fell to Moira's bare shoulders. She felt the urgent rising impulse of desire. "Moira." Eve leant into Moira, kissing her shoulder blade, her neck. Speaking through her kisses, she whispered, "We could just go to your bed."

"I want to show you somewhere special. It's just through the trees." Lightly holding Eve's hand in hers, Moira led Eve out of a gate at the bottom of the garden.

As they emerged through a small gathering of trees, there, deep and powerful, the loch spread itself wide in front of Eve, full and potent in the moonlight.

"Wow." Eve held her palm against her chest.

The air was heavy and rich with the scent of pine and gorse. Moira unrolled the blanket, nodding for Eve to sit with her. Eve sat silently, staring out into the night. The dark shape of the mountains, endlessly repeated into the distance, framed the loch and nearby hills. The lights of the hamlets across the loch could be seen blinking back at them, like stars in their personal universe.

Eve turned to Moira, who looked radiant, beautiful. Eve simply couldn't stop looking at her.

The moon shone in Moira's eyes as she looked back at Eve. "My heart feels so full." Moira's words, like her heart, seemed swollen with feeling.

Eve wanted more than anything to make love to Moira again, to bring her pleasure again. This was her purpose. If Eve Eddison was certain of anything, she was certain of that. At that moment she was fulfilling her destiny, her fate.

"Lie back, Eve," Moira said softly. "Lie back."

Eve swallowed hard. She could see in Moira's intense, almost feral gaze that she wanted to make love to her. *This isn't quite what I had in mind.* Eve glanced around her.

Moira reassured, "It's private, I promise. We can't be seen." Eve could feel her heart pounding.

Looking down, with an intake of breath, Moira let the throw slip off her shoulders, her pale skin illuminated in the half-light.

Eve looked at Moira's naked torso. She felt her body stir in response. She leant in to kiss Moira's neck once more, just under her chin, where her collarbones met.

"Trust me, Eve, you can trust me," Moira whispered, guiding Eve back to lie on the blanket.

Eve could feel the weight of Moira, the soft flesh of her breasts against her half-buttoned shirt. Eve tried hopelessly to control the rush of sensation, which was taking her breath and leaving her weak.

Moira undid Eve's shirt, revealing Eve's breasts, which she caressed hungrily.

"Wait." Eve gently held Moira's face in front of her. She felt a toxic mixture of panic and desire. "Sorry. I did warn you that I'm not very good at letting go. The feelings you make me feel—they're overwhelming."

Moira nodded.

"But I want you so much, Moira." Eve reached up and, lifting herself upright, slipped her arms around Moira's back in order to feel Moira's naked body against her. "I want you to, really I do."

Eve released her hold and lay down.

"I won't let anything happen to you—you're safe, Eve, you're safe." Like a warm breeze on a cold day, Moira's words soothed and eased in the night air.

Eve nestled her hands into Moira's hair as Moira leant over her once more, much more softly this time, kissing Eve's chest, torso, and navel. Trusting Moira, Eve lifted her hips and Moira gently eased Eve's jeans down.

Moira made Eve feel safe, protected, cared for, and this reassurance, this finding a lover who she completely trusted with her heart, her dignity, meant everything to Eve. It meant that night, in the full sight of the moon and stars, witnessed by the hills and mountains, she would give herself completely to Moira.

Eve took a deep breath and tugged her underwear down her legs, closing her eyes as she felt Moira gently slip her fingers inside her. With one hand nestled in Moira's hair and the other grasping the grass to the side of her, Eve let go, embracing the waves of intense sensation, her breath catching at each crest of pleasure. With each slow, deep breath, Eve was engulfed in the intoxicating aromas of pine, fern, sweet dew, and the warm lingering notes of whisky; Eve was engulfed by Moira, consumed by Moira. Moira was the beginning and the end.

Moira felt a strong sense of calm. She knew that she hardly knew this woman, yet she also knew in that moment, that very night, she wanted to be the one Eve trusted above all others, the one she felt the safest with, the one she longed for. She wanted to be the one Eve could let go with.

She kissed the delicate inside of Eve's wrist, her kiss warm and intense. Eve opened her eyes and held the side of Moira's hot flushed cheek. Eve touched Moira's lips, and Moira formed a kiss in response, taking Eve's fingers in her mouth, sucking gently, and mirroring the movement of her fingers inside Eve.

"Moira." Eve's voice arched, desperate with ecstasy and desire.

With this final call, Moira felt Eve's body relax, spent and exhausted, and collapse into the blanket beneath.

Eve lay there on the hillside as her breathing calmed. "That was so…"

Moira lay next to Eve, feeling a sense of exquisite fatigue.

Eve lay naked, watching the crescent of the moon and the shimmer of stars disappear and reappear through the clouds. Her body felt alive, every nerve ending bristling. As the intensity calmed, she shivered as her perspiration evaporated into the cool night air.

"Do you want to go in?" Moira's voice smouldered, smoky with the afterglow of passion.

"Not yet." Eve looked at Moira with heavy-lidded, dreamy eyes. "I just want to be here—with you."

Moira pulled a blanket over Eve and herself, their heads and hearts spinning in time.

❖

Eve opened her eyes and blinked into the early morning daylight. She felt Moira stir and nestle her face into her neck. Eve turned her head gently to glance around the sitting room. The ambling fire Moira had lit when they returned to the croft had gone out. The remnants of tea stained the bottoms of two mugs sitting on the stone hearth. Clothes hung, as if exhausted, from the armchair and shoes scattered themselves over the rug. Her gaze paused sleepily on the mantelpiece clock.

"Oh, shit," Eve exclaimed. "Does that say seven?" Startled, Eve scrambled off the sofa and began pulling on her clothes and shoes.

Moira squinted, bleary eyed, in the direction of the clock.

"It's okay," Moira said, with a voice husky with sleep and the embers of desire. She sat on the edge of the sofa, a blanket tucked around her, watching Eve darting about. "Do you want some coffee?"

With heels barely in her shoes, Eve gasped, "I've got to go. They'll wonder where I am. I have to go, I can't…" Eve stood with her back to Moira, her body facing the direction of the door. "I can't stay." The word *stay* crumbled from Eve's lips as she burst into tears.

"Eve, please don't." Moira held Eve tightly against her. "I know you can't. I know you're leaving. We've always known that, haven't we?"

Eve wiped at her eyes, desperately trying to regain her composure. "But it can't end here, not like this. We can stay in touch, see each other again, can't we?" Eve couldn't tell from Moira's blank expression what she was thinking. "Look, I'll write my number down here." Eve scribbled her number on the back of a leaflet advertising the centre and gave it to Moira. "I'll be home definitely by nine tonight. Will you ring me then?"

Moira studied the number.

"That's a seven, not a one." Eve pointed to the last digit.

Moira nodded and smiled.

Eve hugged Moira, squeezing her, holding her close, as she whispered into Moira's ear, "I'll really miss you."

That evening, staring at her phone, her thoughts full of Eve, her thumb poised to press dial, Moira began to feel a terrible sense of panic. She felt on the edge of disarray, her life unravelling.

This is madness. Where is this going? This has to stop.

Moira resolved right then and there to do everything she could to restore order once more. She would bury herself in her work. Yes. And she would soon forget Eve. As Eve, Moira was certain, would soon forget her.

"Without doubt, it'll all be forgotten," Moira said, with a heavy sigh, as her thumb pressed cancel.

CHAPTER FOURTEEN

D id something happen when you were away, Evie Eds?"
Eve felt her cheeks flush at Roxanne's question.

"Because, well, no offence, Eddison, but you've been a total
space cadet since your hols. And I am now officially bored with it.
And perhaps a little bit concerned, but mainly bored. So spill."

Eve knew that she needed to talk about what happened with
Moira. That she needed to find some way of lifting the emotional
fog that clouded her every thought and impulse. Eve was missing
Moira so much she was left with a constant aching in her chest that
made her feel like she was about to cry. Without question, the last
fortnight had seemed the longest of her life.

Eve slumped next to Roxanne on the sofa, pulling cushions
against her chest.

"Look, you're freaking me out," Roxanne said. "Are you ill or
something? Just tell me what's going on."

"She hasn't rung." *And my life is over.* "I gave her my number
the last time we were together. And then I rang and left a message
on the answerphone for her where she works, to tell her I got home
safely and to ring me."

"What, the chicken"—Roxanne cleared her throat—"the
woman you met on holiday?"

Eve nodded forlornly.

"She didn't give you her home number?" Roxanne asked.

"No, that's the thing, I left in a rush and didn't take it. I only
just had time to give her mine."

"Okay. Well, I don't know, Evie, you never know she may have lost your number. Or one of her hens ate it? Or I'm sorry, mate, but she may not want to see you again."

Eve shook her head. "I don't understand, Rox. It felt real, like she really wanted me. That it wasn't just sex."

"What, you slept together?" Roxanne's mouth fell open. "Wow."

"Yeah, you don't need to sound quite so surprised, Rox."

"Anyone a little oversensitive? *Anyway*. So was she a good lay?" Roxanne smirked.

Eve, ignoring the chicken reference, felt tears rise and sting, as she replied, "Yes. She made me feel...I've never felt that way, you know, with anyone." Tears streamed down Eve's cheeks.

Roxanne put her arm around Eve's shoulders. "I'm sorry, mate."

"Honestly, she only had to look at me, Rox. She has this smile thing going on, melty." Eve drew out the word *melty*. "And when she touched me, well." Eve puffed out her cheeks and sniffed. "And then, when she lay naked on top of me, for God's sake." Eve took off her jumper and looked across to Roxanne, who had shifted in her seat. "Sometimes it can take me ages, you know." Eve blushed, self-consciously. "And then I find it hard to let myself relax."

Roxanne protested, "Oh my God, TMI."

"But with Moira, Rox, it felt different—like it was meant to be." Eve looked away, a wistful expression on her face. "It was magical. She made love to me under the stars, like in the movies—"

"What—you did it outside? Bloody hell."

"I know. It was Moira's idea."

"Really? I thought, you said she hadn't much, if any, gay experience. You didn't think to ask her if she had previous girlfriends or—I don't know—a current girlfriend, perhaps?"

Eve shook her head. "She hasn't, at least, that's what I assumed—"

"You mean presumed?"

Eve frowned. "It all seemed, I don't know, a big deal to her somehow. And she needed quite a lot of reassurance, at least, at first."

Eve shrugged. "So what do you think I should do? I mean, should I ring her again? I don't want to pressurize her if she doesn't..." Eve bit her lip.

There was an awkward pause.

"Well, I guess you could ring again. You don't want to look *desperate* though, Evie." Roxanne sighed.

"No, I guess not," Eve said with a desolate tone, as she watched Roxanne clamber from the sofa and walk over to the front door. "You're leaving already? I thought we were going to the cinema. It's Sunday, we always go. Rox?"

"No offence, but there's only so much sex under the starlight I can take without heaving. And let's face it, we both know you're just going to sit there like a zombie." Roxanne pulled on her coat. "Look, I don't know what to say to you, mate. Ring her, don't ring her— whatever. I don't care. But this whole distracted, sad, anguished thing you've got going on—no offence, but it's kind of a drag."

"Right." Eve lay back on her sofa, listening to her front door closing. She closed her eyes. *Why haven't you rung me, Moira, why haven't you rung?*

It made no difference how much Eve's heart hurt, or how confused she felt that she had misread things so badly, because at the end of the day, it was clearly over. Moira had not rung and that was that. All Eve could do going forward was preserve what dignity she had left, and not bother Moira again.

"Have you heard from our girl, Angus?" Elizabeth asked, dabbing her napkin at her lips.

"No, seen her though," Angus said, matter-of-factly, as he began clearing the Sunday lunch plates from the table.

"Really, where?"

"Back at Foxglove, half an hour ago. She looked tired. I hope she's not working too hard. Why?"

Elizabeth stood to wrap a scarf around her neck and lifted her coat from its hook.

"Where are you going, Betty?" Angus asked, looking at the half-cleared table.

"Moira's."

"Moira's? Wait, I'll give you a lift, woman."

Drawing up to Foxglove Croft, Elizabeth advised, "Wait in the car."

"Why?" Angus asked. "Has something happened? Is Moira all right?"

Elizabeth gave Angus a look.

Angus sighed and rummaged down the side door of his Fiesta, pulling out his pipe and an old book of verse.

"I won't be too long," Elizabeth said quietly, her gaze fixed in the direction of Moira's door as she got out of the car.

"Hello, Moira. Hello." Elizabeth found Moira in her garden attending to her hens.

"Hello there," Moira said with a tired smile. "I'm wondering whether she's egg-bound. I may give her a warm bath in the morning."

Elizabeth looked at Moira studying the hens as they pecked the earth.

"It's been good of Alice to see to them for you," Elizabeth said, stifling the pressing need to ask the questions gathering impatiently at her lips.

Moira looked across at Elizabeth and nodded.

"Whilst you've been so busy, away from Newland." Elizabeth was searching Moira's face, hoping for some betrayal of expression, some indicator of emotion.

"Tea?" Moira suggested, her face unreadably blank. "I've a pot just brewed."

"Aye, yes, that would be lovely."

"I'll bring the tea in. Shall we?" Moira gestured into the sitting room.

"Ah." Elizabeth slipped her shoes off, sinking her elderly frame into the soft cushions of the awaiting armchair. "That's better."

Moira smiled as she handed Elizabeth her tea, served in her favourite china mug.

"You've been missed at the centre. Poor Alice, really, Moira, you need to collect at least a dozen messages from her and that's just from this week. And she's fretting terribly about the preparations for her outreach tour. I could not settle her. She kept repeating that the tour is part of her course assessment and that she was relying on your help. She's convinced she's going to fail."

"I'll call in to the centre first thing tomorrow. I'll sort Alice, don't worry. Angus can come in, you know." Perched on the arm of the chair Elizabeth occupied, Moira nodded towards the window at the red Fiesta and a snoozing Angus.

"Let's not encourage him. Anyway, it's nice for us girls to chat. It's been a little while Moira, hasn't it, since we've had the chance for a good blether." Elizabeth could not help but look at Moira and see in her the young child who'd once needed her so.

"Tell your father to re-warm them in the oven, to eat them at their best. Have you still got that jam I made for you? Please, Moira, do not tell me you've fed it to some animal friend or other." Moira shrugged. "Well. A low temperature mind, they don't need to be the cause of an inferno."

The eleven-year-old Moira was helping Elizabeth to bake a batch of scones. Some savoury, some fruit.

"You've nearly as much flour on yourself, Moira, as in the mixture. Here." Elizabeth brushed away the smudges of flour from Moira's face with the tea towel.

"I'm not very good at baking, am I?"

"Not at all, Moira. It is not that you are not any good—it is that you are learning. And learning is good." Elizabeth paused and smiled gently to herself, continuing, "And, in any case, between us girls, I feel sure that your husband will forgive a less than perfect scone or two."

Moira looked up at Elizabeth and then back down at her floury hands. Picking the mixture from between her fingers, she replied, "I don't want a husband."

"Why ever not, Moira?"

"Because I don't need one." Moira rubbed her hands together to remove the remaining mixture.

"But everybody needs somebody, Moira, everybody."

Moira shrugged. *"I have you."*

Elizabeth quickly swallowed down the emotion rising in her throat. *"Let's get these in the oven, yes?"*

Moira gave a faint nod and took a long, guarded sip of her tea. *What's on your mind, old lady?*

"So the course is going well?" Elizabeth asked.

"Yes."

"Good, good. And you'll be finished soon, then?"

"Yes."

"Good, good." Elizabeth took a sip of her tea.

Moira stood, deliberately disrupting the momentum of questions, and went over to the sitting room window, which faced over the road to the woods behind. "Your front driver's tyre's a little flat."

"Has something happened?" Elizabeth asked cautiously, her voice quieter.

"No, you've likely just run it down over time." Moira knew fully well that Elizabeth wasn't talking about the Fiesta.

"Before you say anything, I know it's none of my business. It's just…Alice noticed—"

"Alice?" Moira looked to Elizabeth. "Noticed what? What does Alice think she noticed?"

"Nothing, Moira. Nothing. It's simply that Alice noticed that you've hardly been home this last fortnight, and that you seem to be a little distracted, not quite yourself."

Moira collected the half-empty mugs, taking them into the kitchen. She called through to the sitting room, "If Alice is concerned about anything, please tell her to ask me directly next time."

Elizabeth followed Moira into the kitchen.

Moira stood at the sink, leaning against the worktop, looking down.

"I didn't mean to upset you," Elizabeth said, standing next to Moira and stroking her arm. "It's just that I don't like to see you so—"

"I'm fine, really. I'm just busy, that's all, and perhaps a little tired. There's no need to worry about me."

"Well then, I'll leave you to it." Returning to the sitting room, taking her coat and putting her shoes back on, Elizabeth held out her hand to Moira, who lent her arm to help her friend steady herself.

"Thank you for calling by." Moira's voice had relaxed slightly. "I'm sorry if I snapped at you. It's been a long week."

Elizabeth gave her girl a hug. "If you need to talk."

"Thank you."

What could she say to those people in her life who meant so much? How could she say, *I am sad because I am missing and longing for a woman I hardly know, and will likely never meet again*? How could she say that but then add, *But I'm fine and I'm still the same*? In fact, Moira thought as she slumped in her armchair and listened to Angus and Elizabeth drive off, how on earth could she say it to herself?

Chapter Fifteen

The Victorian façade of the City Library greeted Eve every day. She loved the old building, its quirks, its readers, and the shabby honesty of it all.

Nursing her recent heartbreak, Eve was only too happy to lose herself amongst the shelves of dusty books, the endless wooden drawers, and the soft tapping of catalogue keyboards. Time passed unmarked, unnoticed. This was the place in which to forget, as hours away from Moira slipped to become a day, days merged to form a week, and weeks blurred to a month.

"Local Community Action—Eve, didn't you go on holiday to Scotland recently?" asked Eve's colleague, Mrs. Harris.

Eve was buried in a family history search. She immediately looked up at Mrs. Harris's question. "Yes, why?"

"Well there's a talk here at the library, a week on Friday, by an Alice Campbell from"—Mrs. Harris lifted her glasses out in front of her face and squinted—"Newland. Well that doesn't sound very Scottish. It's an Eco-House initiative partnership apparently." Mrs. Harris lingered slightly over the word Eco-House to emphasize her inherent mistrust of anything hippy.

Eve said quickly, her voice squeezed in her throat, "Can I see?"

Mrs. Harris held out the leaflet in Eve's direction, releasing an impatient sigh when Eve scrabbled to pick up the files she had dropped on the dusty parquet floor.

"I do not know, Eve, if they spring these ad hoc events at us, how they can expect us to be ready, really. I'll bet they'll ask me to work late, and I've told them, I've my daughter's little ones to care for. What do they expect?" Mrs. Harris closed her eyes and pinched at the bridge of her nose.

Eve stared at the leaflet, picking out every word for deliberation as if it were an ancient script which if deciphered would unlock answers to life's ageless, unanswered mysteries. Scenic rather than revelatory, a picture of mountains and the symbol of a thistle bordered the simple text: *Come and learn about the massive difference one small community has made in the Highlands.*

Eve felt dizzy and sank into the chair behind the reception desk. The chair rolled away from the desk on its castors as Eve made no attempt to stop its travel.

"Are you okay, Eve? You've gone quite pale." Mrs. Harris's tone carried a note of irritation rather than concern.

Eve's hand covered her mouth. She gave a muffled, "Yes, I probably need my lunch."

"Is it that time already? Okay, see you at two o'clock."

Eve rushed from her seat to leave, with her jumper tied around her waist, her lunch box under one arm, and the leaflet folded tight in the fist of her hand.

She headed out into the town square, finding an empty bench in the shade. She read the leaflet for a second time. The talk was the last of a handful of presentations by the Newland Trust taking place throughout the Midlands region. There was no mention of Moira. Alice was the point of contact. Would Alice remember her? Should she ask after Moira? Would Moira be there? Eve had a thousand questions spinning in her head. None of which, she knew, would be answered unless she attended the talk. She needed to think, and she needed her best friend to help.

Eve had enticed Roxanne around to hers with the promise of generous bowls of home-made dessert.

"Bread and butter pudding—this must be serious." Roxanne crammed so much pudding into her mouth that talking was as much chewing as speaking.

As if she'd suddenly put two and two together, Roxanne spluttered, "It's whatsherface, isn't it? You rang her again, didn't you? What did she say? Are you seeing her again?"

Eve solemnly shook her head. "There didn't seem to be any point."

"Well, you know, holiday romances—they tend to come to nothing. It's not you or anything, Evie. It's just one of those things. You might as well forget it."

"That's the thing, in spite of everything, I don't want to forget it. I don't want to forget *her*."

Roxanne shook her head and, speaking through another mouthful of pudding, said, "Whatever...so what's this about then? If it's not *her*?"

"It is her, at least, I think it's Moira."

"Do you know what I think would go well with our pudding?" Roxanne's eyes had grown dangerously wide.

"Cream?"

"No. Gin and lots of it."

Roxanne set her bowl aside and grabbed two glasses, poured two double measures of gin into each, and added a token slosh of slightly flat tonic.

Eve raised her eyebrows. "I've got work in the morning, Rox."

"So have I, drink up." Roxanne slumped into Eve's armchair, and with her pudding bowl resting on her stomach, she took a deep breath and reluctantly asked, "So what exactly do you mean you *think* it's Moira?"

Eve handed Roxanne the leaflet.

"Local Community Action. Blah-blah-blah." Roxanne shrugged. Eve gestured for her to read on. "What? Really? No way. Here in Leicester?" Roxanne looked at Eve. "What the fuck?"

"It only mentions Alice, she's her colleague—there's no mention of Moira." Eve took the leaflet from Roxanne and reread it again, just to be sure. "There would be no reason for Alice to come to see me, would there? I mean unless—do you think something's happened? Oh no, Rox, what if something's happened to Moira?"

"Slow down, slow down. Firstly, what makes you think that Alice even knows about you and fanny flaps? Secondly, and don't be offended, but even if she did know that you two had sex, I can't imagine she would go to the effort of fabricating a talk to come and tell you that Moira's snuffed it."

"Please don't say that, Rox."

"No, no mate, I'm sure Moira's fine."

Eve perched on the edge of her sofa, staring at the leaflet. Roxanne leant over and tugged it out of Eve's hand. "Either way, this can't go on, Eve. I don't know—you need to try and get some resolution or something. And, if not, find a way to get her out of your system. It's boring, Evie." Roxanne fake yawned to make the point.

"Will you come with me then, to the talk? Rox?"

"Couldn't think of anything I'd rather do, mate." Roxanne rolled her eyes and headed to the kitchen. "I'm having more gin."

❖

The talk seemed ages away. Roxanne did her best to distract Eve. They watched films back-to-back, all action, all engrossing, no romance—Roxanne had insisted. Eve had also cleaned her flat from top to bottom. Twice.

"That's enough," Roxanne shouted, as she lifted her legs as Eve attempted to vacuum under the sofa.

"It's just if she comes back to my flat, I want it to be nice, you know, for her to feel comfortable."

Roxanne pulled out the plug from the wall and grumbled, "I doubt she'll make her decision about your future together based on whether you've vacuumed behind your wardrobe. This is new." Roxanne held up a framed photo of Loch View and Foxglove Croft, and asked, "Is that her house?"

Eve took the photo from Roxanne and nodded. "I thought, well, it would show her that I—"

"Can take a blurry photo?"

"It was taken from the loch, on a boat, and it was a surprisingly quick tourist boat, thank you very much. I was going to say, that I wanted it to show her that I remember our time together."

"Right. Well, it looks like you're ready." Roxanne gazed at Eve's flat, every surface dusted, every soft furnishing freshly plumped and preened.

"I hope she comes, Rox."

"I know, mate, I know."

Truth be told, Roxanne didn't know. She didn't know what Eve would do if Moira wasn't there at the talk. She didn't know why out of the blue Moira's Newland Trust would come to their city. What did that say about this Moira woman that she needed such an elaborate excuse to come to see Eve, when the simplest thing would be to pick up the phone? Things didn't make sense to Roxanne. Nothing about Eve and Moira made sense.

When the evening of the talk eventually arrived, Eve was exhausted. She felt rough and sick with nerves as she climbed the stairs to the first floor of the library.

"For God's sake, go and say hello. I'm right behind you." Roxanne's tone made it clear that Eve had no choice.

"Alice?" Eve tapped Alice on her shoulder.

Alice spun around, her face flushed. It struck Eve that Alice's expression at the sight of her was like watching someone's reaction to their newly deceased pet hamster being dug up and brought in through the cat flap by the family cat.

"Hi, it's Eve. Eddison. I don't know whether you remember me—my family, we holidayed in Newland last month? So, well, I thought I'd say hello."

Alice shook her head in a way that suggested she was trying to rid herself of the image of Eve. "I'm sorry. I can't say I really remember you, we get loads of visitors." Alice quickly returned to assembling the equipment for her talk.

"Oh, I know, they're a nightmare," Eve said, gesturing towards the collapsed projector screen which Alice was fighting in vain to erect. "Here, we'll help you."

Roxanne gave Eve a look that meant, *Really, we're helping this rude cow?*

Alice replied coldly, "If you like," turning her attention to the laptop, leaving Eve and Roxanne to struggle with the screen.

"What's the deal with her?" Roxanne half whispered to Eve.

Eve shrugged. "Dunno. She was like it in Scotland. I get the impression she thinks I'm ridiculous."

"Yes, so do I, but I don't treat you like that. Uptight bitch. You don't suppose…"

"What?" Eve asked, at the same time wrestling with the screen.

"She's not Moira's girlfriend, is she?"

Eve let go of the screen, which snapped back closed, narrowly missing Roxanne's fingers. "What, Alice? God, no. I mean…*shit.* Nah."

"Okay." Roxanne sounded unconvinced. "Well, I definitely get a whiff of something."

Fixing the final clips to the screen, Eve nodded in the direction of the audience. "Grab us a seat, Rox, near the front."

Roxanne looked at Eve and then Alice, and moved away, finding two seats near the back.

Alice held the plug of a power cable in her hand and was looking around her for a suitable socket.

"Let me, I work here." Eve held out her hand for the cable.

Alice narrowed her eyes at Eve. "You work here?"

"Yes, I'll just need to find a socket for you." Eve crawled under the table and grappled with the inset socket in the carpet. *Okay, so what's so surprising about me working here?*

"That looks awkward."

The voice from above the table sounded uncannily familiar.

"Moira?" As Eve rushed to free herself, she bashed her head on the table. Eve emerged flushed and rubbing her head.

"Hello, Eve."

Moira?

Alice cleared her throat loudly, then half whispered with a hiss to Moira, "Did you know *she* worked here, that she was going to be here?"

"Let's begin, Alice, yes?" Moira took her seat at the end of the first row.

Eve could sense that Alice was watching her take her place next to Roxanne.

"So that's Moira, eh?" Roxanne asked, adding, "She actually came."

"Yep." Eve was breathing heavily. "Yep."

Alice's talk was surprisingly well attended, considering it was taking place in an industrial Midlands city where any greenery was mainly of a token value for the purpose of showing off concrete buildings. Eve didn't take in much of the talk. She just sat and stared at the back of Moira's head.

"So, counted every grey hair then?" Roxanne smirked.

"I can't believe you just said that."

"Why aren't you sitting with her?"

"She might not want me to." Eve shrugged. "In any case I feel a bit embarrassed."

Roxanne frowned. "You've had sex *outside* and this is more embarrassing because…?"

"Oh my God, Rox, could you say that any louder." Eve sank a little into her chair.

Roxanne joined in loudly with the clapping that signalled the end of the talk. People were gathering around Alice who was handing them various leaflets. As Moira began packing up the equipment, Roxanne grabbed Eve's arm and ushered her to the front.

"Great talk, great talk." Roxanne stood face to face with Moira. "I'm Roxanne, Eve's best friend."

"Hello, Roxanne, I'm Moira." Moira looked directly back at Roxanne, and extended her hand.

Roxanne paused before shaking Moira's hand. "We're going to dinner at Carluccio's. Eve was wondering if you would like to join us."

Eve raised her eyebrows at Roxanne's impromptu invitation and quickly said, "Of course, if you have plans, then that's fine."

Roxanne stood firmly on Eve's foot.

Moira whispered something inaudible to Alice.

Alice scrunched her nose. "I suppose so, but I thought we were eating in the hotel."

"Great." Roxanne grinned enthusiastically. "We'll help you pack up. In fact, why don't you two go ahead to the restaurant, grab a table for us. Alice and I will follow on, yeah?" Roxanne rested her hand on Eve's shoulder.

Alice gasped with barely concealed panic. "No, I need Moira to—"

"I can do that, Alice. We'll be right behind you." Roxanne held her thumbs in the air at Moira.

"It would be good to talk to you." Eve touched Moira's arm. "If you want?"

Moira glanced briefly at Alice and then nodded.

"Great. See you in a bit. Oh, Evie," Roxanne shouted after Eve, "order me a large white wine."

Eve turned around to see Roxanne standing with her hands on her hips, shaking her head at the piles of bags, folders, and equipment scattered over the floor. "Okay, will do, Rox. Thanks."

❖

"I don't know why they couldn't just wait for us. Oh, no way, it's pouring it down." Alice rummaged around in her bag for her umbrella.

Roxanne was trying to balance screen, folder, and leaflets in her arms, whilst holding her jacket over her head.

"It's just here." Alice opened the back door of Moira's Land Rover which had been parked behind a barrier in the library's car park. "They said it could stay here until morning. I've left the laptop in their office. I'll get it tomorrow."

"So you've known Moira long then?" Roxanne asked, sliding the screen into the boot.

Alice frowned with barely concealed irritation. "What?" It was as if Roxanne had asked her the most ridiculous question.

"Moira—you've known her long?"

"Yes." Alice paused, clearly exasperated. "Since I was seven. We moved in with her, and then a few years later she became my stepmum."

Roxanne dropped her coat from her head. The rain splashed into her face. "Your stepmum?"

Alice slammed the door shut and looked at Roxanne with a withering expression. Speaking deliberately slowly, she said, "Stepmum, you know, married to my dad."

"Fuck me." Roxanne leant against the Land Rover. *Oh my God, Eve.* Roxanne looked in the direction of the street which led to the restaurant, which led to Eve and Moira.

"Are we going?" Alice asked, screwing up her face at Roxanne.

"What? Yeah, sure."

Chapter Sixteen

Eve was grateful that the journey from the library to Carluccio's was mercifully short. She hurried with Moira at her side as they silently made their way through the puddled streets to the shelter of the restaurant.

With a chic, informal dining style, Carluccio's was the place to be seen. On reflection, Eve wondered whether it was perhaps not the most private of places to have chosen to eat.

"Would you like to order some drinks to start with, ladies?" A waiter hovered expectantly by their table, his notepad flipped open in his palm.

"Bottle of white?" Eve asked, catching Moira's eye.

Moira nodded. She had been looking nervously around the restaurant.

Okay, Eve say something.

"It's good to see you." Moira spoke softly, as if mindful of the public around them.

"Yes, it's good to see you too," Eve said quickly. "And here too, that's quite a coincidence."

Moira silently stared at her menu in reply.

Eve couldn't help but notice how tired Moira looked. "Moira?" Moira looked up.

Eve took a deep breath. "I hoped, I mean, why didn't you ring me? Return my call?" Eve watched puzzlement wash over Moira's face.

"You rang for me?"

"Yes, I left a message for you—at the centre. You didn't get it?"

"No." Moira's expression turned to a frown as she looked out the window towards the street, which led to the library, which led to Roxanne and Alice.

"Moira?"

"Do you want to try the wine, madam?" The waiter reappeared at their table, tipping the bottle towards Moira.

"No, just leave it, that's fine, thank you." Moira lifted the cold wine bottle from its cooler, melting her fingerprints onto the surface, and poured two glasses.

Eve wasn't sure whether a toast was appropriate, and before she had chance to think of one, Moira had taken a large glug of her drink. She looked serious.

"You okay?" Eve moved her hand across the table to rest beside Moira's. She brushed the edge of Moira's hand with her little finger.

Moira moved it away, looking around as if to check to see if anyone had noticed. She placed her hands in her lap and said quietly, "When you left, I…I just felt so confused."

The waiter reappeared, and before he could speak, Eve said, "We're just waiting for another couple before we order. Thank you."

Moira watched the waiter briskly walk away to a neighbouring table.

Speaking barely above a whisper, Moira continued, "I didn't know what to do. Nothing felt the same after you left." Moira swallowed hard. "I couldn't seem to regain any order. I wanted to see you again so badly."

"Me too," Eve said in earnest. "I thought I was going mad, missing you so much."

Moira took another large gulp of wine. "I've found it difficult to concentrate, to work, to rest. I knew I had no choice but to find a way of seeing you again."

Moira's passionate words filled Eve's heart with joy, soothing the heartache of those lonely nights and distracted days without her. It was all Eve could do not to embrace Moira. *I want to hold you so much.*

"And then"—Moira cleared her throat—"Alice needed my help with the centre's outreach tour and this gave me an idea. You'd told me where you worked, so adding your library, just an extra date at the end of the tour, was achievable and it seemed to make sense. If you'd chosen not to attend the talk…well then, I knew where I stood." Moira held tightly onto the stem of her glass with both hands.

"Right." Eve frowned. "I don't really understand though. If that's how you felt, then why didn't you just ring me? You knew I wanted you to." Emotion caught at Eve's throat. She watched Moira look down again at her menu. "It really hurt not hearing from you."

With a wounded tone, Moira said, "I didn't mean to hurt you, Eve. I'm sorry. Using the phone…just sometimes, sometimes there's too much to say, isn't there? And the phone isn't always best."

"I suppose so." Eve couldn't immediately think of a conversation you couldn't have over the phone—except of course, only the really alarming ones.

Bringing a rush of cold, damp air with her, Roxanne clambered into the seat next to Eve, immediately lifting the wine from the cooler and filling her glass to the brim. She then proceeded to drain the glass dry and promptly refilled it.

"I think we'll need a second soon, yes?" Roxanne frantically waved the wine bottle in the air to attract a waiter.

Moira's attention turned to Alice. Alice's cheeks flushed and glistened under the restaurant lights. Moira stared at her, just stared, her eyes glazed over in thought.

Alice, in turn, simply couldn't take her eyes off Roxanne; it was as if she had never seen a Roxanne species before.

"Everything okay, Rox?" Eve asked, resting her hand on Roxanne's damp shoulder.

Roxanne stared at Moira. "Absolutely, why wouldn't it be?"

Moira looked down at her menu.

"So, what are we eating? I can recommend the ravioli, Alice," Eve said, mustering friendliness. "Honestly, the sage butter's to die for."

Eve's polite attempt at enthusiasm was met with a deadpan, "No. I think I'll have a salad."

"I'll have the ravioli." Moira looked at Eve and smiled, causing Eve to melt.

"So you've had a chance to talk?" Roxanne looked directly at Moira again. "Everything addressed that needed to be?"

Moira didn't say anything. She just held Roxanne's questioning glare.

"Well, we haven't exactly been here long, Rox," Eve said, frowning at Roxanne.

"What do you need to talk about?" Alice looked at Moira.

Eve couldn't decide how much Alice knew about herself and Moira or how much Moira wanted her to know. "Oh, I had some questions about the Trust and, you know, your talk," Eve said, managing a smile.

Alice quickly replied, "I can answer any questions you have, Eve. There's no need for you to bother Moira."

"Thanks, Alice, that's great to know." Eve looked across to Moira who was looking down.

"Let's eat, yeah?" Roxanne waved her arm in the air.

A charming Irish waitress with fiery red curls set off against her black shirt smiled broadly and said, "Girls' night out, is it?" Her question was answered with silence. "Right, so what are we eating, ladies?"

In one breath Roxanne ordered, "One side salad, two ravioli, one large pepperoni pizza with extra salami—and we appear to have run out of wine, thank you."

"You enjoy your food now, won't you?" the waitress said, her warm smile lingering on her lips.

"To be sure." Roxanne winked at the waitress, who gathered the menus and without saying anything hurried off.

Eve looked wide-eyed at Roxanne, who mouthed an exaggerated *What?*

Eve couldn't have been more thankful for her best mate, as Roxanne proceeded to fill the awkward silences with stories of medical mayhem and drunken epiphanies. Roxanne even managed to make Alice laugh with her comment to Moira that she admired her bravery as not everyone could carry off corduroy.

With the meal concluded, Moira watched as Roxanne lay as flat as she could in her chair, having undone the top button of her trousers.

"Oh my God, I may have eaten that a bit quick," Roxanne said with a wince.

"Somewhere in the world I feel sure you have broken a record, Rox." Eve giggled and shook her head.

"I'm sensing that too." Roxanne leant over, whispering to Eve, "A good fart will do the trick."

Eve, who had just filled her mouth with wine, snorted half of it back into her glass and half down her top.

"Oh shit, I'll just go to the loo. I won't be long." Eve spoke in Moira's direction.

Moira nodded and watched Eve weave her way to the toilets at the far side of the restaurant.

"Let's go back to the hotel, shall we?" Alice said, reaching behind her to retrieve her coat and bag. She dug around in her bag for her lipstick. "I'm just going to the loo and then we'll go when I get back, yes?"

"Sure." Moira looked at Alice. "Sure."

Roxanne slid across into Eve's seat opposite Moira, bringing the wine bottle with her.

"You know don't you?" Moira said, taking a sip of her wine and looking directly at Roxanne.

Roxanne took a slug of wine, pouring more wine into Moira's glass, before replying. "That you slept with my best friend? Yes."

Moira placed her hands in her lap to stop them from shaking. She glanced in the direction of the toilets. "I really like her," she said, working hard to steady her voice.

Roxanne shrugged. "She really likes you."

"I want you to know that I have no intention of hurting her."

"And yet..." Roxanne paused. "You clearly have no intention of telling her you're married, do you?"

"Alice told you?"

Roxanne said nothing, her face steely serious.

Moira folded her arms defensively. "You know nothing of my life, Roxanne. Please don't think that you do." Moira's voice bristled with discomfort at Roxanne's interference.

Roxanne nodded. "You're right. I have no clue about your life and no idea what you're playing at. All I care about is Eve." Roxanne pointed at Moira. "You need to tell her before any of this goes any further."

"That's why I'm here. I've come here to tell her, face to face. I couldn't tell her on the phone. And I wanted to see her again, so much." Moira watched Roxanne raise her eyebrows. "I tried to tell her when we first met, several times, but each time I just couldn't."

Roxanne leant forward. "So you lied to get laid."

"No." Moira shook her head. "It wasn't like that."

"Of course it wasn't."

Moira knew that to protest further was pointless and that the cold facts had beaten back the truth. "I'll tell Eve tonight," Moira said flatly as she watched Alice reappear through the dining room.

"You do that. And Moira"—Roxanne slid back across to her chair—"if you don't tell her, I will."

Reaching the table without sitting, Alice pulled on her coat. "Coming?"

"You go on ahead. I just need to speak to Eve," Moira said, standing up from her chair.

"I'll walk you back to the hotel, Alice." Roxanne pulled on her coat.

Alice gasped. "*No.* I mean, you're not coming with me? Moira?"

"You'll be fine with Roxanne," Moira said, looking at Roxanne, who nodded. "I just have some things to talk to Eve about—I won't be long."

Alice asked desperately, "What things?"

Moira replied firmly, "Please, Alice, I won't be long." Moira knew the distress this would cause Alice. But at that moment all she could think of was Eve.

"Oh for God's sake." Alice went puce, her arms stiff at her side, her hands clenched in fists, her knuckles turning white.

Eve arrived back to the table, looking confused. "You're all leaving?" Eve's eyes flickered over the dispersing group.

"No, I thought we could have a coffee. Just you and me." Moira placed her hand lightly on Eve's arm.

Eve smiled and blushed. "Oh. I'd like that." Eve looked at Roxanne. "Although, is everything okay?"

Roxanne shrugged. "You need to talk to Moira, mate. I'll catch you later."

Moira sat back in her seat opposite Eve, folded her arms, and took a deep breath.

"So, shall I order us a coffee?" Eve asked, straining her neck to look for their waitress. "Moira?"

A tear rolled down Moira's cheek in reply. Moira had spent the entire evening willing herself not to cry. She had spent the last six weeks, in fact, willing herself not to cry.

"What is it? Moira?"

"I'm sorry." Moira wiped at her cheeks.

Eve pushed her chair out from under her. "Come on," she said, "let's go." Eve caught the eye of their waitress and signalled for the bill.

"Where are we going?"

Eve looked into Moira's questioning eyes, "My place."

Chapter Seventeen

"This is me," Eve said. "Those are my windows, first floor, third along. It's very different from your croft."

Moira followed Eve's gaze, watching as the street light illuminated her face and neck. "Yes," she said, looking up at the tall façade of red brick that loomed over them, so symbolic of urban industry and far removed from the gentle pastoral slopes of Newland.

Moira took a deep breath as Eve opened the shared front door.

Standing side by side in the lift, Eve held out her hand which Moira took. As she did so, she looked briefly at Eve, smiled, and then looked down. Moira released Eve's hand as the lift doors slid open.

"It's bijou maybe, but I like it," Eve said with a shrug, switching on table lamps in the sitting area. "I guess I worship at the altar of Ikea. It's a Swedish furniture store, so—"

"Yes, I know." Moira smiled at Eve. "I've been to the one in Glasgow. I like the furniture, it's bright, cheerful."

"Cool." Eve smiled sheepishly. "Right. So, erm, coffee?"

Moira looked towards the collection of alcoholic drinks nestled on the corner of Eve's kitchen worktop.

"Whisky?" Eve suggested, blushing.

"Yes," Moira nodded, lifting the bottle, recognizing the brand she drank. It had been the drink that had warmed them in Moira's croft, the drink they'd tasted on their lips when they kissed, and the drink that flooded Moira's feelings with the memories of their magical night together.

Eve confessed with a soppy smile, "It reminds me of you."

Moira's heart ached. She was certain that come tomorrow morning Eve would be doing everything she could to forget her.

"Right." Moira cleared her throat, and turned away to ask, "You've travelled a lot?"

"Sorry? No, not really," Eve said, her expression confused at Moira's question.

Moira gestured towards Eve's fridge door and the many postcards that covered its surface.

"Oh no—they're from Rox," Eve said, shaking her head. "She's always heading off somewhere."

Moira felt her chest tighten at the mention of Roxanne.

Eve straightened one of the cards. "She gets bored easily." Eve shrugged.

Moira held a postcard in her hand studying its picture. She turned the card over. The handwritten scrawl read, *Missing you loads, Evie Eds. My plane gets in at two.* A drawing of a pair of boobs and a kiss replaced Roxanne's name.

"Oh yeah, that's Bolivia," Eve said with a giggle. "When I met her at the airport she was wearing a bowler hat and everything."

"You didn't want to go with her, travelling?" Moira did her best to strike a disinterested, nonchalant tone.

"Nah, it's Rox's thing. And, in any case, I'm a crap traveller. Really, if I'm not asleep, I'm feeling sick. And I've got work. Oh, and then she decided to go to Nepal for some reason—"

Moira turned away.

Eve shut up.

Whilst Eve fixed their drinks, Moira wandered around the living space, taking in each detail that spoke of Eve. Delicate flowered wallpaper enveloped the sitting room area. A slightly worn brown leather sofa, crammed with embroidered cushions, complemented a small purple velvet armchair that was tucked in the corner of the room under a curved standard lamp. A glass vase of cut flowers sat on the windowsill, sparkling in the glow from the street light. The space had an understated beauty to it, just like its occupant.

Moira glanced across at Eve. Never had a moment in time felt so precious.

Eve looked back at Moira, and they shared a self-conscious, tender smile.

Positioned separately on a side table, the photograph of Foxglove Croft and Loch View caught Moira's eye. She picked the photo up and carefully looked at it. "Everything's so crazy. How did everything become so, so complicated?" Moira rubbed her forehead and sat heavily on the sofa. She looked at Eve standing in front of her, her body tantalizingly familiar.

"Here." Eve handed Moira her whisky. She watched as Moira drained her glass dry. With her voice choked with feeling, Eve said, "It doesn't seem complicated to me." Eve reached forward and caressed the side of Moira's head, her fingers massaging through the curls. "I missed you, you missed me. We both wanted to see each other again."

"Eve, I—"

"I'm so glad you're here, Moira."

Moira could feel the warmth of the palms of Eve's hands resting briefly against her cheeks as Eve kissed her. It was a kiss so gentle, so tender. It demanded nothing and promised everything.

Please God. Moira's body ached for Eve's touch.

Without warning, Moira stood from the sofa. "I thought we could have that coffee—before I go back to the hotel." Moira struggled to find the breath for her words as her heart thumped in her chest.

"What?" Eve blinked her question at Moira, her cheeks flushed with desire.

Moira walked over to Eve's kitchen and lifted the kettle. She put the kettle back down and stared at it.

"You okay?" Eve asked, joining Moira at her side.

Moira nodded. "It's just, I need to get back to the hotel soon." She looked at her watch. "And, well, we haven't really had a chance to talk."

"You could text Alice, maybe," Eve suggested with a shrug. "Tell her you'll see her in the morning."

Moira could see Eve searching her face as if trying to gauge what Moira was thinking.

"In any case, we don't just have tonight to talk, to be together, do we? Moira?"

Moira could feel the blood pressing at the walls of her heart. She stared at the floor. She could hear Roxanne saying, *If you don't tell her, I will.*

"I'll text Alice and say that I'm staying a bit longer." Moira looked up at Eve. "Not to wait up for me. She's probably gone to bed already anyway."

Eve said quickly, "Yes. That would be great." Eve's eyes pleaded with Moira. *Please don't go.*

"I thought the hotel was that way." Alice grabbed Roxanne's arm, stopping her in her tracks.

"It is. I need a drink, Alice, and I'm guessing you could do with one too." Roxanne continued walking in the direction of her favourite watering hole.

Alice shouted after her, "You had wine at the restaurant."

Roxanne called over her shoulder, "Yes. That would be what I call a warmer-upper. Come on, it's a great pub, you'll love it." Roxanne disappeared inside the scuffed brass and dark wood doors of The Brewer's Arms.

"What on earth?" Alice followed Roxanne to the bar. "One drink. I am staying for one drink only."

Roxanne nodded, straight-faced, and said, "Absolutely. We'll definitely start with one drink."

"Hi, Roxy." A tipsy Belinda leant heavily into Roxanne, pretty much smothering Roxanne in her cleavage. She then planted a long, lingering kiss on Roxanne's lips.

"Hi"—Roxanne cleared her throat—"gorgeous. Erm, let me introduce you…" Alice's face had completely drained of colour. "Alice, Belinda. Belinda, Alice."

"Hi there." Belinda gave Alice a wink.

"No." Alice gasped in horror.

"No what, honey?" Belinda gave a curious smile, intrigued by Roxanne's guest.

Alice looked around the bar. Men leant against pillars talking to other men. Women were playing snooker, drinking pints, laughing. A tall beautiful female figure languished elegantly on the arm of a sofa.

Alice snapped accusingly, "This is a gay bar, isn't it?"

"Yes. We are all very happy indeed. Good luck with this one, Rox." Belinda mock punched Roxanne on the arm.

Roxanne watched Belinda curve her way over to a group of women, who all turned and looked at her and Alice, and laughed.

"Why would you bring me to a gay bar?" Alice's voice trembled slightly.

"It's where I drink." Roxanne rested her hand on Alice's very stiff shoulder. "It's who I am," Roxanne said gently, watching a flicker of realization pass over Alice's face.

Alice said quickly, "And Eve? Is it who she is too?"

"Yes, it's very contagious."

Roxanne's deadpan mockery was met with an emphatic, "Go to hell, Roxanne." Alice swung her bag over her shoulder and made for the door.

Roxanne grabbed her arm. "And Moira—can she go to hell too?"

Alice wriggled out of Roxanne's hold and stormed off, calling over her shoulder, "I don't know what on earth you mean by that, Roxanne, really I don't."

Roxanne caught the door before it banged and hollered after her, "It's this way to the hotel. And Alice, I think we both know that you do know what I mean."

Alice stopped. When she turned around it was as if someone had let the air out of her; her whole body seemed a little deflated. "No. Moira's not like that. She wouldn't do that." Alice looked at Roxanne, her eyes pleading.

"I know it's all a bit fucked up," Roxanne said with a sympathetic shrug.

"But what about my dad?" Alice asked anxiously.

"Let's take you to the hotel, yes?" As Roxanne walked Alice to the hotel, she checked her phone; there were no messages from Eve.

Alice's phone bleeped. "She's staying a bit longer with her. Apparently, I'm not to wait up." There was a defeated blankness to Alice's tone.

"They need to talk, Alice."

"Does Eve know she's married?"

Roxanne slowly shook her head.

It was obvious to Eve that Moira was troubled. Whatever she had on her mind, however, she was evidently finding it difficult to express. If they were to talk that night then Eve knew she would be the one who would have to begin.

"I was wondering, have you..." Eve paused. Eve knew she needed to know more about Moira, that this was her chance to ask the questions that had waited in the wings like an understudy longing for an audience.

Moira walked away to retake her seat on the sofa. "Have I...?" Her head tilted, waiting for Eve's question.

"I mean..." Eve shook her head. "It doesn't matter." She sighed heavily and filled her kettle. A cold drip of water drizzled down her shirt sleeve, dampening the edges of her cuff. She shivered.

"Leave the coffee. Come and sit with me." Moira gestured to the seat next to her.

Eve settled herself into the opposite edge of the sofa, facing Moira, and tucked a cushion in her lap.

"Ask me what you need to, Eve." Moira's voice was calm, serious.

"Well, I guess I'm kind of curious, just nosy really, whether you've been with a woman before me. You don't have to answer if you don't want to, obviously." Eve hugged the cushion tight against her. She wasn't sure why she felt so nervous of Moira's reply.

Speaking hesitantly, Moira said, "I met someone when I was at college." Moira looked at Eve. "I was in my last year."

Eve nodded. "Right, of course." *Of course you've had girl-friends. I can't believe I thought I was your first.*

"She was a singer. In a band, The Bells." Moira's voice was flat, emotionless. "She was good, she toured."

Eve asked, hesitantly, "Was she your girlfriend?"

"Yes. We were…we were inseparable." Moira took a deep breath. "When we left college we rented a flat in Inverness. We shared it with her band mates, three lads." Moira smiled to herself. "It was fun, lots of music, parties, and lots of alcohol. I'd begun my teaching at the local college, I was doing well."

"I bet," Eve said, her heart full of admiration.

Eve's appreciative response made Moira blush. "And then…" Moira shrugged. "She went on tour with the band and I couldn't go with them, you know, work and everything." Moira stood and went to the window. "Does this open?"

"Oh yes, just release the clip and push, that's it. Not too far, mind. Rox nearly fell out the other day." Eve shook her head.

Moira leant heavily against the frame. It looked as if she was about to light a cigarette.

Eve waited for Moira to begin her story again. She wanted to hear what happened. She felt she couldn't ask.

"It was probably just as well," Moira mumbled into the street below.

"You no longer loved her?" Eve asked, with a shamefully hopeful tone.

Moira's voice hardened slightly, bitterness seeping like black oil at the edges of her words. "It didn't matter whether I loved her or not. The early nineties, they weren't like today. Only the bravest of people came out, lived openly. You felt very unprotected…exposed. And then there was Section 28." Moira looked at Eve, who nodded. "I was teaching, I couldn't risk my career. You see, being a lesbian, announcing to the world that the person you wanted to be with for-ever was a woman, well, it just didn't feel like an option for me." Moira returned her gaze to the pavement outside.

You wanted to be with her forever? Eve pressed her cushion into her lap.

Moira continued, "Whenever we were out together, it felt like I was being watched, judged, that any minute someone would say something hurtful. It didn't bother Iris, but it bothered me. My private life is just that, private." Moira looked across at Eve.

Eve felt herself blush. *Okay, are you directing that at me? Wait a minute—did you say Iris? The Iris in the McAlisters' photo?* Eve tried to recall the detail of Iris. All that she could remember was that she was beautiful, really beautiful. "So are you still friends? I mean, were you able to stay in touch, when she'd finished touring maybe?"

Moira shook her head. "I moved out, I came back to Newland. My father had become ill so I came home, nursed him. And then when he died, I took on Foxglove." Moira walked back towards Eve and sat on the single chair opposite the sofa.

Eve's heart thumped in her chest, as she dared to ask, "So there's been no one else since?"

Moira looked blankly across at her.

"Of course," Eve said quickly. "I mean, I understand you've found it hard. I completely understand."

Eve worried for Moira's heart and felt sorry for her, sorry that she had fallen in love at a time when loving a woman openly would have felt almost impossible. She didn't blame Moira for thinking that she had it easy. In truth, Eve never felt complacent; she shared Moira's mistrust of society in general. It took no imagining to grasp the anguish when the joy and pride of your relationship was so easily overshadowed and diminished by an ever-present sense of menace.

"So what about now? How do you feel when you're with me, do you feel okay?" Eve asked, gently. Gauging Moira Burns's feelings was, for the most part, like gauging wind direction with an empty flagpole.

Moira nodded, her eyes brimming with tears.

"Then stay the night with me. Please." Eve felt emotion tightening at her throat. She knew she couldn't bear it if Moira said no.

"I…" Moira's words failed her, just when she needed them the most.

"You're tired," Eve said, with an understanding nod. "Absolutely. I totally get that. But we don't have to…I mean—"

"No, Eve." Moira shook her head. "It's not that." Moira joined Eve on the sofa, taking Eve's hands in hers. "There's something I need to tell you, that I should have told you."

Eve looked at Moira as a baby lamb looks at the butcher.

Moira stroked Eve's cheek.

Eve blinked. "Moira, what is it? You can tell me anything." Eve watched Moira take a long, deep breath.

"Eve, I'm married."

Although Eve heard the words Moira spoke, the impact, the emotional consequence of Moira's confession seemed unreal, remote, like the approach of something in the distance, just out of focus.

"Eve, did you hear me?" Moira gently squeezed Eve's hands.

Eve freed her hands from Moira's and stood up.

"Eve?"

"I think you'd better leave." Eve looked at her front door.

"Eve? Eve, please, please."

Eve just stared at Moira—her face so familiar and yet so unrecognizable.

"I'll call in the morning, first thing. We can talk properly then, yes?" Moira sniffed hard, as if resisting tears that badgered and threatened. "We'll talk then, Eve?"

"No, I've got work."

"Well, before work then. Please, I need to explain."

Eve mumbled, "No, it's okay, don't worry about it."

Moira gasped. "Don't worry about it?"

Eve shrugged.

Moira held Eve by both arms. "It's not what you think, please, let me explain. I care about you, Eve, I care about you."

Eve, looking down, said nothing.

Moira dropped her hands from Eve's arms and turned away. She silently gathered her things and left, as the stranger, Eve now realized, she had always been.

CHAPTER EIGHTEEN

*C*ome *on Eve, let me in.* Roxanne strained her neck to look up to Eve's window. *Come on, mate.* She checked her phone again. No messages.

She pressed her finger on Eve's buzzer, causing it to ring continuously, while she redialled Eve's mobile number.

"Eve Eddison, you're scaring the shit out of me. Open the fucking door. Now, Eve." As Roxanne shouted into her phone, she kept looking up, pulling furiously at the handle of the entrance door.

"Rox?" Eve appeared around the corner, holding a brown bag of groceries. "Oh my God, what are you doing? I went to get some milk. Wait." Eve opened the main front door. "You were about to pull the bloody door off its hinges. Oh my God, what's wrong?"

"Wrong?" *You don't know I know, do you? Okay, that's good. Yeah, probably best if you don't find out about me outing Moira to Alice either. Nope, you don't need to know about that. Okay. Take a breath.* "Nothing, nothing's wrong. It's just, well, I've been worried, a lot, all day. It was really selfish of you. Why didn't you reply to my text and calls?"

"Worried?"

"Yes, about you and Moira. How it went last night—whether she, whether you...you know."

Eve shrugged her way out the lift and inside her flat. "Soz. I couldn't find my charger. I mean, I had it yesterday."

Eve stood in her hallway, her groceries at her feet, her arms folded in front of her, as Roxanne rummaged in the rucksack hanging from Eve's coat peg. A brolly, scarf, lip balm, out-of-date cinema timetable, and a browning banana were thrown on the floor. Roxanne pushed the missing charger into Eve's chest.

Eve faked surprise. "Oh right, that's great. Thanks, Rox, I'll just—"

"Plug in a fully charged phone?"

"Tea?" Eve filled the kettle, flicked on the switch, stuffed two tea bags into mugs, and grappled with the milk carton.

"Leave it, sit," Roxanne said with a tone that made it clear that Eve had no choice in the matter. "You just have to give me a one word answer to this, right? It's not hard, okay?"

Eve nodded.

Roxanne asked, "Are you still having a Highland fling with Moira? One word reply only—yes or no." Roxanne watched Eve's eyes flood with tears.

Without answering, Eve stood and returned to the kitchen and filled the two mugs with the boiling water.

Roxanne took a deep breath. "Well? Eve?"

"No, okay, no."

Roxanne lay back on Eve's sofa.

Eve spluttered, "Are you satisfied now?"

"Eve, I didn't mean to—Eve."

Eve rushed to her bedroom and shut the door behind her. It was just over two hours later when she re-emerged.

Speaking softly, Roxanne said, "I ordered us a pizza. It's in the oven keeping warm."

Eve replied with an embarrassed, "Thanks."

Roxanne turned off the television. "*Grand Designs.* We've already seen it, that Kevin McCloud's such a bastard. He couldn't have been more delighted when they nearly bankrupted themselves, poor sods."

Eve bit numbly into her pizza, confessing with a full mouth, "She's married." Eve took another bite, even though she hadn't finished her first. "Not divorced, Rox, married, like right now. I slept with a married woman." Eve paused and momentarily stopped chewing. "God, what will my parents say? Oh no, what will Esther think? They must never find out."

"I'm sorry, mate, that's shit. She should have told you the minute she suspected you liked her. To be honest, I think you're better off without her. You're too good for her, Evie. So how did you leave things? Eve?" Roxanne moved the pizza away. "Is it over for good?"

Eve shrugged. "As far as I'm concerned, yes."

"And Moira, as far as she's concerned?"

Eve shrugged again.

Roxanne stared at Eve. "Right."

"I feel a bit sick." Eve's hand lay against her heart.

"I'm not surprised." Roxanne wrapped her arms around Eve and held her tightly.

"How could she do that? I really thought she liked me, Rox."

"She did, I'm sure, Evie."

"Did she tell you that?" Eve's broken expression carried a last glimmer of pitiful hope.

"She didn't have to, mate."

Roxanne could tell that Moira cared for Eve. But it didn't change the fact that Roxanne simply hated what Moira had done to her best friend.

❖

When Moira left Eve's flat, she wandered the streets, numb to the rain against her face, numb to life itself. When she could eventually face returning to her hotel, she hoped to find Alice asleep. She wanted to tiptoe into their twin room and into bed unnoticed. Instead, Moira found Alice sitting up, her bedside light on, speed flicking through the television channels.

"You couldn't sleep?" Moira asked as she took her coat off and hung it up.

Without wishing for Alice to see her distress, she quickly collected her nightwear from her case and hurried into the bathroom.

"Sleep?" Alice said. "How could I? I was worried about you."

Moira looked at her face in the bathroom mirror, at her pink cheeks stained with her tears. Taking a deep breath, she summoned the energy to reply, "There's no need for you to worry about me. So you got back okay?"

"What's going on, Moira?"

Moira came out the bathroom and climbed into bed. "It's been a long day, Alice, let's talk tomorrow, yes?"

Alice turned off the television. "No, let's talk now."

"Really, Alice, I don't want to talk right now. I'm tired and need to sleep."

"Well, I'm tired too but I need to know the truth." Alice paused. "You owe me that much."

Moira switched on her side light. "The truth?" She felt a terrible sense of panic, her chest pressing vice-like around her heart. "What do you mean by the truth?"

"The truth about you and Eve. The truth about what's going on with you. The truth about *you*."

"Please, Alice. I can't—"

"Roxanne told me that she and Eve are gay."

"Right." Moira swallowed hard.

"She took me to a gay bar tonight, would you believe?"

"Roxanne took you to a gay bar?" Anger flamed up in Moira at the thought of Roxanne's interference, but then a sudden self-awareness tempered her feelings, for she couldn't help but realize that she had been the one who had left Alice in Roxanne's care. She had brought Alice here in the first place. What on earth did she think would happen? Had she lost her sense? How was this terrible night not inevitable?

Alice nodded. "Have you been to a gay bar before, Moira?"

Moira shook her head.

Alice scrambled across the gap between them and sat perched on the edge of Moira's bed. "I knew it! I knew Roxanne had got it wrong and that you weren't gay, I knew it. And I bet you didn't know Eve was gay either, did you? I'm sure she fancies you, you know. You'll need to set her straight about that."

Moira said carefully, "I do know about Eve."

"Oh, okay. Well, like I said, I think she has feelings for you, and—"

"She does have feelings for me, yes."

"Exactly, so—"

"And Alice"—Moira placed her hand gently on Alice's arm—"I have feelings for her too."

"What sort of feelings? Moira?"

Moira didn't say anything. She quietly waited for the message to sink in for Alice.

Alice looked at the carpet, staring at an imprint left by a piece of heavy furniture that had since been moved.

Moira watched Alice looking at the floor. She looked at her young face, newly creased with a frown, her hair wavy where it had been tied back, falling free against her flushed cheeks.

Moira's chest ached at her betrayal. The betrayal of the notion of Moira as the woman Alice needed her to be—steadfast, reliable, trustworthy, her compass in life's storm.

The hotel corridor door banged to, and voices whispered and giggled loudly before fading into the distance.

"Is this what you do then—sleep with women behind my dad's back?" Alice's hurt had shaped itself into disgust.

"No, Alice." Moira shook her head insistently. "I've never before, I haven't—"

"So what you're telling me is Eve's the first? You honestly expect me to believe that? To believe anything you say, ever again?"

Moira could see that Alice couldn't bring herself to look at her. "Alice, please. I know this is a shock to you and I'm sorry—"

Alice climbed back into her bed and turned off her bedside lamp.

Before turning off her own lamp, Moira said, "You need to understand, I've hated keeping things from you."

Alice didn't say anything. Moira eventually turned off her light.

❖

Alice lay awake, staring at the ceiling. The red standby light of the television and the green light of the smoke alarm glinted like dying stars in the darkness of the room. Up to this very point, Alice Campbell's life had not made sense. She'd always sensed that something wasn't quite right between Moira and her father. It oddly wasn't the separate bedrooms soon after they were married or even Moira's eventual move to the croft. No. It was the unspoken, intangible distance in their closeness, the disregarded absence of the other, physical touch devoid of meaning, companionship in place of feeling. The emptiness of it all made Alice feel insecure and sad. And cross, it made her feel cross.

And now finally the truth for Alice, this confirmation—this missing piece that brought clarity to the confusing fragments of memory that had pierced her past. And in that very moment, in the darkness of the hotel room, the past became indistinguishable from the present, and Alice was ten again, standing in the McAlisters' dining room, overhearing the whole of a conversation she'd half understood.

"Spring air in the lungs—nothing better." Angus banged his boots at his door. "Well, Moira Burns, soon to be Campbell." Angus shook his head. "Let's get that stove firing for a warming brew."

"I can't take her name, it hurts too much." Moira stood in bare stocking feet in the McAlisters' dining room, looking at the collection of photographs on the sideboard.

"I'm not sure I understand, Moira." Angus dropped his scavenged harvest on the dining table and walked over to Moira to find her staring at the photo of Iris resting in her hand. Angus took a deep breath. "It is not unusual, brave girl, for weddings to bring up all kinds of emotions. It's completely understandable that you should remember your closest friend at this time."

"I miss her so much." Moira's tears dripped onto the polished sideboard, whitening the surface as they dried.

"I know you do, I know you do." Angus held Moira in his arms. "You need to be mindful though, that it must be particularly hard for John too. You must remember, Moira, when you marry John this weekend, you are taking his name, not Iris's."

"I don't have a problem remembering that, Angus. My problem is that I'm unable to forget her." Moira closed her fist around the photo, creasing it in two.

Angus took a seat at the dining table and rummaged in his pocket for his pipe. He placed the empty pipe in his mouth whilst he hunted in his shirt, jacket, and trouser pockets for his tobacco.

With a mouthful of pipe, he mumbled, "We have to let go of memories to be able to forget them, Moira." He lit his pipe and took a deep drag in.

With frustration at the fringes of her words, Moira said, "That's all very well but everything reminds me of her—the sky, the loch, everything around me. And John and Alice—when I look at them, it hurts."

"Moira, you have your future ahead of you, you need—"

"You don't understand, I loved her—"

"They smell funny." Alice revealed herself then, as if from nowhere, and stood smelling at the leaves on the table, at the same time looking at Moira. A cooling breeze blew in from the open kitchen door.

Angus and Moira looked at each other and then at Alice.

"It's wild garlic, young Alice," Angus said, guiding Alice into the kitchen. "And it will make the perfect spring salad. In fact, perhaps you can help me to prepare it."

Alice glanced behind her to see a distraught Moira smoothing the photo of her mother flat and placing it carefully back into place on the sideboard.

"You loved my mum, didn't you?" Alice's words fired out of the dark at Moira, like a sniper's deadly shot at her heart. "Did she love you too?"

"What? How did? I can't…I can't talk about this now, Alice. I'm sorry, please understand."

"That's why you took us in, isn't it?"

"Yes, but please, Alice."

"You never spoke about her. She was my mum and you loved her, and you never said a thing." Alice was breathing heavily. "And

Dad—did he know? About you—about you and my mum? Did he, Moira?"

Moira gave a muffled, "Yes."

"I don't understand. Why?" Alice stared at the blunt shape of Moira. "And Eve? Does he know about her too?"

With a tone empty of everything, Moira said, "No."

"It's all been lies. My whole life—"

"It's not like that."

Alice gasped in distress. "You're lying. Is it like that. And now you'll leave us. You'll leave us for this Eve—"

Moira turned on her bedside light. The agony of the night etched itself across Moira's face. "No. I would never leave you. And I wouldn't lie to you, Alice—"

"But you have lied. You've been lying all these years."

"Please, Alice. I'm sorry."

"Sorry? The only thing you're sorry about is that you've been found out!"

With her face in her hands, Moira released a muffled cry into the room, which reminded Alice of the pain of a wild thing caught in the poacher's net.

Alice clambered out of bed and held Moira. She hadn't meant to reduce Moira to tears, but if she was honest she had wanted Moira to feel her pain. But seeing Moira so distraught only served to double Alice's hurt.

"Don't Moira. Please, don't."

CHAPTER NINETEEN

The week that passed following Moira's return to Newland was marked with a sense of foreboding. Moira was in uncharted waters, the choking fog of uncertainty shrouding any sight of land. She knew she would need to account for herself, she just hoped she would find the words to say and the breath to speak.

"We need to talk, John," Moira said with a heavy sigh, as she stepped into the sitting room of the main house.

The spacious room was the shape of a fifty-pence piece. Long elegant french doors filled the space with a dusty light. Rain drizzled down them like tears.

Moira poured herself a whisky and stood at the window looking out at the loch. It seemed peculiarly dark and moody.

Speaking from the doorway, John asked, "What is it, Moira?"

"I can't do this anymore."

"You can't do what anymore?"

"I can't do *us* anymore." Moira turned to face John. "I'm so sorry."

John awkwardly lit his pipe. He made his way into the room, poured himself a whisky, and sat heavily in the armchair.

He swallowed hard. "So that's what Alice…I just thought she was being melodramatic." John's face drained of colour. "She said I needed to talk to you if I knew what was good for me. She made it sound like you'd met someone." John looked at Moira, his eyes desperately searching her face.

Moira just stood looking at him, unable to speak, her silence in every way her confession.

Swallowing a large mouthful of whisky, John then broke the terrible silence that choked the room. "I want you to know that I love you, Moira. I'm not sure you've ever believed I have."

"Please, John—"

"From the very first day you walked into the Union bar, I've loved you. From the very moment you agreed to be Iris's *S*."

"Don't, please don't." Moira's stomach turned over. She was back at the bar with John smirking at her and Iris.

John said flatly, "It stood for sweetheart."

Moira swallowed deeply.

"She thought you got it, I knew you didn't."

Moira felt her cheeks burn.

"I wasn't surprised she fell for you, I was just surprised..." John paused. Moira held his gaze. "I was just surprised you let her go."

Moira felt weak. She walked unsteadily to the sofa, sinking helplessly into the soft seating, her head resting briefly in her hands. She looked up at John and heard herself ask the one question that had troubled her for too long. "Will you tell me then, why did you go with her, have a child with her, set up home with her, if you've always loved me so?" She had wanted to ask Iris that same question.

"When we all lived in town, it was great, wasn't it? We were all happy, close together, weren't we?" John drained his whisky down. "I stupidly thought it could last forever, the closeness we all shared. And then when we got our break and decided to tour, and you decided not to come, I thought, that's okay because you and Iris, well you were inseparable, and whilst Iris and I were in the band together, I would still see you." John looked into his empty glass.

Moira couldn't quite take in what she was hearing.

"But then one night, Iris came into my room, we were staying in a shitty hotel in Berwick, the..." John scratched his head, trying and failing to remember the hotel's name. "I remember it had no curtains, just cardboard against the windows. Anyway, she was upset. I think you had rowed or something. And then, she just undressed and got in my bed, and…well. I thought when we got back from touring it would go back to normal but you had left and Iris wouldn't talk about it. And then we found out about Alice—we were suddenly parents and things changed, had to change. I knew the right thing was to stand by Iris, to help bring up our daughter." John wiped at his eyes with the back of his hand. "But I never stopped loving you, Moira, neither of us did."

Moira looked at John properly, maybe for the first time since that first night in the Union bar. She watched his greying, receding hairline move up and down as he spoke, the scratch of stubble on his sallow skin. When Moira thought of John, she thought of the young man with shoulder-length hair and full beard, playing his accordion, smoking his pipe. Now sitting opposite her was her companion who had grown old and Moira had not noticed.

Confused, Moira said, "I just assumed, I thought you married me, stayed with me, because it was the right thing to do for Alice, that we helped each other with our grief—"

"Did I? Did I really help you with your grief? I doubt that, Moira. When all you could see was Iris. All you've ever wanted was Iris."

John took a drag on his pipe. He drew in deep, desperate fogs of smoke into his lungs, as if the nicotine offered pain relief. "I wanted you to love me. To look at me the way you looked at her. But you never did."

"Please understand, I wanted to love you, I tried to love you, John, you know that."

John gave a long defeated sigh. "I know. I know you did, Moira. And I've tried to understand. But that didn't stop me hoping like a bloody fool for all these years that if I gave you space and time, somehow you would change, grow to love me, in the same way that Iris and I grew to love each other. But you didn't, wouldn't." John's voice squeezed with the effort of controlling his resentment and hurt.

"*Couldn't*, John. I was never the same as Iris. I can only love women. I told you that—"

"Only women or only Iris?" John's pointed question stabbed at Moira. "I mean, does this new woman of yours know that she's wasting her time, just as I've wasted mine?"

"I never made you stay." Moira gasped in alarm that John had harboured such thoughts.

"But you never told me to leave!"

"How could I? We were a family—"

"But that hasn't stopped you betraying us." John's voice broke and crumbled away.

"I never meant to hurt you, John."

"It strikes me that you never mean to do the things you do, Moira. But it doesn't change the fact they've been done."

John got up wearily from his chair and opened the sitting room doors to the garden. A damp, chilling evening air filled the room.

With a heavy sigh he said, "I've stayed too long. It's time for me to leave."

Moira swallowed hard. "Where will you go?"

"Town, at first, I suppose. It'll be easier for work. I might even head further north, catch up with Hamish. He's always saying he never sees us." John stopped, seeming to wince at the word *us*. "My consultancy work could take me anywhere. A fresh start." Never had those words been said with less enthusiasm.

"And Alice?" The pain rushed at her with the thought of losing Alice. "We'll need to talk to her, John."

John shrugged and stood to walk away. "Yes, I'll talk to her. What you say to her is up to you."

Sitting in the room alone, all Moira could feel was the sting of the salt of her tears at her lips.

Eve had correctly interpreted Roxanne's advice to keep herself busy as, *Come to as many parties with me as possible, get blind drunk, and forget all about her.*

"Who did you say was going tonight?" Eve spat her words into the sink along with her mouthwash. "There'll be lots of hot nurses right, even though it's a Thursday?"

"Guaranteed. Weeknights totally rock. Everyone pops in for one drink only to leave at dawn, slaughtered and missing a shoe. I've invited everyone at the hospital. The only people left on duty will be a junior doctor on the verge of a nervous breakdown and a porter."

"Great. Thanks for inviting me. You know, I may be getting into this fancy dress malarkey." Eve completed the final touches to her cowboy outfit in front of the bathroom mirror.

"Fancy a whisky engine starter, Evie Eds?"

"Nah, you go ahead though, Rox—in fact, finish it off if you like."

"Ta, mate." Roxanne paused. "Eve?"

"What?"

"What's that parcel? No, don't tell me—yet more porn."

"What?" Eve leapt out the bathroom, drew her water pistol from its holster, and aimed it at Roxanne. "Stick 'em up, Officer Barns, or else."

Eve giggled as Roxanne slipped her truncheon from her belt and slapped it against the palm of her hand. Roxanne then used the truncheon to point to a discarded parcel, partially hidden behind an umbrella at Eve's door. "That parcel—you're not going to open it?"

Eve feigned disinterest. "No, it's okay. It's probably nothing."

Even before looking at the postmark, Eve had known that the parcel she had received two days earlier was from Moira. She had simply dropped the parcel on the floor by the door and blocked out the memory of its arrival, just as she had blocked out the memory of Moira standing in her living room, begging Eve to listen. "I was about to throw it away anyway."

Roxanne picked up the parcel, held it to her ear, and shook it.

"You're just going to throw away a parcel unopened?" Just as she spoke, Roxanne noticed the label glued to the side of the parcel. "Inverness?" Turning the parcel over, she read aloud, "Sender:

M. Burns, Foxglove Croft, Newland, Inverness. It's from Moira. God, she's got some nerve. Does she think she can win you over sending you some shortbread?"

"What time's the party at your place. Eight, wasn't it?"

"Yes." Roxanne knocked back the whisky.

"Let's go." Eve patted the thighs of her tan felt chaps and positioned her cowboy hat in such a way that it cast a shadow over her eyes. "I'm a-headin' on over to them thar nurses' lodgings. Saddle up, Barns, we're ridin' out."

Roxanne tossed the parcel back onto the floor. "You had a lucky escape there, mate. She had heartbreaker written all over her."

❖

"Best party ever." Eve hiccuped. "No, wait, I think I've lost my hat." Eve patted her head at the same time tripping up the front step that led into the nursing halls.

"It's here, tit-head." Roxanne lifted the hat that dangled from its strap against Eve's back, and squashed it on her head.

"Oh." Eve looked completely surprised. "Rox, I've got a stitch." Eve bent double. "You're walking too fast."

"Evie, I'm not walking fast, you're not moving. Now shift your arse." Roxanne grabbed Eve around the waist and escorted her, almost in a straight line, back to her room.

Eve stood, rocking slightly, blinking at the sight that greeted her. Eve wondered whether Roxanne knew that someone had ransacked her room. Clothes, shoes, and, it seemed, nearly all of what she owned lay discarded on the floor. If there was carpet, you couldn't see it. If there was a seat, you couldn't sit in it. Underwear and T-shirts were draped, like bunting, over the open drawers. A pair of trainers dangled out of the window, propped open with a beer can, and a pot plant wilted on the sill.

Eve remembered Roxanne joking that one person in the room made it full, two made it crowded, and three people represented a fire hazard.

Eve slurred at Roxanne, "You have a tiny room, Rox. No wonder you're always at mine." Eve wrestled out of her boots and collapsed onto Roxanne's single bed, her cowboy hat squashed under her head. "Your bed's really uncomfortable."

"Yeah, shove over." Roxanne gave Eve a hearty push in the direction of the cold wall.

"Is that your truncheon or are you pleased to see me?" Eve giggled and hiccuped again.

Roxanne pulled her pillow from under Eve's head. "You are totally pissed, Eddison. If you puke on me, you're dead."

Eve rolled into Roxanne and wrapped her arms around her. "Uh-huh." There was a pause followed by an almost inaudible mumble. "You're my best friend, Rox—the very best friend in the whole world, the whole wide universe world."

Eve stood in the middle of her living room, as if waiting for something or someone. It had felt wrong to leave Roxanne without saying goodbye. It had felt wrong to walk away in stocking feet, her boots in her hand. But she had woken with a start, Moira's name at her lips. And then she couldn't stop thinking about the parcel that waited for her. The parcel she couldn't throw out.

Eve's head hurt. She felt sick. Sick and confused. *I need a drink.* She poured herself a glass of water, drinking it down in one thirsty gulping rhythm. She numbly wiped the wet from her chin with her sleeve, her eyes staring, rather than looking, at the parcel. *Moira.*

Dear Eve,

Eve squinted at the sunrise tipping over her windowsill into her living space. She imagined Moira writing the letter, sitting amongst her plant cuttings, the light from her sunroom window fading on the pages as she wrote. Eve lifted the paper to her nose. It smelt strongly of the neat bouquet of ferns, heather, and gorse petals with which it had travelled.

I know I have hurt you. I am very sorry for that. I did not tell you I was married because I thought you would think differently of me. Please understand I never set out to deceive you.

Eve sat pensively on the edge of her sofa, the remnants of the torn-open parcel at her feet. *But you did deceive me though. I trusted you.* The two weeks that had passed since Moira's revelation had done nothing to dull the hurt Eve felt.

A part of Eve didn't want to read on. Reading on somehow felt like a complicit act of forgiveness. *I'm not going to forgive you, Moira. You can send all the letters and flowers you want.* And yet discarding the parcel unopened, the letter within unread, felt equally intolerable.

I need to explain. To explain how I came to marry. I need to explain about my life, about me.

Eve held the letter tightly with both hands, keeping it flat against her lap, almost as if she feared that Moira's words of explanation would slip from the pages and be lost like dropped jigsaw pieces onto the floor.

As a child I played and grew up amongst crofters, my family, and friends. I learnt about life from the natural world around me. I felt safe, I felt free. As I grew older, things changed. I went away to college in Ayrshire to study, to learn about caring for my homeland. It was always my intention, when I graduated, to return to Newland, to Foxglove.

The memory of Moira's croft, the hens in her garden, the magical glade, the image of Moira, spilled uncontrollably into Eve's thoughts. The noise of delivery men unloading in the street outside jolted Eve back to the present, to the letter, to the promise of an explanation.

I didn't plan to fall in love. Iris wasn't part of my plan. It somehow never occurred to me that I would meet someone, fall for someone. I certainly didn't plan to move in with Iris after college, it just happened. Not being with each other, it wasn't an option for us. I couldn't be without her.

Eve shuffled in her seat. She felt her heart quicken as she read the name *Iris*. Eve had thought a lot about Iris—the woman Moira had wanted to be with forever. *Forever.* And every time she thought of Iris it made Eve feel terribly sad, for surely there was no room for Eve, or for anyone else, in forever. Eve took a deep breath and read on.

Over time, Iris and her band, The Bells, became more and more well known, first in Inverness and then the local regions. They were developing a following and the local press were besotted with Iris. Everyone was besotted with Iris.

At first, the press speculated that Iris was dating one of her band mates. Each one was linked to her at some point. And then, out of the blue, an article appeared in the Chronicle, *our local paper. They had taken a picture of Iris, half-naked with her back to the camera, looking at me. We were just talking, but the headline, it read, "Breast of Friends?" My father read the* Chronicle, *Angus and Elizabeth read the* Chronicle, *they all saw the article. It was so humiliating Eve, deeply, deeply humiliating. We denied it, of course, at least to the press and to family. The band was really good, they also denied the story. John even told them he was dating me, you know, to put them off the scent. Whenever we went anywhere, John would put his arm around me. It annoyed Iris, we rowed about it. I thought it was a good idea. John didn't seem to mind.*

Eve's mind was working overtime, reading between the lines of everything Moira was writing, retracing what she had seen, what she had heard. *I bet it annoyed Iris, for John to be all over you. It would have annoyed me.*

Iris tried to tell me that it would be okay if we told people about us, that we were in the music business and that it would be okay. I wasn't in the music business—I was teaching. I was a teacher, not a gay rights activist. I had to think about my job, about my students. I had no choice but to protect my reputation if I were to continue teaching. And there was my father, he was elderly, old fashioned, I couldn't bring him shame. I wouldn't bring shame on Angus and Elizabeth, on Newland. I just couldn't Eve, you have to understand I just couldn't.

The Bells got a manager and he set up tour dates, right across the UK. It would mean that they would be away for months at a time. Iris pleaded with me to travel with them. I felt torn. I couldn't imagine being without her and yet I couldn't get that picture out of my head. That awful picture.

We kept in touch. She would ring me each night before she went onstage. I was her strength, she would say. After six months they were nominated for a newcomer's folk award. It was a really big deal. Iris asked me to come to the ceremony with her. We agreed that I would sit between her and John. They won and when they announced The Bells, Iris went to kiss me, and I panicked, I turned away, and then John was holding me, kissing me. The cameras were flashing, people were applauding—it was chaos.

We didn't speak for days and finally when Iris rang, we rowed. She told me that I had hurt her badly. I told her I would only keep hurting her if we stayed together. She asked me did I mean that it would be better if we ended it. I heard myself say yes. She never rang me again.

Eve realized that she had been holding her breath and that her chest had become incredibly tight. She repositioned herself to lie on her back, her head against the arm of her sofa, Moira's letter resting on her tucked-up knees.

I was in a bad place. I missed her so much, I struggled to work. I struggled to keep going. In the end I packed up, left Inverness, and came home. I came home and never left again. I buried myself in Newland. And then, eight months later, Angus handed me the Chronicle. *The front page read "Ring The Bells, The Travellers Return." I remember looking at the photo, just staring at it. Standing amongst their instruments, Iris and John looked back at me. He had his arm around her. They were both looking down at Iris's pregnant stomach. The article explained that The Bells had returned so that Iris could give birth in her homeland.*

I went to their homecoming concert. I stood at the back of the hall, out of sight. I just had to see her. She looked radiant, beautiful. I knew at that moment I had made a terrible mistake. Everything in me wanted to run to the stage, call her name, tell her I was sorry, beg her to forgive me. And then she kissed John. They looked really happy. I knew I had lost my right to Iris, that I had lost her love. That I had lost love forever.

I left the concert and that was that. And then, thirteen years ago, thirteen years last January, out of the blue, John rang me. He told me that Iris was certain that they would find me in Newland. She'd kept my number all those years. How I had longed to hear her voice—to hear her say my name. But instead it was John speaking to me, with a strange, hollow tone. He told me Iris was very ill and that she had asked for me.

I remember the weather was really bad, I struggled my way to town. When I arrived, John greeted me. A doctor was also present. He had given Iris morphine. She looked a bit high. John left us to see to Alice. We held each other all night. She said she never stopped loving me. I just kept saying sorry.

She slipped in and out of consciousness. Just before dawn, she woke, really lucid and calm. She asked me to look after John and Alice. She made me promise. I promised her I would, I promised her, Eve. I held her hand as she left me. I found it hard to leave her. They let me sit with her for a while longer and then they took her away from me.

Eve looked over to the window, her gaze fixed beyond her living space, beyond the city, to Scotland, to Moira. *I'm sorry, so sorry, Moira.* With an aching heart, Eve read on.

Without Iris there was no Bells, and without The Bells John had no work. I didn't think twice. I took them in and they came to live with me in Foxglove. There was plenty of room for us all. We devoted ourselves to Alice, to bringing her up, in the way we knew her mother would want us to. And then one night, after Alice had won some competition or other, she was so proud, we were so proud, and John kissed me.

Our bond had grown so strong. Even though they were a constant painful reminder of what I had lost, I nonetheless found solace in his company, such joy in bringing up Iris's daughter. We were married in the following spring.

Oh my God. Eve's head spun with everything she'd read.

It felt so good to give Alice a home, stability, but for John and me it didn't work. I tried, for everyone's sake, to love him fully, but I couldn't. It became clear soon after we married that a platonic relationship was all I could give him. All I could ever give a man.

I expected John to move on, for them to leave, but they didn't. John moved back into his own bedroom and we kept ourselves busy. He eventually got a job as a consultant in the Highland Council's agriculture department, which meant he had to work away a lot. I devoted my time to Alice, and to developing the centre. We somehow found a way to make it work.

Eve looked up at the clock on the wall and stared at it as if the hands were marking not minutes, but years that had ticked by. *But weren't you lonely, Moira?* Eve's gaze fell back to the letter.

We reassured Alice that everything was fine and she believed us in the heartbreaking, trusting way that children do. And before we knew it she was eighteen and packing to leave for university. She insisted on choosing the college her mother—all of us—went to. It strangely felt like some sort of circle of life had been completed.

With Alice gone, and John working away so much, the main house that had suited me fine before John and Alice arrived just felt too big somehow. And when John was home, and it was just the two of us, the house felt even emptier. So I turned my attention to renovating the croft and gradually moved in. We did our best to explain to Alice that my move to the croft didn't mean that we were no longer a family. Looking back, I'm not entirely sure who we were trying to convince. Alice was so desperate to believe us and we have been so wrong to let her.

Angus and Elizabeth took the news of my decision to live in the croft with their usual diplomacy. If other people—villagers, acquaintances—wondered at our living arrangements, they had the decency not to ask. That was two years ago. And then I met you.

Eve gripped the page tight in her hand.

I want you to know that John and I have talked, and he has left Newland. We had drifted for years without the courage or impetus to address our relationship, to talk about the future, and I would have carried on in that way, hurting myself, hurting us all, if it wasn't for you. You've shown me that there could be more to me, that there should be more to my life. And for that I'll always be grateful.

I hope that one day you will understand, Eve, and find it in your heart to forgive me.

Moira

Eve's emotions, thrown like a ship in a storm, dipped and rose and dipped again as Eve struggled to anchor her feelings. She could feel Moira's pain, but then there was her deception, her deliberate economy with the truth.

She struggled to digest the fact that the Campbells were Moira's family, that they were living in her house.

And yet Moira must have known that she was risking everything to be with Eve. She must have needed her so much. Eve recalled Moira's deep urgent kisses, the way she touched her, the way she made her feel. Eve's thoughts turned to the night they'd made love, when she had wanted Moira as desperately as Moira had wanted her.

Moira had laid bare her soul, relived her sadness and pain, offered up her life for scrutiny. Eve knew for such a private woman this would have been unthinkably hard.

By rights she should have been appalled by Moira's dishonesty, but she couldn't help but wonder: If Moira had told her then what she was telling her now, would she have wanted Moira any less?

She traced her fingers over the intimate handwriting, over Moira's heartfelt words, and with a sigh, she said, "I want to try to understand, Moira, really I do."

Eve knew there was only one way she would fully understand and that was to see Moira again, if only just for one last time. In fact, if she left straight away she could surely catch a train, and before the sun set she would be in Newland.

Chapter Twenty

A s Eve stood in the driveway of Foxglove Croft, everything about Newland looked familiar, and yet nothing felt familiar. The main road still curved its way past the village hall, past the sheep gathered at the gates and the horses nodding in the fields. The grass edging of the road still brushed against the flower-laden walls of the roadside crofts. Even the sun setting behind the mountains, bleeding blood-orange into the brooding loch, was nothing new. And here at Moira's door were the familiar grains of wood, the worn-down stone step, the threshold to all that had gone before and all that lay ahead.

Please be in Moira, please be in. There was no reply to Eve's knocking. Eve dared to glance into the sitting room. She could see the table full of papers, Moira's armchair, and the whisky decanter catching the glint of the evening sun as it faded through the sunroom windows. She could just make out the hint of the garden beyond. *Ah. The garden.* Eve walked around the croft.

She steadied her voice. "How are your beans?"

Moira looked up and blinked several times as if trying to take in what she was seeing. She leant heavily on her spade, her throat thick with feeling. "Eve?"

"It's okay, Moira. I mean, I've practised this. For us. On the train. I practised what I wanted to say to you."

Moira set the spade firmly into the ground, moving slowly to Eve.

Eve began, "I start off by saying that I read your letter." Eve's chest tightened as Moira stood in front of her. "I read your letter and"—Moira eased Eve's rucksack from her shoulder to rest on the grass—"that I want to try to understand." There was a slight pause.

"And what did I say?" Moira asked. She looked serious.

"That you were pleased I'd come to you." Eve swallowed down suffocating emotion.

Moira stood silently looking at Eve.

Eve couldn't tell what Moira was feeling. "Are you pleased I'm here? I couldn't bear it if you weren't." Never had the word *pleased* felt so inadequate.

Moira nodded.

Eve hugged Moira, holding her tight.

Moira whispered into Eve's ear, "I wasn't expecting you to come all this way."

"No?" Eve asked, confused, releasing her hold to look at Moira. "But how could I not?"

It felt to Eve that all paths seemed to converge on this moment. That if there was an alternate route, then it simply didn't feel like it.

Stepping into the croft, Eve was transported back to that heady June night. With tired eyes, she looked at the floor in the sitting room where she had made love to Moira, where they had lain together.

"It was magical—being with you," Eve said wistfully.

"Until I broke the spell," Moira said flatly.

"No, it was me," Eve said, shaking her head. "I'm so sorry that I sent you away without giving you a chance to explain."

"*No*, Eve. Believe me when I tell you, you have nothing to apologize for. I should have told you I was married. I didn't know how to...I didn't know what we were. And then, everything was moving so quickly." Moira paused and looked intently at Eve. "The very last thing I wanted to do was to hurt you. In fact, I wouldn't have blamed you if you hadn't read my letter."

Eve confessed, "I nearly didn't."

"No?"

Eve shook her head. "I've felt so deceived, and hurt. I can't pretend I haven't. But somehow I had to read your letter. And then reading about your life, your grief—I just wanted to see you again. I had to see you again."

Moira moved away. She sat on the edge of the sofa, looking down, as if entranced by the patterns of the rug.

Eve sat next to her, the edge of her knee just touching Moira's. She said softly, "I can't even begin to imagine how painful that would have been, losing her."

Moira nodded, pulling at a stray thread at the edge of the sofa. She took a deep breath and said, "Eve, I want you to know that I've never done this before—cheated." Moira changed the subject with a deftness of touch that suggested she had guided conversations away from Iris many times before.

"So I'm not another notch on your bedpost of random holiday-makers." Eve quickly shut up at Moira's unimpressed expression. "No. I was joking, obviously. I've never thought I was." Eve quickly looked down. *Oh my God, I can't believe I just said that.*

"No, just you, Eve." Moira sounded tired; at least Eve hoped it was tiredness not exasperation.

"I would never have thought myself capable of it," Moira said, burying her face in her hands.

"Yeah, I know what you mean," Eve said with a nod. "I always thought that people who slept with other people's partners lacked any self-control or common decency. And they always have an excuse—it's somehow never their fault. I mean, look at Esther—she's devastated." Eve's cheeks flushed with feeling.

"Remember, you didn't know, Eve." Moira reassured her with a shake of her head. "And don't forget, I could have said no."

Eve said in earnest, "I'm so glad you didn't. You don't regret it, do you?"

Moira had felt every emotion since meeting Eve. Regret wasn't one of them. "No."

Eve kissed Moira. It was a tired, gentle kiss that tingled on Moira's lips. Eve then nestled into Moira, who wrapped her arms around her as Eve closed her eyes.

"You must be hungry." Moira's voice caught in her throat. She had tried so hard not to think of Eve that she couldn't quite believe Eve was there, in her arms, real and true.

Eve mumbled, "No, I'm too tired. I just need a minute."

"You need to eat something, Eve. I've some stew—it won't take a minute to heat."

Somewhere between stew and heat, Eve had fallen asleep.

Moira rested her lips on Eve's forehead, brushing them gently against Eve's skin, fearing a kiss would wake her.

She hadn't meant to hold Eve all that night, their bodies pressed close, warm upon the sofa. She just found that she couldn't quite let go.

Moira woke to the sound of the dawn chorus, immediately feeling the soft weight of Eve against her. Eve's arm was wrapped around Moira's waist, her head rested against her chest, and Moira could feel Eve breathing in the soft rhythm of sleep.

Moira gently freed herself, placing a throw over Eve. She stood looking at her, still not quite believing that Eve had come all this way. She'd told Moira that she wanted to try to understand. The truth was Moira wasn't entirely sure she understood herself. And then Eve hadn't said anything about forgiving her. But then why would she? Why would she forgive someone who lied to her? After all, Eve had said that she felt betrayed by her. Moira heard herself ask out loud, "Why are you here?"

"What?" Eve sleepily asked.

Moira said quickly, "Nothing, sorry. I didn't mean to wake you."

"It's okay. I need a wee anyway." Eve smiled and stood with a yawn. She nodded in the direction of the stairs. "That way?"

"Yes. Upstairs on the left, opposite the bedroom." Moira smiled broadly. She had forgotten that this incredibly sweet woman could always lighten her heart with a smile.

When Eve emerged from the bathroom, Moira was pulling back the covers to her bed.

Eve stood on the threshold of Moira's bedroom. "I love this room," Eve said, looking out towards the window, to the views of loch and mountains.

"I sometimes wonder whether I should brighten it a little." Moira looked around her. Each piece of furniture had belonged to her father. The surface of the bedside table by the window had faded slightly, and the pastel blue of the wardrobe had become chalky and cracked a little at the handle. Her curtains were plain cream, except for a border of tiny flowers, and her bedspread was made up of a patchwork medley of quilt squares.

"Don't change it," Eve said, stepping into the room. "Unless you want to, obviously. It's lovely."

Moira looked down. She had no idea why Eve could still think anything related to her was lovely. "I thought you might want to rest here. I've made you tea and toast. There's no hurry, come to in your own time." Moira walked towards the door.

Eve stopped Moira in her tracks when she said, "You wanted to know why I was here. Just a minute ago." Moira turned round. "I'm here because just like you said to me at the restaurant, that you couldn't rest or work without seeing me again, well, it's been the same for me. I couldn't seem to think, and at times"—Eve's voice broke—"I've thought I couldn't breathe." Eve wiped at her tears.

Moira moved to her and held her tight.

"I know I should be cross with you," Eve continued, speaking into Moira. "And I have been. I haven't been able to understand how you could hurt me like that." Eve moved away slightly. "But I know you care for me. I can tell you do. Not by what you've said, but because I can feel it—in here." Eve looked down to her heart, pressing her hand against her chest.

Moira lifted Eve's face. "Sometimes your heart isn't the best thing to trust."

"Why not? Isn't the head too clever to be honest?" Eve said with a shrug.

Eve's question had such a simple wisdom to it that Moira found she had no answer. After all, she too had listened to her heart, not her head. And she knew that right now that's all she could rely on too.

"Try and rest, Eve. I'll just be downstairs."

Eve nodded.

Returning to her sitting room, Moira sat in her armchair, and as she stared out through the sunroom window towards the loch, being forgiven no longer seemed that important.

Chapter Twenty-one

It was midmorning before Eve joined Moira in the garden. She had lain down on Moira's bed just for forty winks. Five hours later she had woken and her heart had surged with the realization she was here, here with Moira.

"Wow. I bet you never get used to that view." Eve shaded her eyes with the edge of her hand as the mountains, bustling forests, and gleaming loch bid her a welcome return.

"No." Moira cleared her throat. "I suspect a lifetime of looking wouldn't feel enough. Morning."

"Hi." Eve could feel herself blush at the sight of Moira. She sat dreamily on the veranda steps and watched as the hens scurried and pecked. The loch was still, calm, peaceful.

Moira sat next to Eve and asked, "You okay?"

"Very okay. Thank you." Without thinking, Eve went to kiss Moira, only for Moira to pull away. Confused, Eve said, "I'm sorry. I—"

"No, Eve, it's okay. It's just we're not very private, that's all."

Eve looked across to the main house. It seemed empty. She couldn't quite believe that she hadn't given Alice or John a thought. She had woken with Moira on her mind—only Moira.

Eve tentatively said, "You said in your letter that he'd gone."

Moira nodded. "Yes. He left soon after I got back."

"Because you told him about us?" Eve almost dared not ask the question.

Moira looked away towards the loch as she said, "I didn't know if I would see you again or what it meant for me, so I didn't know what to say to him."

"But you told him, right?"

Moira slowly nodded. "When I returned home, I was a mess. Alice was a mess—"

"Alice knows about me?" Eve raised her eyebrows at the thought of what Alice's reaction might have been. It filled her with dread.

"Yes. Understandably, she's been finding things hard, what with her father leaving and…and everything. I've been trying to give her some space." Moira shook her head. "I told her you were here earlier this morning, though. I couldn't allow her just to bump into you." Moira gave a heavy sigh. "She thinks that I'm making a complete fool of myself."

"Right. Well, I hope you told her where to stick her thoughts." Eve pulled roughly at the grasses at her feet.

"I didn't say anything, Eve—I couldn't. She's hurting—"

"Yes, but that's no excuse to hurt you." Eve looked across again to the main house. "I'm sorry, Moira. That you're going through this. If there's anything I can do, I mean, I could talk to Alice or—"

Moira turned to Eve, her hand resting on her arm. "There's nothing for you to do, really. It's probably best that Alice and I try and work this out together. And if we can't…But there's no need for you to feel sorry for me. Okay?"

"It's not that—I care about you. I care about what has happened to you, what is happening to you."

Moira's voice broke as she said, "I care about you too."

Eve rested her head against Moira's shoulder, her arm tucked around Moira's arm. "And John? When you told him, was it really bad too?"

A wave of agony washed over Moira's face. It was clear that the memory of her last conversation with John still burnt painfully bright for her.

Speaking softly, Eve asked, "Do you think he'll come back?"

Moira put her arm around Eve, holding her tight. "No. No, I don't."

Reassured, Eve asked, with compassion, "Will you miss him?"

"Yes, his friendship—the familiarity of our lives, maybe."

Eve cuddled close to Moira, her gaze resting upon the crests of the distant hills, as she said, "Right, of course. I get that."

Eve's phone burred in her pocket. She pulled it out and looked at it. "I should take this. I won't be a moment." Eve stood.

Moira nodded. Eve's cheeks had gone red, and she seemed to hesitate as if she did not want to answer her phone. "You okay?" Moira asked, as the phone stopped ringing.

"Yes, I'm just going to go to the loo."

"I'll see you inside then." Moira watched Eve walk to the croft, her phone tightly gripped in her hand. Moira heard the phone ring once more and Eve's reply as she disappeared inside.

"Hi, Rox."

❖

Eve was still talking on the phone when Moira joined her five minutes later.

"No, I don't know…No, we haven't worked anything out yet…A few days maybe. I don't know…Yes, I'll let you know… Yes, of course I will…" Eve bit her lip. "Look, I'm sorry…sure. Bye, Rox."

Moira stood leaning against the sunroom door, looking at Eve, wondering why she seemed so sad and concerned. "Everything okay?"

"Yeah, I think so." Eve gave a heavy sigh. "I should have rung her last night, when I got here. She worries about me." Eve shrugged.

"She obviously cares a lot about you."

"Yep, we've known each other since we were kids." Eve shrugged again.

"So what did she say? Did she know you were coming up?"

Eve gave a guilty shake of the head. "I've only just told her. I didn't think she'd approve and would try and talk me out of seeing you again. I was right. She thinks I'm crazy being here and that I shouldn't trust you."

Moira didn't blame Roxanne for mistrusting her and warning Eve to stay away, but she couldn't help but feel angry at Roxanne's continued interference. But at the end of the day, Eve was still here, in her sitting room, smiling at her, with eyes shining with affection and feeling. Nothing Roxanne had said had been able to change Eve's mind.

"I rang my work on the way up here," Eve explained with a guilty smile. "I did fake coughing. I was meant to be working today. Is it wrong that I don't feel bad?"

"Very wrong."

"I stopped myself from saying it was contagious."

Moira laughed and pulled Eve tight against her, and Eve, in turn, pressed her body into hers.

"I'll probably have to ring them again Monday," Eve mumbled into Moira. "I could maybe take some holiday. I've a few days owing me."

Moira replied, her lips brushing against Eve's neck, "August is a busy time for me, but I guess I could ask Alice to cover at the centre. I will have to go in at some point."

"Yes, of course."

Moira whispered into Eve's ear, her breath teasing against Eve's skin, "I'll make time for us."

"Yes, that would be…"

Moira kissed Eve's neck. "A plan?" Moira offered, her hands exploring their way down Eve's body to rest against Eve's bottom.

"What? Yes, a…a plan."

Moira smiled at Eve, at the sight of her struggling to form thoughts let alone words. It never ceased to fill Moira with wonder at how she was able to make Eve feel, and how, in turn, Eve made her want her so desperately.

Moira kissed Eve, a full kiss that spoke of her passion, her overwhelming need. Urged by intense desire, she leant Eve against the trestle table in the sunroom. Pots were pushed aside. Soil spilt.

She wrestled with Eve's trousers, the button, the zip, and Eve took a sharp intake of breath as Moira slipped her fingers, her palm, down Eve's knickers.

Finding breath to speak, Moira urged, "Let's go upstairs."

"What? *No*, please don't stop." Eve pulled open Moira's shirt, kissing her chest.

Moira breathlessly released herself from Eve. "I won't stop. I promise." Moira grasped Eve's hand and led her upstairs.

Barely reaching Moira's bedroom, Eve pulled her buttoned-up shirt over her head. She bent down and pulled at the laces of her shoes, releasing the shoes from her feet.

Moira sat on the bed, watching Eve.

"The first time I fantasized about you"—Eve stood before Moira in her bra, bare feet, and open jeans—"you were watching me undress, like you are now."

Moira looked at Eve's newly exposed body. She swallowed and said, "Come here."

Moira held the warm denim against her palms, leant in, and kissed the soft skin above Eve's knickers. With her chin touching Eve's stomach, she smiled. "So what happens next in your fantasy?"

"This." Eve took a deep breath, reaching behind her, unclasping her bra, and letting it fall.

Moira reached up and cupped Eve's naked breasts in her hands.

Eve closed her eyes as Moira's mouth teased, licked, and kissed at each nipple. Eve's breath caught as Moira's tongue traced its way down Eve's body. Moira could feel the warmth of Eve against her as she eased Eve's jeans down her thighs.

Eve held the sides of Moira's head, running her fingers through her soft curls, massaging, soothing with her touch. Pressing Moira against her, she whispered, her voice grazing against her throat, "I want to be close to you."

"We couldn't get much closer, Eve." Moira looked up and smiled.

Eve looked down at herself and back at Moira. "Kiss me again."

Moira held Eve's bottom, her touch familiar, easy.

"I mean kiss me here," Eve said, blushing deeply, looking down to between her legs, slipping her knickers over her hips, down her thighs.

"What have you done to me?" Moira mouthed quietly between her kisses, as her lips explored the soft curves of Eve's body.

Moira felt her body on fire, her appetite for Eve overwhelming her senses. She pulled Eve into her, enjoying the soft warmth of her, her hands supporting the small of Eve's back.

The wet of Moira's lips formed a kiss as her tongue licked and probed, moving in and out of Eve.

Eve kept swallowing, her cheeks flushed with feeling.

"Moira," Eve managed.

Moira could feel Eve shaking.

Eve shook her head. "I can't keep it in."

Moira guided Eve onto the bed, moving on top of Eve as she reassured, "I don't want you to."

Moira's chest lay against Eve, her lower torso between her legs.

Moira could feel the tension in Eve's body, as if Eve was struggling to control the sensations rushing through her. "You don't need to fight it, Eve. Let yourself enjoy how you feel."

In one impulsive action, Eve rolled Moira over, moving on top of her.

"Eve?"

Eve sat naked astride Moira. Leaning forward, she kissed and caressed Moira's breasts, swollen, aroused under the delicate material of her bra.

Moira stroked Eve's bottom, the inside of her legs.

Eve groaned as Moira's fingers entered her.

Moira reached forward and kissed Eve's neck, her mouth sucking hard at Eve's skin.

Eve pulled Moira into her, rocking her hips rhythmically in time with Moira's fingers.

Moira could feel Eve relax, open up, her muscles giving in to pleasure. She breathlessly asked, "Deeper?"

Eve nodded, her eyes firmly closed.

"Eve?" Moira felt Eve bite her shoulder. "You okay?"

"Yes. Oh my God, Yes!"

CHAPTER TWENTY-TWO

Clouds misted the early Sunday morning sun and the heat of yesterday's passion faded as a cool air nipped in Moira's croft. Moira brushed away the rubble in the grate, adding new kindling. Her phone was tucked between the edge of her jaw and her lifted shoulder, the receiver against her ear. She let the phone slip into her hand. "Please don't go to too much trouble, Betty."

"It's no trouble. So see you both at midday then, Moira."

"Yes, see you then." Moira stared at the phone before placing it back in its holder.

Eve was sitting on the last but one step at the foot of Moira's stairs wearing just her knickers and Moira's jumper. Her hair was wet from showering and a toothbrush stuck out of her mouth.

Briefly removing the brush, Eve said, "Are Angus and Elizabeth well?"

"Yes, they're fine," Moira said, with a distracted tone. "In fact, they've invited us to lunch. Sorry—I heard myself tell them you were here. I was due to go over. I can't believe I was so stupid."

"Right. Blimey."

"I shouldn't have said yes. What was I thinking? We need to cancel. We can't go, Eve. It will be awkward, really awkward."

Oh my God. They blame me, don't they? Eve's heart surged and pounded with panic. *But then why invite me to lunch? Am I missing something?* "So how did they take it when you told them?"

Moira shook her head. "They don't know."

"They don't know?" Eve wiped her mouth with her sleeve. "You mean about us?"

"About anything."

"What, not even about John leaving? But won't they have guessed that something's wrong? I can't believe Alice hasn't told them—"

"I begged her not to say anything. It's not unusual for John to work away."

Eve, dumbfounded, stood and joined Moira at her side. She placed her hand on Moira's forearm and said, carefully, "Yeah, that's kind of a lot to ask of her—"

"It's important to me that I tell them myself!" Moira took a deep breath to steady herself. "I'm sorry, Eve, I didn't mean to raise my voice at you. It's just I haven't been able to find the right time, because I know that once I tell them about John leaving then they'll ask why he left—it'll all come out. *Everything.*"

"Everything? So they never knew about Iris? But they have her photo—I just assumed—"

"For Alice. We put it there for Alice."

Eve looked at Moira's anguished face. "Right. I see. So they have no idea at all about you?"

Moira shrugged. "It never came up."

"Yeah, the whole *I'm gay* thing rarely just comes up in conversation."

With a weariness that seemed to weigh down her words, Moira said, exasperated, "You don't understand, Eve."

"What's there to understand? They love you. You love them. I'm sure they'll just want you to be happy, Moira." Eve gesticulated with her toothbrush as she spoke.

Moira snapped, "That may be the case in your world, where everything's so simple, so—"

Eve gasped. "*My* world?"

Moira shook her head. "Look, let's not talk about it."

"But if we're having lunch with them…?"

Moira walked off to the sunroom. "We're cancelling." She paced up and down, shaking her head. "I can't do this, I can't."

Eve called after her, "It's okay. Surely, we don't have to cancel—we just need a plan. If you can't face telling them yet, then all we need to do is agree why I've come up. If you want we can just be friends until you talk to—"

"Friends? We're hardly friends, Eve."

Eve looked into the sunroom, to Moira refilling the pots with yesterday's spilt pebbles and soil. *Yeah, but I'm not exactly your girlfriend either, am I?* Eve sat pensively on the edge of Moira's sofa, feeling the adrenaline high of her rush to Moira draining away.

A terrible, silent five minutes passed. Eve had honestly never felt so alone. She folded her arms across her chest and fixed her concentration on the floor. She traced the edges of the floorboards, the indents of half-moon holes left by wood knots, the swirling patterns of the grain. The dried drips of wood stain—a silent reminder of work undertaken, of the life lived before her. Eve held her body taut, almost as if relaxing would be the end of it all.

Moira appeared in the sunroom doorway. Her words, as if sodden with pain and sadness, sank heavy into the sitting room air.

"I can't bring myself to tell them. They'll know I've lied to them. I let them think that Iris and I were just friends, that I married John because I loved him." Moira's face creased with pain. "So much deceit, so many lies."

"No, Moira." Eve rushed across the room to Moira and held her tightly, rubbing her back, soothing her. "You didn't set out to deceive them, to hurt them. They'll know that. My guess is that they won't think you've lied to them. All they'll know is that you couldn't tell them the truth."

"You think?"

"I'm certain."

"I wouldn't know where to begin."

"The beginning is normally a good place to start. Look, I can help you tell them, if you like."

"No, it's okay. I'll talk to them." Moira stroked Eve's cheek. "Soon. I promise."

Eve nodded. "Okay."

"You really want to go to lunch?" Moira asked, a smile at the edge of her lips.

Eve shrugged. "Well now I know they don't hate me—yet."

"Something tells me you're not that easy to hate."

"No?"

Moira's slipped her arms around Eve. "No."

"So was that our first row?" Eve asked, her cheeks tingling with the fading glow of confrontation.

With a soft kiss on Eve's neck, Moira whispered, "I like you wearing my jumper." Moira eased her hands beneath the jumper and lifted it over her head. "But I like it even better when you're not."

Eve stood just in her knickers. Moira cupped Eve's breasts and kissed them.

Eve held Moira's head with both hands, breathlessly asking, "So everything's okay. With us. Moira?"

"You taste soapy," Moira said with her face buried in Eve's chest.

Eve lifted Moira's face to hers. "You can talk to me about things, you know."

Moira nodded, her eyes cloudy in the first mists of passion.

Eve kissed Moira. It was a kiss she hoped would say to Moira, *I am here for you. All of me.* Eve felt her legs weaken as Moira returned her kiss deeply.

"And toothpaste, you taste of toothpaste too," Moira said, running her tongue over her lips and smiling.

Eve brushed at Moira's mouth with her thumb. "Come with me?" Eve said softly, as she slipped her hand into Moira's and led her upstairs to the bedroom.

Eve stood by the bed, half-naked, her body pressed close against Moira's. She felt Moira's hands against her bottom, pressing her yet closer still. Eve struggled to catch her breath, the air suddenly too thin—she was at altitude, heady, high with Moira.

Eve held Moira's intense gaze as she undid each button of Moira's shirt, slowly, deliberately, almost as if she was releasing the chains that had bound Moira for so long. Eve bit her lip at the sight of Moira's soft breasts rising and falling, at Moira's aroused nipples. She felt on the emotional edge with Moira, the dizzying feelings so intense.

Moira shrugged her shirt to the floor, and Eve reached behind Moira to unclasp her bra. Moira released a whimper as Eve caressed Moira's naked breasts, Eve's lips soft and warm against Moira's skin, her tongue teasing, licking, sucking.

Eve could feel Moira's fingers stroking at the nape of her neck before Moira's hands slipped beneath Eve's knickers to rest against her naked bottom.

"You're everything to me," Eve whispered, as she undid the zip of Moira's trousers and eased them down her thighs.

Silently, Moira stepped out of her trousers, moved towards the bed, and lay down, removing her knickers, as Eve discarded hers.

Eve lay on top of Moira, her mouth searching out Moira's as if Moira's lips would quench her thirst. Eve could feel Moira's body beneath her, restless, writhing with pleasure.

"I want to know what you taste like," Eve said in between kisses that made their way down to between Moira's legs.

In steady rhythms, matched by the motion of Moira moving against her, Eve immersed herself in Moira, losing herself completely.

Eve's tongue then traced its way from inside Moira to the smoothness of her inner thigh, to the curve of her stomach, to the swell of her chest. Eve sought Moira's neck, kissing, licking at her skin, as her hand slipped between Moira's legs.

Moira arched her hips into Eve as Eve pressed deeply, rhythmically inside Moira. She could feel Moira's body push against her for one last time, and then sink, spent beneath her.

Eve held Moira until their breathing calmed and the heat of their passion cooled.

And as the morning sun rose yet further in the sky, Moira asked, her head rested against Eve's chest, "What do I taste like?"

"Like Newland," Eve said sleepily. "You taste like Newland."

Chapter Twenty-three

W elcome, both. Welcome," Elizabeth called down the lane, appearing from behind her cottage wall.

"Hello." Moira raised her hand and waved. Moira glanced to her side at Eve, who was blushing and waving. It was impossible for Moira not to feel joy and pride at the sight of her.

Moira handed Elizabeth a bouquet of flowers from her garden. Her gesture was met with a long, tight hug.

Elizabeth smiled broadly at Moira. "Thank you. Just beautiful. And, Eve, how wonderful to see you again." Elizabeth held Eve's hands and kissed her lightly on her cheek.

"Hi," Eve said, with a self-conscious smile. "Thank you for your lovely invitation."

"Well, we would have been very disappointed to have missed seeing you again. Shall we?" With effortless grace, Elizabeth tucked her arm into Eve's and guided her inside the cottage.

Moira just caught the words, "I hope you're hungry," as she followed behind.

Elizabeth and Angus's Sunday lunches had a warmth and familiarity about them that made Moira feel safe, reassured. The vegetables were always from their garden, and they took great trouble to source the rest of their meal from local producers. As a child Moira had spent many a Saturday with Elizabeth at the local market, or standing in the slurry of a farmyard with Angus puffing on his pipe, chatting to the farmer and his wife.

"She slept with that ewe for three nights until it lambed, three nights in the barn, in the hay. I knew from that day she would be a crofter, a woman of the land. She was ten, Eve, ten." Angus puffed proudly on his empty pipe.

Eve nodded, looking across to Moira who seemed embarrassed. Eve took a large slug of her wine, catching Angus's eye and blushing as he smiled back at her.

"I'll help you with the dishes." Moira gathered the plates from the table.

Eve rose to lend a hand.

"No, no, stay, you are our guest." Elizabeth disappeared into the kitchen with Moira. "Pudding won't be long."

In the kitchen pouring cream into a jug, Elizabeth asked, "So, how is everything?"

Moira slipped the plates into the suds foaming in the washing-up bowl, her hands turning pink in the hot water.

"We missed you and John at the meeting Wednesday. Margaret had got quite a bee in her bonnet, really, I think John is the only one who can settle her—"

"He's left." The words fell from Moira's lips as if they had been teetering there perilously.

"Left?" Elizabeth set the cream jug aside.

"We've called it a day."

"I'm so sorry, Moira." Elizabeth steadied herself against the worktop.

"Don't be, it's fine. I'm fine."

"Why didn't you tell us? And poor Alice—how is she coping?"

Moira sighed. "I don't know. We're struggling to talk."

"Oh, Moira, I wish you'd felt able to say something. You shouldn't have to go through this alone."

"I'm not."

"Oh." Elizabeth's gaze fell away to the dining room, to Eve.

"I mean, I have you and Angus, and Alice, of course." Moira's heart thumped so fast it hurt. She felt her eyes smart.

"Of course," Elizabeth said. "You know how we feel about you, don't you? You're in every way our daughter."

"I know." Moira held Elizabeth's soft bone-white hands in hers. "And you're in every way my mother." Moira choked back tears as she pulled Elizabeth into her. "I love you, old lady." Moira could feel Elizabeth's delicate frame in her arms.

"It's lucky we had the main course." An impatient Angus called into the kitchen from the dining room.

"Well, we have been summoned. I hope Eve likes rice pudding—"

"Wait. There's something else…I…I like her. Eve, that is."

"So do we, Moira."

Moira shook her head. "No—that's not what I mean. I want you to know that I *really* like her." Moira dropped her chin into her neck, only for it to be lifted by Elizabeth, who brushed Moira's newly tear-stained face with the tea towel.

Elizabeth tightly held Moira's hands, the tenderness of her expression and the firmness of her hold reassuring Moira of the strength of her love.

"Let's take this through, shall we?" Elizabeth suggested, smoothing her apron flat against her waist. "After you."

Moira nodded. There was no plan for what she had said and now no plan for what she would feel.

"Do you cook, Eve?" Angus asked, pouring Eve another glass of wine.

"Yes, just simple stuff. I particularly like to bake." Eve looked at Moira and smiled as Moira sat down next to her.

Moira looked away from Eve, certain that if she caught her eye her best efforts not to break down would be undone.

"Aye. And you enjoy your work?"

Eve nodded, swallowing a large glug of wine. "Yes. I work in a library."

Angus took a sip of his water. "Aye. Very good. Betty loves to read—"

"What's that?" Elizabeth arrived at the table, oven gloves gripped around a large glass dish, brimming with bubbling rice pudding.

"I was telling Eve how much you like to read," Angus said with an admiring smile.

"Oh yes, I'm quite the bookworm. There's nothing I enjoy more than to be taken on a magical adventure by a good book. I'm not sure Angus understands."

"Not at all, I just don't need books to whisk me away when I have you."

"Stop that nonsense, I'm sure Eve doesn't want to hear—"

"She has been my magical adventure, Eve. My embarkation and now my destination."

Elizabeth shook her head at a beaming Angus.

"That's beautiful, Angus," Eve said, wistfully.

Angus looked across at Eve and smiled.

Eve took another large slug of her wine. "That's how I want to feel about someone one day."

"I'm sure you will, Eve," Angus said with a soft kindness to his voice.

"I hope so," Eve said.

In that moment, Moira had no sense of what she wanted. She sat at the table, absently watching Angus and Elizabeth chatting, sharing their stories, and laughing with Eve. All Moira could think about was all that had been lost, all Iris had lost, their love, omitted, invisible in the closeted silence. Moira's heart ached for all the invitations for two Elizabeth would have been delighted to send, if only she'd known she could, for Iris's unspilt laughter to the jokes that Angus never told, and for the bracing hilltop Newland paths that Iris never walked, her breath untaken by the view she never saw. It was all too late and all too sad for words. Moira looked at the pictures on the sideboard, and her gaze fixed itself to the snap of Iris. *Iris...*

Elizabeth caught Moira's eye. "I'm going to dish up some pudding for Alice. Will you take it with you, Moira? I know it's not much, but it's a start. Poor thing."

Angus and Eve looked up.

Eve turned to Moira and whispered, "Is everything okay?"

❖

It was early evening before Moira and Eve returned home. Dusk had begun to shroud Newland in a hazy half-light, and Eve could sense that Moira's mood had fallen silent, introverted.

"You were quick. Did Alice like her pudding?" Eve followed Moira into the garden.

"She wasn't about. I just left it in the fridge."

"Are you okay?"

Moira closed the henhouse. She didn't say anything.

"You know, I never actually told my family that I was gay," Eve revealed, watching the hens pecking at their food. "Roxanne blurted it out to Esther one day. Esther told my parents. My mum Googled *lesbian* and that was that. I hadn't said a word. Crazy, hey? Moira?"

"I'm tired, Eve. I can't chat now." Moira went into the sitting room, turned on a side lamp, poured herself a whisky, and sank into the single chair.

Eve curled up on the sofa opposite. The room felt cold. Eve half expected Moira to light a fire or something but she just sat absently nursing her drink.

Moira's silence frightened Eve. "Are you cross with me that I encouraged you to tell them?" It was the only reason that Eve could think of that might explain Moira's sombre mood. Had she overstepped the mark in trying to help and had Moira resented it?

"What?" Moira shook her head. "*No.* Look, let's go to bed."

"Oh, right. An early night." Eve winked mischievously, hoping to lighten the mood.

Moira gave Eve a blank look in response and turned away to turn off the lamp, plunging Eve into darkness.

Moira silently got undressed, went into the bathroom, and closed the door.

Eve lay under the bedclothes and shivered.

The sheets felt cold. Eve shivered again. *I wonder if Moira has an electric blanket?* Eve rummaged around the sides of Moira's bedding, finding a T-shirt under her pillow.

"Can I borrow your T-shirt?" Eve called through to the bathroom and received no reply. She pulled on the T-shirt, squinting at her chest to read the faded writing. *Is that an* S*?*

"What are you doing?" Moira reappeared in the bedroom.

"Oh, I'm sorry, I was cold."

"Take it off," Moira said sharply, her tone colder than the room.

Eve quickly pulled the T-shirt off. Resting the T-shirt on the bed sheet, Eve felt sick as she read the back. *The Bells.*

Eve stammered, "I'm so sorry, Moira, I didn't realize—really I didn't. I wouldn't have put it on had I known. I wouldn't be that disrespectful, really."

All of the warmth, the life, seemed to drain from Moira's face. She looked at Eve as if Eve was a stranger, trespassing, unwelcome, and intruding where she was not wanted.

Eve quickly folded the T-shirt, put it back under the pillow, and tucked the bedclothes close around her. She felt her pillow dampen at the side of her face.

Moira got into bed, turning away, her back towards Eve.

"Moira?" There was no reply. "I'm sorry."

Moira whispered, "Let's not talk about it."

"Right, okay."

Eve lay still, fearing that even the motion of her breathing would be too much for Moira. It made no sense that Eve could feel so alone when the person she cared for most in the world lay next to her.

Eve hadn't intended to oversleep, and when she woke mid-morning Moira had already left. She lifted Moira's pillow. The Bells T-shirt was no longer there. The note Eve found on the kitchen table read, *Gone in to work. Back at five. Can you feed the hens? And dig up some potatoes for dinner.* To the point. Eve flicked the paper over in case Moira had left a cross for a kiss. Nothing.

Dig up some potatoes? Eve looked outside at the confusing patch of green shoots, stakes, and netting that made up the vegetable garden. The truth was the only digging Eve had ever done before was for gossip. *Hens. I'll do the hens first.*

As Eve opened the henhouse, the hens flapped, squawked, and pecked around her. She flicked their food at them more to keep them away from her as to feed them.

"Oh God. Just fuck off, will you, just…" Eve stood amongst the hens and could not help but cry.

"Why don't *you* just fuck off." Alice appeared in the garden, looming over Eve, and growled, "Leave them, for Christ's sake. I'll see to them."

The hens scuttled away.

Eve wiped her eyes with her sleeve. "I'm not here to cause trouble—"

"Why are you here then? You've got some nerve turning up. You've ruined everything. You know my dad's left because of you? It's only a matter of time before Moira realizes you're not right for her. I mean, how could you be?"

"I'm just visiting for a few days, so there's no need—"

"Good, so you're not staying then. I'm glad."

"Staying?"

The thought of staying, of leaving her home, her family, Roxanne, of leaving for good, had simply not occurred to Eve. She hadn't anticipated the panic the notion now filled her with.

Eve said hesitantly, "Well, we haven't talked about it."

Alice walked away without waiting for Eve's full reply. "You're pathetic."

The ferocity of Alice's words left Eve stunned. Dazed, she turned her attention to the vegetable patch. She had no idea where to begin. *What am I doing here?*

It had taken Eve a couple of hours to build up the courage to dig up her first potato. The run in with Alice had done nothing to boost her confidence. She stood, frowning at the ground, trying to identify leaf shapes with the help of a book entitled *Eat Your Garden* that she found underneath a plant pot in the sunroom. She suspected that the title was more apt than it should be as the chances of Eve digging up an ornamental hardy perennial instead of something for dinner was alarmingly high. But if Moira came home to Eve admitting she couldn't even dig up potatoes, then what would that mean?

It was nearing five when an exhausted Eve walked inside the empty croft, the harvested potatoes in her arms. Dumping the vegetables on the trestle table, she looked at her soil-covered clothes. She was a mess. Everything felt like a mess. She looked into the sitting room, at her mobile phone amongst Moira's papers on the dining table.

She reached for the phone, reassuringly familiar in her hand. She opened an unread text. *You okay? Call me. R X*

"Hi, Rox, it's me. I guess you're at work or something. Can you give me a ring back?" Eve felt emotion choking at her throat. She gripped her mobile phone tightly. "I'm okay and everything, it's just, well, it would be nice to talk to you." Eve didn't mean to burst into tears—to sob down the phone like a fool. She rallied to say. "Speak soon. Bye."

Eve jumped, spinning around, as Moira tipped the potatoes into the sink.

"I didn't hear you come in. You frightened the life out of me." Eve held her palm against her chest, trying to calm her racing heart. She quickly wiped at her tear-stained cheeks with her cuff.

Without looking away from the sink, Moira said, hesitantly, "Sorry about last night. I didn't mean to…it's all a bit overwhelming."

Eve sniffed. "You and me both. I had a run in with Alice in the garden."

Moira turned to look at Eve. "What did she say?"

Eve took a deep breath. "That I'd ruined everything. That you'd soon regret being with me. She wanted to know whether I was staying. God, she was really angry." Eve watched Moira's face drain of colour.

"I'm sorry." Moira gave a heavy, tired sigh, leaning for a moment against the sink. She asked quietly, "What did you tell her… about staying?"

Eve lifted peeled potatoes from the sink for chopping, trying to remember what, in the heat of the moment, she had said and, moreover, what she now wanted to say. Her hands ached in the cold water. She leant across to turn on the hot water tap. There on the window sill, in a small china dish, cherished in the shade of rosemary and sage, sat a gold ring.

Eve swallowed hard. She could feel her chest squeeze as if caught in a vice. She stammered, "Do you still wear it—his ring?" She nodded towards the dish.

Moira's cheeks flushed. She shook her head.

"Right." *Why haven't you put it away then, Moira, got rid of it or something?* Eve cleared her throat. "You're going to put it away now though. Now that it's over officially."

"No, Eve, I'm not."

"No?" They stared at each other, Eve's pain reflected in Moira's eyes. "Why would you keep his ring? I don't understand."

Moira said firmly, "Exactly, you don't understand."

"I've tried to. I'm trying to now, Moira."

"Because it's not his ring."

Eve blinked. "What?"

Moira dried her hands against her trousers, and without saying anything left the room.

Eve stared at the plain thin band of precious metal, glinting like a beacon of truth in the early evening light.

"Moira. Wait." Eve's chest tightened at the sound of the front door closing and the crunch against gravel of Land Rover tyres.

CHAPTER TWENTY-FOUR

Without thinking, Moira drove to the education centre. She turned the engine off and sat gripping the wheel—her head resting against her seat, her eyes firmly closed. The confrontation with Eve kept playing over and over in her head.

With a burst of urgency she jumped out the Land Rover and clambered, almost desperately, into the hills. Reaching the pinnacle, by the tor, Moira stood tall.

The hills in the foreground and mountains in the distance seemed to be wrapping Moira up, enclosing her, protecting her. It felt like they were listening, like a wise and patient counsellor, poised to hear her woes.

The wind whistled through the stones of the tor, playing an ancient, timeless melody, the high notes floating in the ether between the present and the past. Moira sat amongst the stones with her eyes closed. She could swear she could hear drums beating out a furious rhythm, and an audience clapping, shouting for more.

Moira opened her eyes. The wind had dried her tears to salt, just as time had crystallized her past into jewels of memory, glinting clear and bright. She closed her eyes again. Iris's face shone back at her, thrilled with life, thrilled with love. Moira's lips moved in time to their conversation which came rushing back at her, word for word.

"Will you marry me, Moira Burns?"
"Don't be silly. We can't be married."

"We can in our hearts, Moira. So will you?"
"But people will ask who gave it me. What would I say?"
"Then just keep it, Moira. Keep it knowing that I gave it you.
That it tells you that you are mine."

Moira opened her eyes, the word mine lingering on her lips. She'd kept the ring Iris Campbell gave her. She kept it in spite of everything, because to give it back or to throw it away would have implied she no longer loved Iris and that simply wasn't true. Their love, like the band of metal that symbolized it, would not be smelted in the heat of their arguments, or turned to ash by the cruel whims of fate.

She rarely felt the need to wear it, but somehow always felt the need to have it near.

And here was Eve, asking her about it, demanding to know what the ring was, and why it meant so much. And to have to explain, what would Moira say, what could she say?

Moira stood and looked out across Newland. It had grown dark, and time had passed unnoticed. She knew she should return home, but she simply couldn't, at least not that night. She would go to the main house, slip into the sitting room to rest and maybe sleep, and in the morning she would face Eve.

"Moira? Is that you?" Alice stood on the landing, blinking with sleepy eyes at Moira.

"Yes, it's me, Alice. I'm sorry, I didn't mean to frighten you."

"What are you doing here? It's late. Is everything okay?" Alice looked at the pillow and blanket underneath Moira's arm.

"Yes, of course, everything's fine. I just needed to borrow these. Go back to bed. I'm sorry to have disturbed you."

"Are you sleeping here? Has something happened—with you and her? I knew it."

"Goodnight, Alice."

Alice said, smugly, "The bitch has told you she's not staying, hasn't she?"

"Alice!"

"Well, she is. Coming here, making you think she was interested. Playing with your life, our lives, like it's some sort of game.

Her and that Roxanne, I bet they're laughing right now. Just laughing at us."

"I don't know what you're talking about. Please go to bed, Alice, I won't ask you again. I am not in the mood."

Like a dog with a bone, it was as if Alice couldn't stop gnawing at Moira. "I knew she was trouble. The way she kept chasing you, leaving messages, even after she left—"

Barely containing her anger, Moira swallowed hard to say, "Never interfere like that again, Alice. I can't believe you had the nerve to delete a message intended for me. You were wrong to do that."

"With everything you've done, how can you say *I'm* wrong."

Moira shouted, "That's enough."

Alice stood in front of Moira like a child who had been scolded, her face creased with indignant hurt and fear.

"I'm sorry, Alice—"

"Go to hell!"

Alice slammed her bedroom door and a heart-shaped woven wicker ornament once fixed to the outside of Alice's door fell to the floor. Moira picked it up, rested it against the wall, and walked away.

It was not the first night that Moira Burns had sat, nursing a whisky, in the armchair of the sitting room of the main house, watching the sunrise over the distant mountains. It was not the first time she could have begged the awakening birds not to sing. It was not the first time that she didn't think she could find the strength to begin a new day.

Moira stayed awake all night, thinking about Eve, worrying that she had left her alone. Yet she knew Eve would want—no, need—Moira to talk, to talk about Iris, to talk about them, and she couldn't, she just couldn't.

Moira rested her head, heavy in her palms, unable to face the pain she felt and the pain she knew she was causing.

"Did you stay up all night?" Alice leant against the door of the sitting room, dressed in her pyjamas.

Startled, Moira struggled to gather her thoughts to speak. "Yes, I'm sorry for last night…for everything, Alice. Please believe me."

"How can I believe you? You've done this to us. You've chosen her, over Dad, over me. Don't pretend you care."

"Of course I care, Alice, I care that you're upset, hurting. But you have to try to understand."

"*I* have to understand. You're joking, right? I don't have to do anything you say—you're not my mum!" Alice stopped herself short with her words. The shock of them silenced the room.

Moira sat, numb, looking at her hands resting in her lap, tracing each fine vein, each freckle, each crease of skin from knuckle to fingertip.

Alice said, her voice calmer now, "That's all I've ever wanted to do is understand—understand about the past, about me, my mum, my life. You and Dad, you've kept the truth away from me for all these years. And now it's too late."

Moira looked at Alice, confused. "Why is it too late?"

"Because of her. Dad's lost you, I'll lose you, I'll lose everything because of her."

"*No.* I'll always be here for you. Whatever happens between Eve and me, you won't lose me. I promise."

"But Dad's lost you."

"It's not like that. In the end…we needed to let each other go."

"Because you don't love each other any more?" Alice asked, guarded curiosity replacing the accusation in her voice.

"Because it was time."

Moira followed Alice's gaze to a beaten-up cardboard box tucked at the side of the sofa.

Alice said quietly, "It's Mum's stuff. Dad thought I might like to have it. Do you think he's letting Mum go too?"

Moira stood unsteadily to her feet to comfort Alice, standing at her side, her arm resting loosely around Alice's waist. "All I know is that he wanted you to have her things, Alice. And I think he's right."

Moira felt her chest tighten as Alice walked over to the box and lifted it onto the sofa.

Alice leafed through concert programmes, tickets, music sheets. She lifted a black T-shirt from the box and held it against her. A white letter *B* caught the light of the sunrise. Alice discarded it back into the box. "She's got loads of these, notebooks. She was quite arty, wasn't she?"

Moira nodded, waiting for the pain to screw into her.

Alice looked at Moira and took a deep breath to ask, "What was she like?"

Moira swallowed, holding herself stiff. "Musical, a good singer."

"No. I know that. What was she like as a person—when she was younger, my age?"

Moira sat on the arm of the sofa, looking at the pile of note-books. A purple cloth covered book caught her eye. Distracted, she replied, "Passionate. She was always campaigning. She despaired at people's apathy. She cared about her homeland, politics, nature."

"Wow, is that you?" Alice held up a photo of The Bells. The photo showed Moira standing next to Iris. Iris had her arm around Moira's waist.

Moira felt her heart pounding insistently in her chest. "Yes, they were just starting out. We'd all just finished college. The house in the background was where we lived in town."

"Wow." Alice looked at Moira and smiled. "She was so pretty, wasn't she? Dad's hair is a shocker. Uncle Hamish looks so different now."

Moira nodded.

"And then I came along." Alice's tone became flat. "I'm having a tea. Want one?"

Moira nodded. "Thank you. I might stay here a little while longer, I'm not sure I can…I'll get some sleep. Would that be okay?"

Calling from the kitchen, Alice shouted, "Yeah, sure. I'm going into work first thing. I'll come home at lunchtime. I've got that stupid assignment to finish. Maybe we can go through some more of Mum's stuff together again at some point."

Moira could tell in the hint of relief that softened the air, that albeit a fragile beginning, it was nonetheless a start of finding a way through with Alice. And a start was all Moira would hope for.

Moira's tired eyes fell once more upon the box. "Yes, if that's what you would like." She gently lifted the purple notebook, brushing her thumb lightly over the raised surface of the hand-painted fabric. A sprig of heather, the brown spray of a fern, protruded from between the cloth and the hardback book, and crumbs of lavender filled the crevices of the binding at the turn of each page.

A green leather bookmark with the gold embossed image of a grand building, with the letters *SAC* beneath it, half slipped from the book. Tucking the bookmark back opened the page it marked. Moira stared at Iris's handwriting, at the inky soft curves and sharp edges forming the word *Highlander*. Moira swallowed.

Alice reappeared in the sitting room with two mugs of tea and two large slices of cake. "Elizabeth's started bringing me food over. Does she think Dad was the cook in our house? Before you say it, I know she's just trying to help…Moira?"

Moira stood at the doors to the garden, her arms folded in front of her. She was sobbing.

"Moira, are you okay?"

Moira's tears were her only reply.

Eve had spent the long night alone curled up on the sofa, a blanket tucked around her, the terrible ache in her heart her only companion. If she had slept, it didn't feel like it. Every time she heard a noise, her heart would pound, her eyes would dart to the door, and she would hold her breath, her ears straining to make out the sound—her mind spinning to find the first words to say. But it was just the breeze blowing against the door. It was always just the careless breeze.

All morning through to lunchtime, Eve busied herself tidying up the vegetable patch after yesterday's debacle with the potatoes. She knelt amongst the vegetables, diligently patting the ground.

Her phone burred in her pocket. Eve's heart surged. *Moira?* Eve brushed the soil from the screen. *Rox.*

"Hi, Rox."

"You okay?" Roxanne asked. "I've been on night shift. I've only just got your message. Has something happened? Why were you so upset?—A pint please."

"Are you at The Brewer's?"

"What? Yes. Anyway, don't change the subject. What's happened?"

"It's nothing really, Rox. I didn't mean to worry you."

"Nothing? Eve, you were sobbing down the phone."

"Well, it's just…"

"Just what? Eve, it was easier to get poor Mrs. Smith to pass her kidney stone this morning than it is to get information out of you."

"We've been rowing, all right? She's been away all night. I was thinking I should probably tell someone. Although my gut feeling is that she's fine and she won't want the fuss." Eve did her best to keep it together as she said, "I think she's going to dump me, Rox."

"Well, that might not be a bad thing, you can move on."

"What? I don't want to move on. I want *her*. Remember what I said at The Brewer's when you asked me about my ideal woman? She's the one. Don't you get it, Rox?"

"No, as you're asking, I don't get it. Because unless I'm misunderstanding something here, you ring me in floods of tears because of her, and then she storms off and leaves you on your own all night in the middle of fucking nowhere. And all that's okay with you because…?"

Eve walked over to the veranda and sat wearily down.

"Oh, and let's not forget, Eve, she lies. She lied to you, she's lied to everyone. Are you honestly telling me you don't care about that?"

"No, of course I'm not, Rox, but I kind of understand why she did. She's hurting and lonely. I told you what the letter said, about her past, about Iris. She never meant to hurt me."

"No, Evie. She's messing with your head, and she'll break your heart all over again."

"You don't know that. You don't know *her*."

"And neither do you. For fuck's sake, Eve."

"I *do*. I do know her. I know her in my heart."

Roxanne let out an exasperated, "Whatever."

"You don't understand, Rox, when she looks at me, when she kisses me, I can tell she cares. And when we make love, she's with *me*, completely. I've never felt this way about anyone before, really I haven't. I can't even bear the thought of spending another night without her." Eve's voice broke.

"So have you spoken about the future?"

"No, everything's been a bit tense to talk properly. She's struggling with her feelings, coming to terms with her past and stuff. It's like she can't move on. And I want to help her. I want to make everything okay for her."

"So what are you going to do?"

"Wait for her."

"You might be waiting a hell of a long time, Evie. And in the meantime she's hurting you."

"It doesn't feel like pain so much. It feels more like—"

"You're going to say love, aren't you?"

"Yes."

"Oh God, I need more beer."

"So shall I ring you later then?"

"Tonight. Ring me tonight. Right?"

"Yes and thanks for being there for me. For always being there for me. You're the best mate in the whole—"

"Wide universe world. I know. Talk soon, mate. And get yourself on the train if it gets any shittier."

"Bye, Rox."

Eve held her mobile in her hand and sat looking out to the loch. She had spoken with such conviction about her feelings, about her hopes. And yet Eve knew that hoping wouldn't bring Moira home. And hoping wouldn't make everything right.

Chapter Twenty-five

M oira told herself to expect to find that Eve had left. That love, once again, had left. She had spent the afternoon at work, delaying the inevitable. She steeled herself for the sight of the empty sitting room, the single glass by the decanter, the unintended order of a home lived in by one. She had not prepared herself for soil prints, muddy clothes, and the warmth of life waiting for her return.

"Eve?"

"Moira? I'm up here. I hope you don't mind, I thought I'd take a bath. Hi."

"Hi."

"Are you okay? I was worried. I'm sorry for what I said. I thought it was John's ring. Is it Iris's? If it is, I'd never ask you to get rid of it. I wouldn't do that to you, honestly. I know how much she meant to you. I know you think I don't understand but really I'm trying." Eve splashed out of the bath, the unrinsed soap shimmering over her body.

"Slow down, Eve, slow down." Moira's voice shook with tiredness. Her eyes briefly flickered over Eve's body.

Eve bit her lip.

Moira turned away and went to her bedroom, and sat heavily on the edge of her bed, her head in her hands. "Why are you still here?" Moira asked, shaking her head.

Eve followed Moira into the bedroom and stood in front of her. "What?" Eve said, her voice trembling with alarm.

"It makes no sense," Moira said, looking at Eve. "When everything seems so…"

"Stressful?"

Moira nodded. She could see that Eve's face had drained of colour. Looking down at the floor, she said quietly, "I don't know why you didn't go home."

"Is that honestly what you think? That I should have gone home?" Eve reached for Moira's hand.

Moira stood to walk away.

"Then tell me to go, Moira. Have the guts to look me in the eye and tell me to go."

Moira stopped but didn't turn round.

"Tell me to my face. Tell me that everything we've been through so far was for nothing." Eve's voice broke. "Tell me that you don't want me, that you don't want to hold me ever again, or kiss me, or wake up in my arms…ever again. Tell me, Moira."

Moira turned round. "Stop talking, please, Eve."

"No." Eve placed her hand on her hips. "No. It seems you can say what you like and I'm meant to somehow suck it up. Just so you know, I'm not still here because I'm some pushover you can treat like crap. I'm here for us. Yes. I'm being strong for us, because I believe in us, even if you—"

Moira stood in front of Eve. "Did you want a towel?"

"A towel?" Eve swallowed. Eve had been arguing naked, standing in the middle of Moira's bedroom, dripping on the floor, a puddle of bathwater at her feet.

Moira collected a towel from the bathroom and wrapped it around Eve. She placed her palm at Eve's cheek. "I'm sorry for treating you this way."

Eve hugged Moira, whispering into her chest. "Sorry is a start but it's not an explanation. We need to talk."

Moira held Eve tightly in her arms. "In the morning. I promise we'll talk in the morning."

❖

"Are you going to work?" Eve fumbled for her watch on the bedside squinting at the hands that read eight thirty. "Don't you have time for some breakfast?"

Moira pulled on her jumper. "I've eaten. There's coffee in the pot and I've cut some bread for toast. I'll see you later."

"When exactly? Will you be away all day again? It's just you said we'd talk. We need to talk. I'm going to have to go back soon and I *need* to know what's going on between us. What's going on with you."

"I'm not sure I know what to say, Eve."

Eve climbed out of bed, struggling into her jeans and T-shirt. "Then just tell me how you feel, how you *really* feel—what's going on in your head."

"I'm going to be late."

"Talk to me, Moira."

Eve watched as the dark around Moira's eyelids grew darker. It filled Eve with an awful sense of dread. She bravely continued, "You won't let me in."

Moira looked down.

"What kind of relationship can we have, Moira, if you won't—can't—talk to me? Or is it just about sex? Are we just sex?"

Moira's face creased with hurt. "Is that what you think?"

"No, it's how you make me feel."

"Then leave."

"What?" *Please, no.*

Not bearing to see Eve's face Moira turned away to say, "I think you should go home, I'll give you some space to pack your things." Without pausing to look at Eve, Moira left the room, but Eve followed.

"Moira, I haven't said these things because I want us to split up. Wait. I've said them because I want us to have a future, to be together."

"How can we have a future? You're half my age, for God's sake."

"What? I don't care about that. I just want you." Eve's words travelled with her down the stairs as she followed Moira out into the garden.

Moira stood looking at the newly organized vegetable patch.

Eve said, "I didn't know where everything went. But I'm willing to learn, really I am. Please let me try—"

"It's not about the vegetables, Eve."

"I know that. I'm just saying…please, Moira."

"What? You're saying what? You'll live here in Newland, leave your family, Roxanne? You'll be content without the daily buzz of the city? Your gay bars? Will you?"

"I…" Eve desperately searched for words. Tears were all that came.

Moira looked at her vegetable patch, her hens, at Foxglove, and then at Eve crying. "It's too much to ask you to cope here and I won't leave Newland. You need to know that, Eve. You need to know that about me. I can't leave here. I won't leave. I won't change."

"I don't want you to—please—I *love* you."

"How can you?" Moira's heart broke as she turned and walked away.

CHAPTER TWENTY-SIX

Moira hadn't gone to work. Her breaking heart instead led her to the only place where it knew it could be safe, where it had always been safe.

She stood in Angus and Elizabeth's dining room, and had intended to calmly explain that she had asked Eve to leave and that this was for the best, and would it be possible to spend a little time with them to give Eve a chance to pack her things. She'd gotten as far as hello before crumbling in front of them. Elizabeth held her in her arms as Moira sat sobbing at the dining table, her head buried in her hands.

"Why don't you make us some tea, Betty." Angus swallowed several times to find his voice. "I'll stay with her."

Moira tried her best to rally, taking a handkerchief from Angus. "I'm sorry, I can't seem to stop. I can't…"

"Let it all out, Moira. It's perhaps time you did, don't you think?"

Angus and Elizabeth sat with Moira, Angus holding Elizabeth's hand. They sat watching Moira cry, waiting for her to be able to talk.

"I've told her to leave." Moira took a deep breath and wiped at her cheeks with the back of her hand. "It's for the best. I also wanted to say that I'm sorry"—tears glistened down Moira's cheeks—"if by not handling things very well, I've caused you distress."

"How have you not handled things well?" Angus shook his head. "I don't understand." He looked at Elizabeth and tightened his hold of her hand.

Stifling her embarrassment, Moira said, "My feelings—the dishonesty of it all."

"Oh, I see." Angus lit his pipe and slipped it into his mouth. A mist of sweet smoke clouded the air, drifting and gathering like his thoughts. He looked closely at Moira. "Aye, well, if life has taught me anything, Moira, it is that honesty is sometimes overrated."

Moira blinked several times, surprised at Angus's words. She would have thought that honesty would have meant everything to him.

Angus continued, "Yes, I think you'll find there is a good deal more decency in a well-meaning omission and far more cruelty in so-called honest words." Angus took a long drag on his pipe.

"Right." Moira nodded slowly, her brow furrowed in thought. "So you don't feel deceived—that I couldn't tell you everything about me, the truth of my situation?" Moira looked at Elizabeth.

Elizabeth replied gently, "Deceived? No, Moira—confused perhaps, worried about you at times, yes. But we have no right to expect you to tell us everything about yourself. After all, everyone has things that, for whatever reason, they don't feel they wish to share with others. We understand that you value your privacy. We've always understood that. We've always tried our best to understand you, brave girl—so that we would know how to help."

"So are you saying you've always known about me?" Moira asked tentatively.

Elizabeth nodded. "That you would follow your own path, definitely—that was obvious in your independent spirit that shone out in you so brightly, even as a young child. It was clear to us that you would never follow the crowd, and we were, *are*, so proud of you for that. But if you're asking Angus and me whether we knew about your feelings for young Iris, and what that might tell us about you, then I can only say this—that it was less what you said, or perhaps tried to say, and more…" Elizabeth's voice began to tremble.

"We watched you grieve, Moira." Angus quietly continued for his wife. "It was your terrible, terrible grief that gave your feelings away. For it wasn't the grief of someone who had lost their best friend. It was clearly the grief of someone who had lost a love."

Elizabeth stroked Moira's tear-stained face. "You've lived with that grief every day, Moira. And no one, it seemed, not John, nor Alice, nor us, could help you."

Angus took a deep breath of tobacco, breathing it out, the smoke escaping from his lips like the truth, as he said, "That is, until Eve."

Moira looked at Angus. "I don't want to talk about her, please." Moira stood up.

"Please, sit down, Moira. I wasn't going to tell you what to do." Angus's words were firm but kind, and not for debate.

"Do you know what struck me when I first met Eve? It wasn't, as it happens, that she wasn't wearing any trousers." Angus shook his head. "No, it was the way she looked at you, the incredibly tender way you looked at each other. I'd never seen you look at anyone that way, Moira. And how much she admired you, it made me feel proud to know you, so I can only imagine how she made you feel. I don't have to tell you, Moira, that love is a precious thing and all too easily lost."

Moira gasped, "You honestly think I want to lose Eve, her love?"

"Well, in that case, I'm not sure we understand," Elizabeth said, confused.

"It's just, what can I offer her? How can I be her future? She's so much younger, so much more life—"

"Nonsense," Elizabeth intervened with a shake of the head. "You're talking as if you think you've had your life—as if it's over." Elizabeth watched Moira take a deep breath in. "Is that it? Is that what this is about? I think Eve would disagree. It's blatantly obvious how fond she is of you. The poor thing, she came all this way, which I think was very brave indeed, to be with you, leaving her friends and family behind. All she seems to want is you, Moira, a life with you. Why on earth don't you simply let her?"

"Because we're so different, there's no way she can cope here."

"Have you told her that?" Elizabeth asked, with a questioning frown.

"Yes."

"And what did she say?"

"That she wanted to try, but it's clear she has no idea what this life would mean for her."

"Are you sure she has no idea? And for that matter"—Elizabeth took a deep breath—"are you sure she couldn't love you as much if not more than Iris?"

Elizabeth stood and rested her hand on Angus's shoulder, steadying herself, as she concluded her thoughts. "When someone we love dies, we don't remember them as flawed and real, we remember them as we need to remember them, in ways which comfort us. They become not as they were but how we need them to be. Eve cannot compete with an idealized memory, Moira. No one can. And no one should have to."

Moira sat, staring at the ground, lost in the words she had waited too long to hear.

"Well, Betty," Angus said, "I think we've said all we can for now. It is up to our girl to find her way."

❖

Startled by the front door opening, Eve stood from the sofa, her packed rucksack resting against her legs. "Moira?"

"No." Alice stood scowling at Eve.

"Is Moira with you?" Eve asked, looking past Alice, hoping that Moira was just behind her. She wasn't. Eve folded her arms. "What do you want?"

"I just wanted to drop off these things for Moira. I didn't realize you'd still be here." Alice rested a notebook, accompanied by a chocolate cake wrapped in cling film, on the table. She placed a note on top of the book.

"Why did you think I wouldn't be here?" Eve asked, fearful of the answer.

"Well, Moira couldn't have made it clearer that she doesn't want you. I heard you rowing in the garden—it was impossible not to hear you." Alice shrugged. She then narrowed her eyes and asked with a suspicious tone, "Why haven't you left?"

"Sorry to disappoint you, Alice." Eve looked at the cake. "I can see you've come ready to celebrate."

"If you must know, I came to see how Moira was, she wasn't in work. God only knows what state she's in. I hope you realize how much you've hurt her."

"What? How much I've hurt *her*? Take a look around you, Alice, I'm not the one who's stormed off because she wouldn't talk."

"That's because she doesn't, she doesn't talk. Certainly not about anything that matters. Take it from me, if you're expecting her to pour out her feelings, then you'll be waiting a very long time. So why don't you go home. Go on, just go!"

"Fuck off, Alice! You don't get to tell me what to do."

"Go home, *please* just go home." Alice's voice wavered.

"No, Alice."

"Why not?"

Alice's pleading tone prompted Eve to sit down. She replied, exhausted, "Because I love her."

"I know. I heard you tell her," Alice admitted, the merest hint of pity in her voice. "And I didn't hear her tell you she loved you back. That's why you might as well just leave. There's no point." Alice quickly turned to leave.

"But there's no point to anything without her," Eve said, trying desperately not to cry again in front of Alice.

Alice glanced back at Eve, and then left without another word.

When Moira finally summoned the courage to return home as dusk fell over Newland, her heart sank into her stomach when she saw the note on her table. The croft was empty. The note would be from Eve. It would contain her parting words, wounded and cold.

Just stopped by. Thought you might want this—it didn't seem right for me to keep it. It seemed to mean a lot to you. Let me know if you want anything else. I'm putting the rest in the loft. Alice. X

No note, then. Eve had left without even a hurt goodbye. But what did she expect? What on earth did she expect? Eve had given her a second chance, many chances in fact, and she had blown them one by one.

Moira scraped a chair out from the table and sat heavily down. She placed the note aside and looked at the cake, missing a large slice, crumbs scattered on the table, and over the purple cloth cover of the painfully familiar notebook.

She rested her palm flat against the embroidered cover. The book, its spine, its bindings, felt cold and hard, lifeless like a carcass bereft of a soul. The text inside, the fading ink, in every way the fossil imprints of words imagined and spoken long ago.

For too long Moira had lived in the cold shadow of the past, in the futile search for comfort amongst the emotional ruins and relics of love. She realized that now, now when it was too late.

Moira shivered.

She wanted warmth, laughter, hands in her hair, kisses on her lips, blushing cheeks, a sweet smile, her name spoken in passion, the beating heart of love. She wanted Eve.

But with Eve gone, she had no clue in that moment where she could find her or whether she would want to be found.

"You don't have to store them away," Moira said, standing at the sitting room door of the main house.

"I wasn't expecting to see you tonight," Alice said. "You look tired, Moira."

"It's been a long day."

Alice nodded and turned away, her gaze falling on the box of her mother's belongings resting on the sofa. "You don't think I should put them away?"

"Not unless you want to. She's your mum, Alice. She'd have wanted you to have her things around you. You should keep this too."

Moira dropped the notebook gently into the box. At the same time, she tucked her Bells T-shirt underneath Iris's T-shirt, to rest, as it should, with all the other memories of the past.

"And…" Moira hesitated.

Alice looked up.

"I have something which I would like you to have—which I think you should have. If you'd like to."

Moira unfurled her fist to reveal a delicate band of gold. "Your mum gave it me many years ago. It was your great-grandmother's."

Alice stared at the ring, her face lit by the beauty of it.

Wide-eyed, Alice whispered, "It's beautiful."

"Yes."

"To give you this—she loved you so much, didn't she?" Alice's voice crumbled with distress.

"Yes, but—"

Alice spluttered, "I ruined your life, her life. Didn't I?"

Moira gasped. "*No*, that's not right—"

"You would have been with her until the end though. She wouldn't have stayed with my dad, would she, if she hadn't fallen pregnant? I'm not stupid, Moira."

"Please, Alice. Here, sit with me a moment." Moira gestured to the sofa.

Alice sat next to her, tears glistening in the lamplight.

"It's not as simple as that. Nothing ever is, Alice." Moira took Alice's hands in hers. "I once asked your mum what she was most happy doing—caring for the environment, like you and me, or singing. She said singing. She *chose* to be a singer. She lived the life she wanted. And it wasn't the life I wanted. After all these years, it's only in the last few months or so—"

"Since Eve?"

Moira nodded. "Spending time with Eve, talking with her, just being with her has forced me to face things I find hard. So much of my life I've felt burdened with the belief that I somehow failed your mum. That I couldn't be braver about my sexuality—that I wasn't prepared to give up my teaching, what I cared about. And now"—Moira swallowed deeply—"I'm beginning to wonder that even though your mum and I loved each other very much, I think we had different destinies."

"But you always told me we make our own fate. That you don't believe in destiny, Moira."

"I don't, at least I didn't. But it's somehow"—Moira shook her head—"the only thing that seems to make sense these days. Because I want you to know this, Alice, understand this: your mum, your dad, and I were destined to parent you, to love you, and we have, and we do, with all our hearts. My only regret is that I haven't told you that more."

Alice nodded, retightening her ponytail and wiping her eyes with her sleeve.

Moira wasn't sure whether her words had made any sense, or any difference. "I'll leave the ring here." Moira placed the ring gently on the sofa. "I'll see you tomorrow, Alice."

As Moira stood, Alice reached out for Moira's hand. She squeezed it and said softly, earnestly, "Thank you…for everything."

Emotion muffled Moira's words as she said, "You're welcome, Alice. Goodnight, then."

Just as Moira reached the door, Alice sniffed hard. "I can't believe she waited for you."

"Sorry?" Moira's chest tightened.

"Eve. I overheard you rowing. You think she'd take the hint, wouldn't you?"

You overheard? "No, you're mistaken, Alice. Eve has gone." The words caught in Moira's throat. "She wasn't there when I got home."

"Yes, but she was definitely there when I called by a couple of hours ago."

"But…she was still there? What did she say? Was she all right?"

"I tried to make her leave. I thought that's what you wanted."

Moira felt sick, terribly, terribly sick. She asked quietly, hesitantly, "And what if I don't want her to leave?" Moira held Alice's questioning stare.

Alice shrugged, standing to close the lid on the cardboard box. She looked at the ring on the sofa. "I guess that's up to you."

Chapter Twenty-seven

Returning to her croft, Moira's heart ached with all that she had said, all that she had felt, all that she was feeling now. *You waited for me? You didn't leave?* It was too much to hope that Eve was still there and too much to quite believe.

Moira quickly glanced around the sitting room. Urgency rose in her as she hurriedly checked each and every room in her croft. She pushed open the sunroom doors and rushed into the garden. She stood still, listening, her heart beating like a drum sending a message into the evening air.

She desperately cast her gaze into the distance, towards the blowing grasses disappearing on the horizon, where garden met meadow met glade. *The glade.*

"Eve."

Eve looked around to find Moira standing over her.

Moira had found Eve nestled amongst the grasses in the glade. She was sitting with her knees tucked under her chin and her arms wrapped around her shins, looking out at the loch. Her rucksack lay on the ground at her feet.

Moira sat down next to her.

The air was cool and fragrant, and the evening sky was lit with glinting stars and the glimpse through drifting clouds of a crescent moon.

"I haven't left yet," Eve said matter-of-factly.

"No. I can see that."

"I know you want me to leave."

Moira said quickly, "I don't. I don't want you to leave. I can't begin to tell you how I felt when I saw that you were still here."

Eve looked intently at Moira. "Try, try and tell me. Please. I need to hear it."

"I thought…I thought I'd lost you, driven you away. I've been so stupid, I lost sight of us, of you. I love you, Eve, so very much."

Eve asked, "Why couldn't you say that before? You let me think you didn't love me. You hurt me, Moira. You really hurt me."

"I know I have. And that it's unforgivable. The truth is I've always loved you, from the moment I first saw you. But I didn't feel it was right to tell you because in the end we're so different, Eve. I was worried it couldn't work."

Eve frowned. "But is being different a bad thing? Doesn't that just make us interesting to each other? And at the end of the day doesn't everyone just hope that they'll be happy, healthy, and have someone to share life with?"

"But that's the point, Eve. I'm a lot older than you. You've got your whole life ahead of you."

Eve replied, "Yes, and I'd like to spend it with you."

"But I won't be here to share your whole life with."

"Why, where are you going?"

Moira said with a heavy sigh, "You know what I mean."

Eve shook her head to say, "No, I don't. I don't know why you think life offers anyone any certainties. We could be the same age and I could die before you. All we have in fact is right now. And I want to spend every one of my right nows with you."

Moira didn't know what to say. There seemed to be no defence against such sense. Instead, she watched Eve tip her chin to look at the sky.

"When I was a little girl," Eve said, her voice distant, wistful, "I used to wonder where the stars went during the day or on those nights they didn't seem to shine."

Moira looked up, her eyes tracing the pinpricks of light suspended in the sky.

"When I was young," Moira said, "I thought the brightest star was my mother looking down on me." Moira glanced at Eve, who in turn held her gaze. "If I'm honest, I still do."

"So she'd be that one." Eve pointed to a star glistening brightly above their heads.

Moira nodded. "I guess."

"And Iris? Which one is she?"

Moira felt her chest tighten. If this was a test to see whether she would talk about Iris, then she would not fail again. She would talk about her, she would talk about everything.

Moira lay down on the ground, the earth holding her close. "That one."

Eve lay down next to Moira. "It's beautiful."

"Eve, I know that the stars we see at night are dead or dying. They offer us no warmth and only the memory of life."

Eve turned on her side to face Moira, her elbow propped, her hand supporting her tilted head. "But it will always be in our sky, won't it? Her star?"

"Yes," Moira confessed, with the saddest of tones. "I'll always love her. I can't pretend to you that I won't."

This was it, the impasse that would mean the end for them. Moira was certain.

"I know you will," Eve said stoically. "But, for me, somehow what matters is not whether or not you love Iris, but whether you love *me*. And you've told me you do." Eve smiled and shrugged, nestling her head into Moira. "And I love you, Moira."

Moira kissed Eve's forehead, her lips lingering against her skin, Eve's wise words soothing Moira's bruised heart. Moira struggled to ask, "What now?"

"We go forward loving each other."

"Okay." Moira laughed. Only Eve could make things seem so uncomplicated. "We could, I don't know, divide our time—"

"A long-distance relationship?" Eve rested up on her elbow to look at Moira. "Yep, that would go well, what with your love of chatting on the phone and my easy-cheesy attitude to leaving you."

Moira couldn't help but laugh again. "Yes, you may have a point."

Eve kissed Moira, a quick, soft kiss. "I know it seems soon for us to live together. That everyone will wonder what the rush is," Eve said with a shrug. "But I want to be with you, so much. Really I do."

Moira stroked Eve's flushed cheek. "I know, Eve. I know."

"So I've been thinking. Funnily enough, I've had a lot of time to myself to do that. You see I visited Inverness with my family, and they have these new apartments that look out over the river. I thought I might take a look. I could try to get work in a library or at the university, and I'm used to renting on my own. If I remember correctly, around the corner's the cinema and restaurants. As it's a city I can't imagine there's nothing gay going on. You never know, they might even have a Pride festival."

"That's a big step, Eve. It's a long way for your family to visit."

"Yep." Eve gave a mischievous grin. "My plan has many plus points."

Moira laughed and shook her head.

Eve continued in earnest. "It gives us a chance to get to know each other, doesn't it? To take our time. To just enjoy each other, without the pressure to immediately know what we are, or what we might become. What do you think?"

"I think as plans go it's a pretty good one. If that's what you feel you're able to do. You'll be leaving a lot behind."

Eve said simply, "I know."

Moira cleared her throat, her words faltering as she spoke. "In the future, if things go okay, if you wanted, then we could, perhaps, live together in the city. I could continue to work in Newland and commute. I don't know what Alice's plans are yet for after college but I want her to always have a home in Newland. I could ask her if she'd like to have the croft. I could rent out the main house. That would go towards our rent—"

"What, you'd give up your home for me?"

Moira could hear the surprise and emotion in Eve's voice. "Yes."

"What about your hens?" Eve asked, straight-faced.

"I don't know, Alice, maybe?"

"Wouldn't they miss you? I feel certain they'd miss me," Eve said, smiling.

Moira laughed again.

Eve cuddled close to Moira. "We wouldn't be able to watch the sun set over the loch. We'd lose this place."

Moira held Eve tight against her. "I guess."

"It would be harder just to drop in for tea with Elizabeth and Angus."

Moira could feel Eve's breath against her neck. She half whispered, "What are you saying?"

"If you can commute for work between Inverness and Newland, then couldn't I?"

"So, what, you would consider living in Newland?"

"I want to be with you, Moira. And I know enough to understand that Newland is your home."

Moira struggled to digest what Eve was saying. "But do you not want to get away from…memories?"

"Only if you do. I don't mind that you have a past. I only mind if it hurts you, if it hurts us."

Moira shook her head. "I won't let it any more, Eve, I promise."

"How about you just promise to talk to me if it ever does?" Eve stood, brushing at her clothes. "Will you come with me tomorrow to look at flats before I go back?"

"Yes, of course, you need to go home."

"I am home."

Moira felt her eyes sting and mist with tears.

"You know what we could do now." Eve gave a slow, suggestive nod.

Moira stood to face Eve, smiling in recognition. "I don't think I can—"

"Put the bloody heating on. Oh, and we can finish that cake I started, it's delicious."

Moira shook her head and laughed as she watched Eve weave her way through the grasses back to the croft.

Moira heard a hen squawk and Eve swear in surprise. Never had Moira Burns known such peace.

About the Author

Anna has a degree in English Literature and master's degrees in museum studies and the word and visual imagination. She has written and curated a permanent exhibition of LGBT voices and memorabilia, based at Leicester's LGBT Centre, one of the first permanent exhibitions in the UK. As a former member of the Steering Committee for the Leicester, Leicestershire, and Rutland LGBT History Project, Anna is passionate about preserving LGBT history and ensuring that LGBT voices are heard.

Books Available from Bold Strokes Books

Escape in Time by Robyn Nyx. Working in the past is hell on your future. (978-1-62639-855-9)

Forget-Me-Not by Kris Bryant. Is love worth walking away from the only life you've ever dreamed of? (978-1-62639-865-8)

Highland Fling by Anna Larner. On vacation in the Scottish Highlands, Eve Eddison falls for the enigmatic forestry officer Moira Burns, despite Eve's best friend's campaign to convince her that Moira will break her heart. (978-1-62639-853-5)

Phoenix Rising by Rebecca Harwell. As Storm's Quarry faces invasion from a powerful neighbor, a mysterious newcomer with powers equal to Nadya's challenges everything she believes about herself and her future (978-1-62639-913-6)

Soul Survivor by I. Beacham. Sam and Joey have given up on hope, but when fate brings them together it gives them a chance to change each other's life and make dreams come true. (978-1-62639-882-5)

Strawberry Summer by Melissa Brayden. When Margaret Beringer's first love Courtney Carrington returns to their small town, she must grapple with their troubled past and fight the temptation for a very delicious future. (978-1-62639-867-2)

The Girl on the Edge of Summer by J.M. Redmann. Micky Knight accepts two cases, but neither is the easy investigation it appears. The past is never past—and young girls lead complicated, even dangerous lives. (978-1-62639-687-6)

Unknown Horizons by CJ Birch. The moment Lieutenant Alison Ash steps aboard the Persephone, she knows her life will never be the same. (978-1-62639-938-9)

Divided Nation, United Hearts by Yolanda Wallace. In a nation torn in two by a most uncivil war, can love conquer the divide? (978-1-62639-847-4)

Fury's Bridge by Brey Willows. What if your life depended on someone who didn't believe in your existence? (978-1-62639-841-2)

Lightning Strikes by Cass Sellars. When Parker Duncan and Sydney Hyatt's one-night stand turns to more, both women must fight demons past and present to cling to the relationship neither of them thought she wanted. (978-1-62639-956-3)

Love in Disaster by Charlotte Greene. A professor and a celebrity chef are drawn together by chance, but can their attraction survive a natural disaster? (978-1-62639-885-6)

Secret Hearts by Radclyffe. Can two women from different worlds find common ground while fighting their secret desires? (978-1-62639-932-7)

Sins of Our Fathers by A. Rose Mathieu. Solving gruesome murder cases is only one of Elizabeth Campbell's challenges; another is her growing attraction to the female detective who is hell-bent on keeping her client in prison. (978-1-62639-873-3)

The Sniper's Kiss by Justine Saracen. The power of a kiss: it can swell your heart with splendor, declare abject submission, and sometimes blow your brains out. (978-1-62639-839-9)

Troop 18 by Jessica L. Webb. Charged with uncovering the destructive secret that a troop of RCMP cadets has been hiding, Andy must put aside her worries about Kate and uncover the conspiracy before it's too late. (978-1-62639-934-1)

Worthy of Trust and Confidence by Kara A. McLeod. FBI Special Agent Ryan O'Connor is about to discover the hard way that when you can only handle one type of answer to a question, it really is better not to ask. (978-1-62639-889-4)

Amounting to Nothing by Karis Walsh. When mounted police officer Billie Mitchell steps in to save beautiful murder witness Merissa Karr, worlds collide on the rough city streets of Tacoma, Washington. (978-1-62639-728-6)

Becoming You by Michelle Grubb. Airlie Porter has a secret. A deep, dark, destructive secret that threatens to engulf her if she can't find the courage to face who she really is and who she really wants to be with. (978-1-62639-811-5)

Birthright by Missouri Vaun. When spies bring news that a swordswoman imprisoned in a neighboring kingdom bears the Royal mark, Princess Kathryn sets out to rescue Aiden, true heir to the Belstaff throne. (978-1-62639-485-8)

Crescent City Confidential by Aurora Rey. When romance and danger are in the air, writer Sam Torres learns the Big Easy is anything but. (978-1-62639-764-4)

Love Down Under by MJ Williamz. Wylie loves Amarina, but if Amarina isn't out, can their relationship last? (978-1-62639-726-2)

Privacy Glass by Missouri Vaun. Things heat up when Nash Wiley commandeers a limo and her best friend for a late drive out to the beach: Champagne on ice, seat belts optional, and privacy glass a must. (978-1-62639-705-7)

The Impasse by Franci McMahon. A horse packing excursion into the Montana Wilderness becomes an adventure of terrifying proportions for Miles and ten women on an outfitter led trip. (978-1-62639-781-1)

The Right Kind of Wrong by PJ Trebelhorn. Bartender Quinn Burke is happy with her life as a playgirl until she realizes she can't fight her feelings any longer for her best friend, bookstore owner Grace Everett. (978-1-62639-771-2)

Wishing on a Dream by Julie Cannon. Can two women change everything for the chance at love? (978-1-62639-762-0)

A Quiet Death by Cari Hunter. When the body of a young Pakistani girl is found out on the moors, the investigation leaves Detective Sanne Jensen facing an ordeal she may not survive. (978-1-62639-815-3)

Buried Heart by Laydin Michaels. When Drew Chambliss meets Cicely Jones, her buried past finds its way to the surface—will they survive its discovery or will their chance at love turn to dust? (978-1-62639-801-6)

Escape: Exodus Book Three by Gun Brooke. Aboard the Exodus ship *Pathfinder*, President Thea Tylio still holds Caya Lindemay, a clairvoyant changer, in protective custody, which has devastating consequences endangering their relationship and the entire Exodus mission. (978-1-62639-635-7)

Genuine Gold by Ann Aptaker. New York, 1952. Outlaw Cantor Gold is thrown back into her honky-tonk Coney Island past, where crime and passion simmer in a neon glare. (978-1-62639-730-9)

Into Thin Air by Jeannie Levig. When her girlfriend disappears, Hannah Lewis discovers her world isn't as orderly as she thought it was. (978-1-62639-722-4)

Night Voice by CF Frizzell. When talk show host Sable finally acknowledges her risqué radio relationship with a mysterious caller, she welcomes a *real* relationship with local tradeswoman Riley Burke. (978-1-62639-813-9)

Raging at the Stars by Lesley Davis. When the unbelievable theories start revealing themselves as truths, can you trust in the ones who have conspired against you from the start? (978-1-62639-720-0)

She Wolf by Sheri Lewis Wohl. When the hunter becomes the hunted, more than love might be lost. (978-1-62639-741-5)

Smothered and Covered by Missouri Vaun. The last person Nash Wiley expects to bump into over a two a.m. breakfast at Waffle House is her college crush, decked out in a curve-hugging law enforcement uniform. (978-1-62639-704-0)

The Butterfly Whisperer by Lisa Moreau. Reunited after ten years, can Jordan and Sophie heal the past and rediscover love or will differing desires keep them apart? (978-1-62639-791-0)

The Devil's Due by Ali Vali. Cain and Emma Casey are awaiting the birth of their third child, but as always in Cain's world, there are new and old enemies to face in post Katrina-ravaged New Orleans. (978-1-62639-591-6)

Widows of the Sun-Moon by Barbara Ann Wright. With immortality now out of their grasp, the gods of Calamity fight amongst themselves, egged on by the mad goddess they thought they'd left behind. (978-1-62639-777-4)